Pra
L.L. Bartlett's Je

DARK

"The Jeff Resnick series is going nowhere but up. Conflicts swirl like the SHATTERED SPIRITS of the Niagara in this one."
—*Feathered Quill Book Reviews*

BOUND BY SUGGESTION

"This fast-paced paranormal thriller will keep everyone wanting to see a LOT more of Jeff Resnick. If you love a good mystery, especially a paranormal thriller, this series is one you need to tune into!"
—*Feathered Quill Book Reviews*

CHEATED BY DEATH

"This tough, but somehow vulnerable, psychic detective has just the right amount of edge to his personality to make him extremely appealing. This book just sizzles hot, asking to be read in a single sitting!"
—*The Feathered Quill Reviews*

ROOM AT THE INN

L.L. Bartlett has done it again. The action never stopped in this gripping tale of murder. I applaud the author for delivering a riveting read. Can't wait for the next book in this exciting and wonderful series.
—*Dru's Book Musings*

DEAD IN RED

"Bartlett's hero is complicated and mesmerizing ... a gripping and energizing mystery."
—*Booklist*

"Bartlett has a deft touch and makes psychic abilities very real."
—*Library Journal*

MURDER ON THE MIND

"This is a high-powered drama filled with interesting characters that add dimension to a tightly paced story with a good kick at the end."
—*RT Magazine*

"This fine paranormal amateur sleuth will send readers shuffling off to Buffalo to accompany Jeff on his investigation."
—*Midwest Book Review*

"Nicely written and quite twisty."
—*The Book Bitch*

"I sincerely hope after reading Murder on the Mind by L. L. Bartlett that I've just witnessed the birth of a new mystery series."
—*Books N Bytes*

Other Books by L.L. Bartlett

The Jeff Resnick Mysteries
    Murder On The Mind
    Dead In Red
    Room At The Inn
    Cheated By Death
    Bound By Suggestion
    Dark Waters

Collections
    Evolution: Jeff Resnick's Backstory
    A Jeff Resnick Six Pack

Short Stories
    When The Spirit Moves You
    Bah! Humbug
    Spooked!
    Crybaby
    Eyewitness

    Abused: A Daughter's Story
    Off Script

Writing as Lorraine Bartlett

The Tales of Telenia (Fantasy)
    Threshold
    Journey
    Treachery

The Victoria Square Mysteries
    A Crafty Killing
    The Walled Flower
    One Hot Murder
    Dead, Bath and Beyond

Recipes To Die For: A Victoria Square Cookbook

Short Stories
    We're So Sorry, Uncle Albert
    Blue Christmas
    An Unconditional Love
    Love Heals
    Prisoner of Love

Tales From Blythe Cove Manor
    A Dream Weekend
    A Final Gift

Writing as Lorna Barrett

The Booktown Mysteries
    Murder Is Binding
    Bookmarked For Death
    Bookplate Special
    Chapter & Hearse
    Sentenced To Death
    Murder On The Half Shelf
    Not The Killing Type
    Book Clubbed
    Title Wave
    A Just Clause

A JEFF RESNICK MYSTERY

SHATTERED SPIRITS

by L.L. Bartlett

 Polaris Press

Polaris Press
P.O. Box 230
N. Greece, NY 14515

ACKNOWLEDGMENTS

My thanks go to Loremil Tan Jensen and Beth Paull for information on fractures, and to the nice people at Forest Lawn Cemetery. Thanks to Linda Kuzminczuk, Amy Connolley, and Judy Beatty for proofreading the manuscript.

ONE

I'd seen the headstone before. Once, when I was about to take a bite of toast on a Sunday morning. Another time it happened when watching a member of the Jazz miss a free throw with only seconds left in the game. And then that sunny Tuesday morning at the corners of Kensington and Fillmore Avenues.

I get these flashes without warning. Insight some might call it. It's damned aggravating if you ask me. It's been more than two years since the mugging that nearly killed me—fractured my skull and broke my arm—but I'd pretty much recovered, except for the flashes and the stuff that came with them. Precognition some call it. I call it a pain in the ass.

That day I was sitting on my new-to-me Schwinn Prelude racing bike. It was a recent purchase and I was riding alongside my co-worker, Dave Morris, from The Whole Nine Yards. Back in my high school days, I rode a used ten-speed I'd bought for twenty bucks from a schoolmate. It served me well for more than two years and I'd ridden it to school and my various part-time jobs. I don't know whatever happened to it. I'd left Buffalo for the army at eighteen and when I'd returned eighteen years later to my brother Richard's home, it was gone.

Dave was into bicycle racing big time and had tried to get me hooked on the sport ever since I'd come to work at the bar. I'd finally caved just three weeks before. It was, after all, good exercise and there was a kind of freedom associated with riding with the wind—and actually faster than it. I'd joined Dave several times on long rides through most of the cemeteries nearest my brother Richard's home, as well as a couple of forays to Forest Lawn Cemetery farther along. Dave liked Forest Lawn because it was such a challenge with its hills and valleys, and the beautiful park-like scenery was easy on the eyes, as well.

We were on our way there when I got that same flash of the headstone. This time it was different. More detailed. The stone was granite, and the grass around its base was shaggy. No flowers. Odds were nobody had visited the grave for years.

"Light's changed," Dave called as I lagged behind.

I had to scramble to get going and catch up with him. We moved to the side of the road and rode single file.

The rides in the cemeteries were peaceful, although getting there could be nerve wracking. Dave usually rode to Richard's house, where I lived in the apartment above his three-car garage, and we'd set off to a pre-determined destination. That morning, Forest Lawn was again our target. I preferred to take the back route, especially since this cemetery was farther out and we had to contend with commuter traffic.

Bicycles have to obey the same laws as motorized vehicles and Dave and I drew abreast at the next light. We still had a couple of miles to go before we arrived at the cemetery, which was sure to have little to no traffic—just what I liked.

I adjusted the strap on my helmet while we waited for the light to change, pulled it a little tighter, then gripped the bike's handholds, getting ready to take off again. Then suddenly there was the roar of a powerful engine to my right. I started to turn my head when the handlebars on my bike were wrenched out of my grasp. I tipped to the right and the bike and I were dragged into the intersection. The big black vehicle sheered away and the bike and I went down, sliding across the sea of asphalt, which was littered with dirt, pebbles, and shards of glass—ripping open my T-shirt and tearing the skin on my face and shoulders until I slammed into the granite curb on the west side of Fillmore Avenue.

That's when everything went black.

"Your résumé is very impressive, Dr. Alpert," Mark Jordan, Personnel Director of Buffco Diagnostics said, looking over the crisp white piece of vellum on the tidy desk before him.

But. Here comes the but, Richard thought bitterly.

"But we couldn't possibly pay you what you're worth."

"I'm negotiable on salary," Richard said, keeping his tone level.

Jordan shook his head. They weren't going to hire him, and salary had nothing to do with it. It was the zero he'd acquired behind his age on his last birthday that was the stumbling block. He was too damned old. Washed up at fifty.

"Besides," Jordan continued, "I'm sure your volunteer activities must take up a lot of your time."

That was an excuse. Jordan was less than a decade younger than Richard. Would Buffco Diagnostics decide he was too old in the not-too-distant future?

Richard didn't bother to offer a smile and stood. "I can see I've wasted your time."

"Not at all. It's just that we're looking for someone a little bit—"

"Younger."

"We don't discriminate by age, race, or sexual orientation," Jordan said with conviction.

Yeah, and they probably had a bridge in Brooklyn for sale, too.

"I'll see myself out," Richard said, crossed the room, and opened the door to the neatly appointed anteroom where several other men in suits waited their turn for interviews. There wasn't a gray hair on any of their temples.

Richard passed the security checkpoint at the company's main entrance, heading for the visitor's parking lot. Scratch one more possible place of employment. Not that he needed to work. He had more money than he knew what to do with or could ever spend in a lifetime. What he wanted was something meaningful to do to occupy the long hours of the day. He missed the routine that accompanied gainful employment. He loved his wife, Brenda, and their eight-month-old daughter, Betsy, but he wanted more. He just wasn't sure what "more" should entail.

Already the temperature had risen on that morning in early June and Richard peeled off his suit coat, then retrieved his keys as the reached his car. His cell phone gave a jangle as he unlocked the driver's door. He grabbed it from his slacks pocket and glanced at the unfamiliar number. He opened the car door, tossed his jacket onto the passenger seat, and got in the Mercedes before tapping the talk icon.

"Hello?"

"Richard? It's Dave—Jeff's friend from the Whole Nine Yards."

There was something amiss about the tone of Dave's voice. Richard's gut tightened. "What's wrong?"

"Jeff and me were riding our bikes—heading for Forest Lawn."

"Cut to the chase," Richard said firmly.

"An SUV clipped Jeff while we were waiting for a red light."

"My God. Where is he?"

"Sisters emergency room."

"And?" Richard asked, dreading the worst.

"He's pretty bashed up. They won't tell me how bad."

"When did this happen?"

"A couple hours ago. I called the bar, but Tom didn't come in until about ten minutes ago. He called your house, and your wife gave him your number, and he just called and gave it to me."

"I can be there in about twenty minutes."

"Okay, I'll see you here."

Richard tapped the end call icon and sat there, staring at his phone, stunned—his own disappointment already forgotten. Should he call Brenda? Yeah, call her and tell her what? *Jeff's banged up—I don't know how bad. Go ahead and panic.*

He felt panicky enough for both of them. Still, after getting a call from Tom at the bar, she was probably already frantic. He hit the call button, flicked through to his landline's number, and hit call.

Brenda picked up almost immediately. "What happened?" she asked, obviously upset.

"Jeff was on his bike and got hit by a car."

"Is he alive?"

"Yes."

He heard her let out a relieved breath. "Where is he?"

"Sisters."

"I can be there—"

"No. I'm on my way there now. I'll give you a call as soon as I know anything."

"Okay," she said, but she didn't sound it. "Go!"

They didn't even say good-bye.

Richard tossed his phone on top of his jacket, started the car, and put it in gear.

The drive across town might well be the longest twenty minutes of his life.

Richard stormed through the emergency room doors of Sisters of Charity Hospital, waved his hospital ID at the guard on duty, and stopped dead, looking around. His first instinct was to head straight for the receptionist, but he caught sight of Dave seated in one of the ubiquitous plastic chairs in the crowded waiting area, head down and looking pale.

Dave glanced up, his expression grim, and practically leapt to his feet, none too steady. Richard charged forward, then hesitated and turned back to the receptionist's desk.

"I'm Dr. Richard Alpert. My brother, Jeffrey Resnick, has been admitted. Can you tell me his condition?"

The pretty Latina consulted her computer before answering. "Serious condition. If you'd like to see him, he's in unit three. Through those doors to the left."

He knew the way. "Thank you." But before he left the waiting room, Richard turned back to meet Dave. "What the hell happened?"

Dave placed a hand on Richard's arm, pulling him aside. "It was an accident. It wasn't anything Jeff did. It was just an accident," he said, but it sounded more like he was trying to convince himself. "Hit and run, too. The guy behind the wheel never even stopped."

"I'm glad you were with him, Dave."

"It could have been me," Dave said sounding shell-shocked. "I've been riding for twenty years and ... it could have been me."

Yeah, but it wasn't.

"You don't have to stay. If you want to leave—"

Dave shook his head. "Tom is okay with me being here until we know...." He let the sentence trail off.

"I'll see what's what and come back to let you know how he's doing," Richard promised.

"Thanks," Dave said, but his expression was still shadowed by guilt.

The ER was bustling and Richard headed straight for unit three, but instead of entering the cubicle, he paused to grab Jeff's chart, giving it a quick read through. He let out a long breath. Things weren't great, but they weren't horrible, either.

"Excuse me," said a twenty-something nurse in pink scrubs, "but you shouldn't be looking at a patient's chart."

"Sorry. I'm Dr. Richard Albert. I'm affiliated with the hospital. Mr. Resnick is my brother."

"Sorry, sir. It's just that—"

"Has he been scheduled for surgery?"

"Not yet. It's been a hectic morning."

Richard nodded and replaced the chart. "I'd like to speak to the resident on duty."

"I'll let her know, sir."

"Thank you."

The nurse nodded, and stepped away.

Richard turned back to the draped cubicle before him, steeled his courage, pulled the privacy curtain aside, and entered.

Jeff lay on the ER gurney, his face a swollen mass of raw pink flesh, swathed in a sea of blue: blankets and hospital gown, and surrounded by white—sheets and gauze. Richard had seen plenty of fractures during his internship at this very same hospital, and was thankful because despite the damage to Jeff's femur and ankle, it could have been much worse. An IV bag hung over the bed, dripping into the back of his hand. Eyes glazed, Jeff lay semi-inclined, staring into space.

"Jeff?" Richard called, stepping close to the bed.

It seemed an eternity before Jeff swung his gaze in Richard's direction. He seemed to have a hard time focusing. "What are you all dressed up for?" he asked, his words slurring.

"I—I had to be somewhere this morning. How do you feel?"

Jeff's laugh was half-hearted. "I can't feel a god-damned thing. I don't give a shit about nothing ... 'cept...." He frowned. "Now I've fucked up your day. Your week. Prolly your year, too."

"You haven't fucked up my year. The day, maybe the week, but not the year," Richard said, pulling up another one of those horribly uncomfortable plastic chairs. He sat down, practically shoulder-to-shoulder with his younger brother. "Do you remember what happened?"

Jeff's eyes closed and he shook his head ever so slightly. Then his brow furrowed, and he seemed to struggle to concentrate. "A tombstone. I saw a tombstone."

Richard's heart froze. "Was there a name on it?" he asked, dreading the answer.

Again, Jeff barely shook his head. "No. Jus' from the back. Been seein' it for a week or two. Seems like somebody—or thing—wants my attention."

"What do you mean?"

"Not the first time I seen it...." He reiterated, closed his eyes, and was asleep.

Richard bowed his head and rubbed his eyes with both hands. He should ask to see the x-rays. He should call Brenda. He should walk back into the ER waiting room and give poor Dave an update, but he didn't. He sat for long minutes, not thinking, just listening to the cardiac monitor behind the bed, knowing it was going to be one hell of a long day.

TWO

Welcome home, Jeffy!" Brenda squealed as she approached Richard's Mercedes with little Betsy Ruth attached to her left hip. She circled around to the passenger side of the car and pulled open the back door. My crutches were on the floor, and I wasn't sure how the hell I was going to extricate myself from the car without a hell of a lot of help thanks to the calf-to-toe cast on my right leg, and the hinged brace on my knee. I hurt just about everywhere. I wished I had a date with a deep soaker tub, but that wasn't going to happen anytime soon.

"Ja-Ja!" Betsy called. She knew Ma-Ma and Da-Da for her mom and pop, and that I was her Ja-Ja. I'm surprised she wasn't freaked by the road rash wounds on my face, but she held out her little arms for me. Unfortunately, there was no way I could hold her.

"I'm gonna need some help," I admitted.

Richard got out of the car and circled around to join Brenda. "Can you scooch forward?"

It was a painful trek across the seat, and it took more than a minute. The effort and discomfort to wiggle forward enough to get my ass poised on the edge of the seat and my legs out of the car left me panting and sweating.

"My life is in the toilet," I muttered.

"You're lucky to be alive," Brenda said.

Betsy reached for me yet again. "Ja-Ja!"

"No, no!" Brenda said and moved behind Richard.

He grabbed my crutches and leaned them against the car before helping me to stand.

I'd thought a broken arm was inconvenient after I'd been mugged a little more than two years before—but four days into it, I could see a broken ankle and fractured femur was going to be much, much worse.

"God, this sucks," I managed with a grimace, and looked up to the big picture window of my apartment over the garage. My cat, Herschel, sat behind the glass—another part of my welcoming committee, but I wasn't going to stay in what I'd come to feel was my home. No way was I going to be able to navigate those stairs, at least not for another six or eight weeks.

I tucked the crutches under my arms and hobbled across the short expanse of driveway to the two steps that led to the back door of Richard's house. Brenda held it open and I carefully stepped up into the butler's pantry. I'd once again be staying in the bedroom right off it that years before had been occupied by the chauffeur who had driven Richard's grandparents around town. It was known as Curtis's room—after Curtis Johnson—but it bore no resemblance to the place where he'd lived for more than a decade. When I'd returned to Buffalo some twenty-seven months before, Richard, Brenda, and I had repainted it a calming beige. Since then, it had undergone a total transformation from a bedroom to Brenda's craft room.

The room contained a twin-sized daybed, but the bolsters and frilly spread were gone, replaced by a couple of standard-size pillows, sheets and a light blanket. Her crafting supplies had been put away in wicker baskets on the built-in shelving, and her gift-wrapping station had completely disappeared. The room was also a warehouse of baby equipment: stroller, toys, and a playpen that could double as a place for Betsy to nap, but they had been folded up to take up less space. The walls were all pink floral chintz and girly as hell—not my style at all.

I turned in the opposite direction toward the kitchen, shuffling toward the maple table and collapsed into one of the chairs, setting my crutches aside. Richard took his usual seat, and Brenda placed Betsy in her highchair. "Want some coffee?" Brenda asked.

I was going to have to crash soon, so coffee was out of the question. It amazed me how exhausting it was just to maneuver around. And though the morning was warm— soon to be hot—I didn't want anything cold to drink. "Cocoa?" I asked.

"Coming right up."

Betsy flexed her fingers, reaching for the small Tupperware container that sat in the middle of the table. Richard made a grab for it and spilled Cheerios onto the highchair's tray.

Brenda got to work making cocoa with milk and expensive powdered chocolate, and I looked out the window toward my apartment. I was too far away to see if Herschel was still sitting on the window sill. I turned to Richard. "Any chance Herschel can come across the driveway to stay while I'm here?"

He frowned. "We can feed him while you mend."

"I'm gonna be in this cast for at least a month and a half—maybe longer."

"We don't mind."

Yeah, but there was no way I wanted to let my cat live alone for that length of time. I decided not to push it on day one of my recovery in their home.

"Maggie's coming for dinner," Brenda said, stirring the pot of warming milk. "I bought a chicken and thought I'd roast it. But we've got steaks—or we could get a few lobsters. You can have anything you want," she offered.

"Chicken's great," I said, my gaze straying back to the window and the garage apartment beyond. And then I was hit by that stinking vision of the back side of a tombstone. It had happened so many times that I knew I was going to have to address it soon. I got the feeling that the grave might be somewhere in Forest Lawn Cemetery—Dave's and my destination on the day of my accident. I needed to go there, but there was no way I could do it on my own—not in my present condition. And how was I going to convince Richard—or anyone else—to take me there?

Richard must have noticed my suddenly vapid stare. "Jeff, are you okay?"

I shook myself. "Sorry. I got lost in thought."

"Ja-Ja!" Betsy cried, and offered me a Cheerio. I let her feed it to me—which made her giggle.

"We're glad you're here," Richard said, taking in his wife and daughter. But this was his place, not mine. All I wanted was to just go home to my own couch or bed.

"Oh, I almost forgot," Brenda said as she took a big blue mug from one of the cabinets. "There was a message on your phone. The bank called. Something about your credit card. They want you to call them ASAP." She reached into her pocket and withdrew a slip of paper. "I wrote down the number."

My cell phone had arrived at the hospital DOA, and I couldn't reach the phone on the wall across the way. "Can I borrow your cell?" I asked Richard.

He retrieved it from his pants pocket and handed it to me. I punched in the number, sorted through the options, and surprisingly enough got a live person in no time flat. After giving them answers to my security questions, and supplying the last four digits of my Social Security number, the woman on the line got down to business.

"There's been a charge against your account made in Florence, Italy."

"When?"

"Yesterday."

I sighed. "I broke my leg and have been in the hospital since Friday, so it wasn't me."

"That's what we thought. We put a freeze on the account and will now cancel it. You won't be responsible for the charge, and we'll send you a new card."

"Thank you."

"You should receive your new card in seven to ten business days. And please let us know if we can assist you in any way in the future."

"Thank you. Bye." I hit the end-call icon and handed the phone to Richard.

"What was that all about?"

I shrugged. "My credit card was compromised. They're going to send me a new one."

He shook his head. "That seems to happen way too often these days."

"I guess it's better it happened now—when I'm not likely to have to use it for a while. Otherwise, it could be really inconvenient."

Richard nodded.

Betsy offered me yet another Cheerio, which I gladly received.

Brenda finished making the cocoa and brought the mug to me. "Do you want some cookies to go with that?"

"What kind?"

"Oatmeal."

"Sounds good."

She headed across the kitchen, snagged a handful from the jar on the counter, placed them on a plate, and brought them to the table. I took one, and so did Richard. Brenda sat at the table and did likewise.

I nibbled on my cookie, sipped my cocoa, and looked out the window once again. I still couldn't tell if Herschel was in the window.

"Have you got any plans for the day?" Richard asked.

"You mean besides crashing?" I shook my head. "But I don't want to go to bed, and I'm afraid I might fall off the couch."

"Then it's a good thing we bought a new recliner for the living room. It arrived just this morning," Brenda said.

I knew that Richard despised the idea of a recliner. He associated them with lower middle class TV stereotypes—think Archie Bunker from a million years ago. He preferred to use a hassock, which matched his favorite chair in his study.

"Whoa, what great timing." My bum ankle began to throb. I might have to switch chairs at the kitchen table so that I could rest it on the unused one.

I sipped more of my cocoa. Richard and Brenda polished off their cookies while CP tossed Cheerios onto the kitchen floor. We seemed to have lost the art of conversation.

And then I saw it ... again. That damned, stinking tombstone! But this time there was movement off to the left. I wasn't sure what it was—maybe the swish of fabric—but the vision winked out before I could be sure. I hitched in a breath.

"Is that leg bothering you?" Brenda asked.

"Yeah."

"We should have stopped at the pharmacy to get your meds," Richard said. "I'll do that right away." But probably not soon enough to stop the pain that was already escalating.

I drained my cup. "I'd sure like to try out your new recliner, if you don't mind, Rich."

"Not at all." He stood and handed me my crutches. I still didn't feel comfortable using them, worried they'd slip out from under me and I'd fall. The last thing I needed was to take a tumble and break something else. As it was, the helmet I'd worn the day of the accident had probably saved me from suffering a concussion, but it hadn't done a thing to save the skin on my face. Thanks to the ointment that covered my cheeks, chin, and nose, I looked like some kind of gunky monster.

A nurse at the hospital had gone over a long—a very long—list of things that I would need done for me in the next few weeks. Richard had assured her that Brenda would be up to the task. I hadn't heard Brenda's take on that pronouncement.

I struggled to my feet and Richard led the way to the rather gloomy living room. It wasn't my favorite room in the Alpert family manse. Later, when the sun swung into the west, it would be a more welcoming place. But at just after eleven in the morning, it was a rather depressing space.

The couch and other chairs had been moved to accommodate the rather large, dark brown leather wing chair that faced the big plasma TV. It didn't look at all like a recliner, which I'm sure was the point. Brenda joined us, with CP straddling her left hip.

"Take a seat," Richard invited.

I did, and was surprised at how comfortable the chair was.

"Just push back and the leg rest will pop up," Brenda encouraged.

I did so. Not bad.

Brenda handed the baby to Richard. "I've got a nice fluffy pillow over here to prop up that leg." She retrieved it, gently moving my leg, making sure I was comfortable.

"Is there anything you want—need?" Richard asked.

I let out a long breath. *Yeah, a fully functional leg.* "Just a nap."

He nodded.

"Thanks for the chair. It's great," I said, feeling guilty at how they'd had to change their lives to accommodate me once again.

"We needed a new one," Brenda piped up, which was a lie since now the symmetry of the room was totally off balance. Brenda would figure out how to fix that—but not anytime soon. "Would you like me to draw the drapes?"

I shook my head. "I'm good. I just need to crash."

Brenda made a grab for something on the coffee table and pressed it into my right hand; a little brass bell. "Just give a ring if you need anything, okay?"

I could have used a trip to the john, but things weren't dire, and really, it was getting difficult to keep my eyes open. I pushed back farther in the chair until it was in the full reclining position. "I feel rotten putting you guys to so much trouble."

"It's no trouble at all," Richard said, but again, I knew a lie when I heard it. At that moment, there was nothing I could do to alleviate the problem, and that's just what I had become to them once again: a big fucking problem. The thought made my throat constrict, but before I could say anything, I'd fallen into an exhausted sleep.

I awoke with a start, realizing someone was holding my hand.

"It's okay," said a familiar voice. "It's just me."

Maggie—my lady of two years.

She'd been a regular visitor at the hospital, but had never stayed long. Same with my friend Dave, whose visits I'd come to dread. He felt terrible about my accident, blaming himself, which was just ridiculous. It was an accident. *Period.* He wouldn't listen to me. When he wasn't apologizing, he was talking about life at the bar. How our boss, Tom Link, had been interviewing potential bartenders to take my place. I didn't like the sound of that, either. But there was no way I was going to be able to go back to work for at least two months—and it wasn't likely there'd be a job for me until I was able to stand on my own two feet for several hours on end. The thought depressed the hell out of me and I tried to put it out of my mind.

"Brenda says supper's going to be ready in a while. Do you need anything right now?" Maggie said.

I wanted to stop hurting. I wanted to be whole again. I wanted the past few days to have been just a terrible nightmare that I'd awaken from and all would be well.

"No, thanks."

I still hadn't gone to the can, but I got the feeling Maggie wasn't going to be too interested in taking me there. Or rather, helping me once I got there.

I pushed myself up into a sitting position, which made the situation all the more urgent. Maggie removed her hand from mine. "I guess I should hit the can." I could see by the angle of the sun that I'd slept far later than I'd expected.

"Sure." Maggie stood. Back at the hospital, she had at least learned the basics of helping me to stand, and had my crutches at the ready. Too bad the doorways were the narrow standard of the nineteen twenties; it would've been cool to zoom around the floor in one of those motorized scooters, but it was going to be crutches or nothing.

Maggie followed me out of the room but stopped me. "You're going the wrong way."

I craned my neck to take her in.

"The powder room's over there," she insisted.

"There's not enough room for me to maneuver. I'll have to head for Brenda's craft room."

She nodded. We continued down the hall that led to the kitchen, where Brenda was stationed at the counter making a salad, and CP was strapped in her highchair, taking a snooze.

"Hey, sleepyhead," Brenda called. "It's about time you

woke up. Want a beer?"

"A real one?" I asked.

"Well, no. Non-alcoholic. But you can pretend."

"Maybe later. I'm heading for the bathroom."

"I spread your meds out on the dresser. You're in line for a pain pill if you want it."

Did I ever. "Thanks."

I nodded and hobbled through the butler's pantry and into Brenda's craft room. I noticed and stopped in front of a newly installed dresser and pulled open a drawer. Brenda had already filled it with clothes—none of which I recognized. There seemed to be about a dozen pairs of shorts and sweatpants, and I guessed that would be my wardrobe for the foreseeable future. I'd have to thank her. She'd gone to a lot of trouble to accommodate me.

Leaning half on the crutches and half against the dresser, I shook out a pain pill. Once in the bathroom, I washed it down with water. Maggie hung back while I took care of business, and seemed antsy to get back to a part of the house that wouldn't be used as a sickroom. Truth be told, I felt the same way.

We made it back to the kitchen and found Richard had joined Brenda and had made himself a drink. "What can I get you, Maggie?"

"A G and T will work fine."

"We're going to have dinner in the dining room. Would you like to have your drinks there or in the living room?"

Everyone looked at me, and I felt like a pinned bug. "The living room, I guess."

"Go on in, and I'll bring them out," Richard said.

"Can I help you with anything, Brenda?" Maggie asked, sounding just a little desperate. Thanks to my funny feelings, I can tune into Maggie pretty well, but I wasn't sure what was going on with her just then. I wasn't sure I wanted to, because it didn't exactly feel good.

"If you want, you can set the table."

"Sure thing."

"I'll meet you in the living room as soon as I finish Maggie's drink," Richard said.

I nodded, heading in that direction.

I'd barely gotten settled in the recliner by the time my brother arrived with my so-called beer. He handed it to me. "Thanks."

He sat down on the couch, took a look around the room, and frowned. He didn't like the furniture placement, either. He sipped his scotch. "You mentioned something at the hospital the day of your accident. Something about a tombstone."

"Yeah," I said, and took a swig of my pseudo beer and fought against a grimace. It wasn't very good. "I saw it a few times before and several times since that day."

"What does it mean?"

"I have no idea. I'm thinking it might be a while before I have an opportunity to figure it out, too."

"Do you know where this tombstone is?"

I thought about it. "Not exactly."

"Have you ever been there before?"

"Maybe."

"You don't sound at all sure."

"I'm not. But once these things start, they keep bugging me until I figure them out."

"Maybe when you're feeling up to it, we can take a drive around the cemeteries you and Dave rode your bikes through."

"Maybe," I said. The thought of ever riding a bicycle again didn't exactly thrill me. "Have we heard from the cops about the accident?"

Richard took another sip of his drink. "Not since the first time I spoke with them. Unfortunately, my guess is it's not a high priority."

"That's occurred to me, too."

We sipped our drinks. The silence felt awkward.

"By the way, Dave called," Richard said at last. "He wants you to call him. I guess Tom hired someone to take your shifts."

"It was bound to happen," I said, and wished the damn pain pill would kick in. My leg hurt so much, and in two different spots, and I wondered if I'd be able to eat the dinner Brenda had gone to such trouble to prepare. I changed the subject, looking on the bright side. "I'm so glad to be out of that lousy hospital."

"Now, now—you got great care."

"But it wasn't home. And as much as you guys have done for me—and I sincerely appreciate it—when can I go home to my cat?"

"At least six weeks," Richard said, but he didn't face me. He didn't seem all that crazy about the idea of me being his guest for the bulk of the summer, either.

"That's an awfully long time for Herschel to be separated from me."

"It'll go by in the blink of an eye."

Considering the time I'd spent in the hospital had gone by at glacial speed, I doubted that. I glanced at the clock on the mantle. It was just after seven and I wondered how long it would be before I could make my excuses and hit the sack. But what if I couldn't sleep? There was no TV in my recovery room. At the hospital, I'd left the TV on all night long so that when I awoke—which seemed like every fifteen minutes or so—I could flip channels until I found something to interest me, and then conk out for a few minutes before waking with a start once again. There wasn't even a book or magazine to help pass time in Brenda's craft room.

The next couple of months looked pretty damned bleak indeed.

"Supper's ready!" Brenda called from the open doorway, then turned and disappeared.

"We'd better go," Richard said and stood. He took the half-empty bottle from me and picked up and handed me my crutches. God, how I hated those damn aluminum sticks. That I had to depend on them for the next six to eight weeks made me loathe them even more.

I made my way to the seldom-used dining room. The overly bright chandelier over the table scorched my retinas. "Where should I plop?"

Richard shrugged. "Anywhere."

I plunked down on the next-to-last seat on the right side and somehow managed to maneuver my injured leg onto the chair where Richard's wizened grandfather used to sit at the head of the table. Richard took the seat where his nasty grandmother had resided at the west end of the table. Brenda came in with Betsy on her hip once more, while Maggie hauled in the highchair. The baby's chair went on Richard's left.

It took another couple of minutes to bring all the food to the table, and then the passing of bowls and platters commenced. Again, the conversation was virtually nil as we chowed down. I still couldn't understand what was going on with Maggie, but maybe it was because the pain pill had begun to kick in.

Something felt wrong—very wrong—but then everything felt wrong from the time the handlebars of my bike got snagged by that damn SUV.

I had a feeling it was going to take an awfully damn long time for things to feel right again.

THREE

I didn't catch up with Dave at the bar for another couple of days. I just didn't feel like calling him. Thanks to damn Vicodin, I didn't feel like doing much of anything except lying in that recliner with the TV on. The pills made me feel all gummed up, but going without them made me feel even worse.

Maggie called me a couple of times a day, but seemed distracted—or maybe it was me who couldn't focus. The days ran into one another with no real start or end.

I waited until dinner that night to broach the subject so near to Dave's heart; me checking out my replacement at the bar. That night, Brenda made scampi, but my stomach roiled at the thought of garlic, so my evening meal consisted of buttered slices of Italian bread and a bite or two of salad.

"Are you doing anything tonight, Rich?"

My brother's gaze seemed focused on his plate, but he'd only been toying with his entrée. I don't glom onto what he thinks or feels like I do with so many others, but I could tell he'd been preoccupied by something for days and that whatever it was had been eating at him. No doubt he'd kept it to himself to spare me, but I didn't need coddling. Maybe we'd get to it later, but first I needed to placate Dave.

"What have you got in mind?"

"Dave's pretty upset because Tom hired a woman to

take my place at the bar."

"Male chauvinist pig," Brenda muttered, and stabbed a grape tomato in her salad.

"I don't think so. Dave's sister is a Special Ed teacher in the Iroquois School District and he couldn't be more proud of her. He even speaks well of his ex-wife."

"Then what's the problem?" Richard asked.

I shrugged and offered a wry smile. "He said that woman gives off bad vibes."

"That I can understand," Brenda said. She too had a smidge of what she called 'the second sight.' Not as pronounced as my own so-called gift, but enough to make even Richard a believer.

"I wouldn't mind a night out of harness," he said.

"Oh, yeah?" Brenda asked. So far, she'd been my primary caregiver, as well as taking care of CP and the house.

"I'm not sure I could stay much more than half an hour," I said, "but I'd like to go—if only to shut Dave up."

"Brenda?" Richard asked.

"You don't need my permission," she said, but the three of us knew that wasn't exactly true. Still, I was happy she wasn't opposed to us having an abbreviated boys night out.

It was just after eight when the two of us left the house and I wedged myself into the front seat of Richard's Mercedes. It wasn't comfortable because I had to recline the seat in order to accommodate my leg, but I hadn't taken my scheduled pain pill because I wanted to be acutely aware of what was going on at The Whole Nine Yards. I'd probably be sorry about that decision, but I was also curious to learn about the person who had superseded me.

Richard pulled up to the driveway in front of the bar's parking lot and stopped. "Do you want to get out here?"

Since it was easier to hobble an extra ten or twenty feet than struggle out of the car on my own, I shook my head. "Grab the handicapped spot in the lot and we'll go from there." I grabbed the red temporary parking tag Richard had acquired on my behalf, ready to hang it from the rearview mirror, but the spot was taken by an illegally parked Jeep. We ended up leaving the car two blocks out. He helped me get out of the car, handed me my crutches, and we started down the sidewalk.

During the past two years, my schedule at The Whole Nine Yards had pretty much been in flux depending on Dave's whims. He'd worked for our boss, Tom, for nearly ten years. Tips were better on the weekends, so Dave worked those evening hours. He also worked the more lucrative evening shifts on days when there were likely to be more customers. It wasn't fair, but that was the way it was. If I didn't have a wealthy brother who cut me tons of slack, I'd have been up shit's creek.

Then again, the sliding schedule had actually worked to my advantage, since I might have to call in sick if I got one of my skull-pounding headaches thanks to the mugging that had nearly killed me a little over two years before. But they'd diminished with the ever expanding span of time between them.

A creeping uneasiness began to inch up my spine as we approached the bar's front door. We could hear boisterous laughter and saw the bar was packed, which was unusual for a Tuesday night.

"I'll get the door," Richard said, and held it open as I staggered up the steps and into the tavern. The joint was really hopping. All the stools at the bar were full, as were a majority of tables. Both of the big-screen TVs were tuned to competing baseball games, with the sound off and closed-captioning on, while satellite radio played adult-contemporary music booming from a stereo on a newly installed shelf on the western wall.

"Hey, Jeff!" called my boss, Tom, from across the crowded room. He had to elbow his way through the mob to join us. "Hey, how ya doin'?" he asked, taking in my cast, brace, and crutches.

"Better," I had to practically shout.

"Hey, Richard," he greeted my sibling, who nodded in return.

"Siddown, siddown," Tom encouraged me, but we had to struggle to find a place to perch. Richard took my crutches and stood them against the nearest wall before he took his seat. "Let me get you guys a couple of beers. Be right back." He turned and made his way through the throng once more.

My mouth had gone incredibly dry and I felt a little queasy, but it had nothing to do with my fractured bones or psychic vibrations.

"Wow," Richard said, his expression subdued. "I've never seen the place so busy."

"Yeah. Me, either." My gaze traveled to the bar where a pretty brunette with bared shoulders covered in lacy black tattoos stood in my usual spot, pouring Pilsner glasses of draft. She seemed to be keeping up with a conversation or two as she worked. She set three glasses of amber on a tray and handed it to Tom. Seconds later, he rejoined us, setting the beers on the table in front of us and taking one for himself. He sat down.

"Can you believe this?" He grinned as he took in the crowded room.

"Business sure has picked up," I agreed, but it didn't make me feel good.

Tom positively beamed. "It's all because of Maria." He gestured toward the bar. "When she interviewed, she told me if I hired her she'd bring her clientele with her. Business is up over two hundred percent."

"You've made other changes." Richard indicated the stereo.

"Yeah, and there's more in the pipeline. Maria has lots of great ideas."

I took a look around the place and didn't see one familiar face. Not even Tom's cronies, whose ass cheeks had molded permanent dents in the padded bar stools over the years.

"Doesn't Dave usually work evenings?" Richard asked and took a sip of his beer.

"Maria's customers are night people. We haven't closed the bar before two since she came onboard. We went to four on Saturday night."

I usually never had to work beyond one—or after Tom had closed the place if it emptied out before that.

"I may end up hiring someone else in the evening when the traffic is heaviest."

I swallowed. Although the possibility had loomed, I now realized that my days working at The Whole Nine Yards were effectively over. I had no charisma. No one ever came to the bar because I was there—except the occasional visit from Richard or my friend, Sam Nielsen, from *The Buffalo News*—which was inconsequential compared to the business Maria attracted.

Tom looked back to the bar and caught my replacement's gaze. He raised his glass in a toast. She gave him a nod and her smile was positively predatory.

I finally picked up my glass and immediately let go after getting hit with a stinging blast of—something.

The glass shattered—splashing beer and hunks of glass everywhere.

"Whoa!" Tom called, as a stream of the brew cascaded off the table and onto his lap. "Have you had a few too many already?" he said and laughed nervously.

"God, Tom—I'm sorry!"

There was nothing to mop up the mess, and Tom was already on his feet, heading for the bar to get some napkins.

Richard looked at me critically. "What happened?"

I had to swallow a couple of times before I could answer. "I felt something when I touched that glass. Something very not nice. Tom was the last to hold it, but it wasn't his aura I was reading."

Richard's gaze flicked to the bar and Maria and back again. "Touch a piece of it again."

"No."

"Why?"

"Because it was creepy."

"Touch it," he insisted.

"You touch it."

"Don't be a wimp—touch the damn thing, and fast. Before Tom gets back."

I did, laying a finger on the biggest chunk of glass—hoping the shock wouldn't be as great—and a shudder of revulsion cascaded through me.

"What?" Richard persisted, but Tom had returned with a replacement beer and a fistful of paper napkins and mopped up the mess. They were embossed in gold with the name of the bar and a logo of a football goalpost with a ball sailing through it. Another of Maria's bright ideas?

Tom tossed the sopping napkins onto the tray that still sat on the table. Like Richard, he eyed me critically. It seemed as though he wanted to quiz me on what had just happened, but then he seemed to reconsider. I wasn't even sure how to interpret what I'd felt when touching that glass. On more than one occasion Tom seemed to allude to my empathic—psychic ... whatever it was—ability, but had never come right out and talked about it. He'd been damned kind to me during the past two years, but there was no way he was going to trade the jump in income to make a space for me, and I guess I couldn't blame him. My misfortune—the accident—had been his very good luck.

I forced a smile and grabbed one of the unused napkins, wrapped it around the glass and raised it, feeling heartsick. "To the future."

Tom's eyes practically glowed as he clinked his glass against mine. "May it be lucrative."

Funny ... I didn't see much of a future for him at all.

"So?" Richard asked as he pulled away from the curb and looked for a place to make a U-turn. He didn't have to elaborate.

"That bitch who took my job is bad news."

Richard made a left into a side street, did a K-turn, and then drove up to Main Street and turned right. "Tom can't fire you because of your accident. That's illegal."

"But he isn't going to want me back, either. Dave is already sweating bullets—worrying that he's the next to go."

"What did he tell you the last time you talked?"

"That he hates the bitch." I shook my head. "He feels guilty about me getting hit by that SUV—and guilty because he feels relieved it didn't happen to him instead."

"What do you think about that?"

I shrugged—not that Richard could see. "It wasn't his fault. It just happened."

Richard braked for a red light. "Let's get back to the bitch bartender. What was it you felt when you picked up that glass?"

That was a hard question to answer. "It's not clear to me. I might have to think about it some more." I paused. "Or not at all. I mean ... I'm never going to work there again."

"Are you sure?"

"Yeah," I said sadly. "And once again I've become a giant turd of a problem to you, Rich, and I'm sorry. God-damn I'm sorry." I had to swallow a bunch of times so that I didn't start bawling. Why the hell had I bought that stupid racing bike? Why the hell couldn't I have just let well enough alone and kept plugging away? I gazed down in the darkness to where my cast resided, but couldn't focus on it in the dim light and the blur of tears that threatened to overtake me.

A hand rested on my shoulder. "Don't be so damned hard on yourself," Richard said kindly. "You know, we're kind of in the same boat."

I took a ragged breath. "Oh, yeah?"

He nodded. The light went green and he hit the gas. "I haven't mentioned it to you, but, I've kind of been looking for a job."

"A job?"

"Yeah. I've got a headhunter and everything. But the thing is—nobody wants me. I'm too friggin' old."

"You're not old," I countered automatically, but the truth was at fifty his chances of getting hired at any place other than the likes of Walmart were against him.

"Yeah, I'm not old—except to potential employers," he said bitterly.

"You—of all people—don't need to work," I pointed out.

"Need and want are two different things."

"I thought you enjoyed your volunteer job at the hospital foundation."

"I do, but that's five or ten hours a month—not nearly enough to keep me occupied."

"So what can you do?"

We must have driven half a mile before he answered. "I was thinking...." He stopped again. We drove another couple of blocks.

"What?" I demanded.

"Just don't blow me off without considering what I have to say."

"Which is?"

"What do you think of the two of us going into business together?"

I blinked. Talk about coming in from left field. "And do what?"

"Consulting."

"On what?"

"Cold cases."

I blinked again. "Cold police cases?"

His gaze remained fixed on the road. "I'm not sure, but that might be a place for us to start."

I couldn't believe what I was hearing. "Explain."

"Well, look what you did for Paula Devlin."

Paula had been one of Richard's patients at the low-income clinic where he'd volunteered the year before. Her son had gone missing. He'd asked me to meet her to see if my insight might prove useful in finding the boy. Yeah—I'd found the kid in less than an hour, whereas the cops had been stumped for almost eight months.

"And what roles do we play?"

"Well, you're a trained investigator. Your specialty was crime scenes. And you've got special insight. That could be a big plus."

"And what about you?"

"I'm an experienced researcher. And I'm good at logistics."

"He said modestly," I commented.

"I'm well aware of my strengths and weaknesses. Yours, too."

Oh, yeah? "And where do we find clients? Hang out a shingle?"

"We'd have to offer our services gratis for a while—until we acquire a reputable reputation—but I don't see a problem."

No? I could see all kinds of problems, but I wasn't about to mention them just then. "Sounds like you've put a lot of thought into this."

He braked for the red light at the top of LeBrun Road and flicked the car's left turn signal—not that there was anyone around to see it. "I keep remembering what your friend Sophie told me."

Richard had met my psychic mentor once—and only once—the year before. She'd told him that the two of us were destined to work together. I hadn't taken that to mean a financial alliance, since all the investigating I'd done since my return to Buffalo had been related to the weird vibes I'd felt, and most of the time were related to death and destruction. It wasn't exactly fun to experience, and those flashes of insight often brought on painful consequences in the way of skull-pounding headaches. But ... what else was I capable of doing?

Richard never had to work another day in his life, but I knew it wasn't just boredom that gnawed at him. He needed a purpose above that of being a husband and father. Having a purpose? I hadn't had the luxury of that aspiration. Since the mugging, I'd downgraded my life's goal to just making it through another day, another week, another month, another year.

"What does Brenda think about this?"

"I haven't mentioned it to her yet."

"And why's that?"

It was his turn to shrug.

I had a feeling she might not be happy with this great idea. After all, so far Richard had been a victim of repeated collateral damage due to my crime-fighting sprees.

It was all too much to take in right then and our boys-night-out foray had exhausted me. "I'm sorry, Rich, but I don't think I'm capable of wrapping this idea of yours around my brain right now."

"Of course not," Richard agreed as the light turned green and he turned for home. "And I won't push it."

"I appreciate that." Still, he'd given me a lot to think about. A hell of a lot.

Richard pulled into the driveway. It seemed as though every light in the house was ablaze and almost immediately Brenda darted out the back door. "Did you have a good time?" she asked after yanking open the car door. She saw that my crutches were in the back and grabbed them before helping me exit the car.

"It was weird," I admitted.

She frowned. "Well, I'm not surprised." She patted my shoulder and followed a step behind me, holding the door for me to enter the house. I paused in the butler's pantry. To the left was the kitchen—to the right my temporary digs.

"Are you okay?" Brenda asked, concern evident in her tone.

"Yeah. I'm just really tired. It's been a long day. I think I'll turn in early."

"It's probably a good idea," she agreed.

I shuffle-hopped to the door of Brenda's craft room. It was embarrassing to have to have help to get up in the morning and ready for bed. As an RN, Brenda was used to patient care and she and Richard traded off helping me with such tasks.

I aimed for the day bed, which had already been turned down. I backed up and pulled down my sweatpants, letting them fall to the floor before I sat. Brenda crouched before me and I lifted my legs so she could tug them off.

"I'm sorry you have to do this," I said yet again, embarrassed.

"Shut up." She collected my pants and stuffed them into the hamper.

"Do you need help going to the john?"

"I only had one sip of beer."

She placed the plastic urinal next to the bed. "Your little buddy is here if you need it."

I felt my cheeks grow hotter. "Thanks." I changed the subject. "Brenda, how long has Rich been looking for a job?"

"He finally told you about it?"

I nodded.

She sighed. "Almost six weeks."

I felt bad that he hadn't felt comfortable sharing that with me. And why was that?

"What do you think about it?"

She hesitated. "I guess I can understand it. Right now I'm happy being a wife and mommy, but once Betsy goes to school I'll be beating the bushes to find a job, too."

I nodded again.

She turned for the dresser and pulled out a T-shirt, handing it to me to use as a sleep shirt. "Do you need anything else? Cocoa? A hot toddy? Something to eat?"

Again I shook my head. "No, thanks."

She bent down and kissed me on the cheek. "I love you, Jeffy."

"I love you, too. See you in the morning."

"I was thinking about making oatmeal for breakfast."

I frowned, remembering the sticky goo old Mrs. Alpert used to make me eat.

"It'll have raisins, and you can put real maple syrup on it if you want."

"Okay," I said, resigned. Oatmeal was supposed to be good for you.

She switched on the bedside lamp. "Sleep well." She hit the switch that turned off the overhead light as she left the room and closed the door.

Brenda had installed one of Betsy's baby monitors in the room and I could see that she'd switched it on once again. She was worried that I might fall in the night. I appreciated her concern, but saw it as another infringement on my privacy. I turned it down to next to nothing. Did they need to hear me fart and snore during the night? That would be a big no! I kept my replacment cell phone close at hand. If I fell, I could call them and I would. Well, maybe.

I stripped off my shirt, tossed it on the floor out of reach of tripping me, and donned the T-shirt, then strained to haul my legs up and onto the bed. Once in, I knew I wasn't going to move for many long hours. I usually slept on my stomach, but the cast made that too difficult.

I turned off the light and the soft glow of a night light Brenda had installed between the bed and the bathroom illuminated the gloom. She was a great mommy—much better than the one I'd had. I didn't bother to pull the covers over me. The house was warm. Maybe in the middle of the night I'd need them, but not now.

I stared at the dark ceiling above me and my thoughts turned back to Richard's proposition. Could we be an effective team? Yeah, he'd been right. We both had strengths. We worked well together. But could we make a living at solving cold cases?

From his perspective, it didn't matter. He had money up the wazoo. If we went into business together, would it end up being a hobby for him; something to keep him busy, but no real income. And would I end up living on his generosity only? I hated that idea. But then … he didn't give a shit about money. If he had to support me for the rest of my life, it wasn't something he worried about.

Was it time for me to make a major mind shift? Should I look at this business deal Richard offered as some kind of karmic payback? In many ways, I'd had the shittiest luck in recorded history, and yet what if I could pay forward the good luck I'd had with being reunited with my brother? If I couldn't bring back someone's long missing, or dead relative, friend, or lover, perhaps together Richard and I could bring closure to people who'd waited years—maybe decades—for justice.

The image of the tombstone on the grassy knoll flashed once again before my mind's eye.

That was it, nothing more. Virtually nothing to go on.

Who did it belong to? How had he or she died? What would it cost me—in time and emotional involvement—to look into it? Could Richard help me find out what was behind the vision?

Could investigating that image be our first cold case?

I had a feeling pondering those questions might keep me awake for some time.

Richard sat at the kitchen table, waiting for Brenda to return. As soon as he'd parked the car in the garage, he'd entered the house and headed for the Scotch bottle. What the heck; he hadn't finished his beer at the bar and he needed a shot of courage to bring up the whole idea of going into business with Jeff.

He hadn't done more than wet his lips when a somber Brenda returned to the kitchen.

"Is Jeff all tucked in for the night?"

She nodded and took her usual seat at the table. "He seemed really down and didn't have a lot to say."

"Yeah." This time he took a real sip of that fine breath of the heather.

"He said he only had one sip of beer."

"That's right," Richard agreed, "and I didn't have much more."

"Did something bad go down?"

"The woman his boss hired to take Jeff's job seems to have taken over. The place was jammed—all people she brought in. Tom's probably making money hand over fist and Jeff's sure he's lost his job. He thinks Dave will be the next to go. Worse, he freaked just touching the glass the woman held."

"Surely he'll be able to find another job."

"I don't know. Tom cut him a lot of slack. The odds of finding a job with that kind of flexibility could be hard—if not impossible."

Brenda scrutinized his face, and her expression wasn't at all encouraging. "You've got something on your mind," she practically accused.

"I do," he admitted. "And tonight I shared my bright idea with Jeff, but now I see I should have run it by you first, because if you don't approve, then nothing will come of it."

Brenda's expression darkened. "Start talking."

Richard took another fortifying sip of Scotch. "It's become obvious to me that ageism is alive and well in America. I've had twelve interviews for jobs in the last six weeks and not one of the companies are going to hire me—no matter what my capabilities. So, this last week I've been trying to think outside of the box."

"I hate that expression," Brenda commented.

"I'm not fond of it, either, but it does convey the idea that what once worked no longer does."

"So what are you proposing?" Brenda asked, sounding none too friendly.

"That Jeff and I go into business together."

"And do what?" The edge in her voice grew sharper.

"Become consultants."

"On what subject?"

"Well, that's the thing. Crime, most likely. Jeff is a skilled investigator, and I'm an experienced researcher."

"And you'd do what?"

"Investigate cold cases."

"How cold?" she demanded.

"I don't know."

"What kind of time commitment are you talking about?"

He shrugged. "I don't even know if the idea is viable."

"And what's the danger factor?"

"Danger?"

"Yes. Since Jeffy came home to Buffalo, you've been shot, exposed to HIV; someone died in our backyard; people were killed in your car, and your boat was destroyed. What other calamities are we going to have to face?"

That all did sound terribly negative.

"As I mentioned, my thought was that we'd concentrate on cold cases. Cases where the cops have no leads, and that Jeff's special insight might prove useful."

"How old a cold case?" Brenda asked again.

"The older the better, because there's less likely to be pushback."

"Pushback?" Brenda asked.

"Danger," he admitted, using her descriptor.

Brenda nodded, her gaze fixed on the table in front of them.

Richard sipped his Scotch.

The refrigerator's motor kicked in, making a bit of a racket.

The quartz clock on the wall ticked loudly.

Brenda sighed. "What does it matter what I think?"

"Of course it matters. If you say no, then we'll figure out something else to do."

Brenda's gaze shifted to the floor. "It's not just you and me to consider. It's Betsy I'm worried about. Have you considered what this could mean to us as a family?"

"That's why I think we should concentrate on old—*really* old—cases."

"And where would you find these cases?"

"Probably via the cops."

Brenda chewed at her bottom lip for long seconds. "Is there likely to be any money in this?"

Richard's gaze dropped to his drink. "Not really."

"Jeffy is a proud man. He hates being the recipient of charity."

"Yeah, I know."

"Cold cases—old cases—aren't likely to be hot commodities. This sounds more like a hobby than a career—and don't you think that's what Jeffy longs for?"

"I agree it might be an adjustment for him to make."

"Because he wants to support himself. He doesn't want to have to rely on you forever."

"I thought about that. I don't care if we make a living doing this, as long as we can make a difference—we can help others—what we can offer would be a valuable service."

Brenda shook her head, and Richard's gut tightened. Why hadn't he talked this over with his wife *before* he'd mentioned it to his brother?

Brenda looked thoughtful.

"Like I said, if you say no—that's it. We're done."

"It feels wrong that you're throwing all this on me now."

"I—we—just need you in our corner. If you're not, then we won't do it. No hard feelings."

"I've heard that before," Brenda muttered. "How long do I have to consider this?"

It was Richard's turn to frown. "To be honest, Jeff seemed a little overwhelmed by the idea. I don't even know if *he's* in. Let's face it, using his psychic abilities isn't something he likes to do. And yet, he's a sucker for hard-luck cases. He's had enough shit thrown at him that he's willing to do what he can to spare another from a similar fate."

Brenda twisted the engagement and wedding rings on her left hand. "I can't stop you from doing whatever you want to do. I wouldn't want to. But you have to put self-preservation above all else or I can't sanction it. And you have to protect Jeffy, too, because he doesn't seem to have a self-preservation chip."

"I swear, I'll look out for all of us."

Brenda nodded. "Then ... I guess I'm okay with this."

"That's good enough for me." Richard reached across the table to take her hand. "Thank you."

Brenda shook her head. "I have a feeling there'll be

days you'll regret ever taking this on."

"That may be, but this feels *right* to me."

She nodded and got up from the table. "I'm going to check on Betsy and then head for bed to read for a while."

"I'll be up soon," he promised.

She bent down to kiss him. "Good night."

Brenda left the kitchen and Richard listened until her footfalls faded.

Now that he more or less had her on his side, he only had to convince his brother.

FOUR

It was Richard's turn to check on me to make sure I'd made it through the night unscathed, and he showed up at my door a little after eight the next morning. "Ready for some breakfast?"

I'd been awake for more than an hour—bored out of my skull. Anything was a welcome diversion. "Sure."

I hoped Brenda was kidding about serving oatmeal for breakfast, but when I came to the table there it was; gray, sticky, and totally unappetizing. Even the lure of raisins and maple syrup couldn't raise its appeal.

I propped my broken leg up on the extra chair while Richard stood the front section of the newspaper against his coffee mug and absently dug into his bowl. Meanwhile, Betsy banged her sippy cup on the tray of her highchair and seemed to be trying to mimic a hit from Sesame Street.

I picked up my spoon, took a small bite of oatmeal, and shuddered. Disgusting. I put my spoon back down.

"Coffee?" Brenda offered.

"Yes, please."

Seconds later, a steaming cup of joe sat before me, already doctored the way I like it. I took a tentative sip. Too hot. I set the cup back down. "Um, Rich, what we talked about last night—or rather, didn't talk about," I began.

Richard looked up from the newspaper. "Brenda and I discussed it. She's okay with it. How about you?"

I looked over at Brenda, who stood by the counter sipping her coffee. She nodded, but didn't look at all enthusiastic.

I looked back to my brother. "I'm not sure I want to commit."

Richard's hopeful expression disappeared.

"There's an awful lot to talk about," I continued.

"I've got all day," he offered.

Yeah, and I had nothing else to do, either. Except....

"Maybe we should try a sample case and see where it goes before we talk about this to the world at large."

"What did you have in mind?"

"Remember I told you about that flash I keep getting about a tombstone?"

He nodded.

"Maybe that's a place to start."

"I'm listening," he said sounding cautious. "Have you figured out where to find it?"

"Something tells me I need to go to Forest Lawn Cemetery."

"That hardly narrows it down. The place is massive."

"Yeah. But I have a feeling that I could find it ... if we drove around long enough."

"The gas tank's full."

"I don't know if we'll find what I'm looking for, but maybe we can talk while I look."

"Then it's a plan," he said, sounding more optimistic.

I nodded and my gaze sank back to the bowl of pseudo barf before me.

"You don't have to eat it," Richard said.

"It would be wasteful not to." I picked up my spoon and let out a shaky breath, wondering if I might gag if I had to eat the entire bowl.

Then suddenly Brenda swooped in and grabbed my breakfast. "I'm sorry, Jeffy. I thought if I made oatmeal the way I like it, then you might, too. You can have anything you want."

"Even Eggs Benedict?"

"That would be a stretch," she admitted.

"Then how about a couple of pieces of dry white toast."

It was Brenda's turn to shudder. "If that's what you want."

"Sounds like heaven to me."

"Then dry white toast it is."

"Ja-Ja!" Betsy called, and gave the sippy cup another good whack on the tray before her.

"Atta girl, Betsy," Richard called, and all four of us laughed. But I had a feeling I wouldn't be laughing when Richard and I went to Forest Lawn later that morning. Still, I wasn't going to dwell on it, either. I picked up my coffee cup as Brenda pushed the lever down on the toaster and smiled. It felt good to be in that kitchen surrounded by three of the four people I loved most on the planet.

The crap I had yet to endure could wait a few hours.

Getting in and out of Richard's Mercedes was a major pain in the ass. Once again, I nixed the idea of lounging on the back seat. It wasn't exactly comfortable, but it worked.

Richard took the same route to Forest Lawn as Dave and I had traversed on the day of my accident. I found myself swallowing a lot as we approached the intersection of Fillmore and Kensington Avenues, but Richard had Vivaldi's *Four Seasons* playing on the Mercedes' sound system—his good luck/most favorite piece of music—and since we didn't have to stop at the light, I got past it without a meltdown.

To distract myself further, I decided to bring up a not-so-popular subject and lowered the volume on Vivaldi.

After all, if Richard wanted me onboard for his little entrepreneurial plan, it might be time to do a little negotiation on terms.

"I was just wondering," I said, trying to sound innocent, "why you don't like Herschel."

"Herschel?" He said the name as though he'd never heard it before. "Oh, you mean your cat."

I nodded.

"I don't dislike it."

"*Him.*"

"Him."

"Then why can't he come stay with me while I recover?"

Richard's gaze remained on the road, but I could see the muscles around his jaw tighten. "It's because of Betsy."

Liar.

"Cats have been known to sleep on infants' faces and smother them."

"That's an urban legend. Name one incident."

"Of course I don't know anyone who's personally experienced it. I'm sure if I Googled it I could come up with a handful." He braked for the next light.

"I'm in cast prison," I said looking down at my lower leg, "but Herschel has been sentenced to solitary confinement until I can go back to my apartment."

"Brenda goes over to feed him twice a day."

"Yeah, and probably spends an entire five minutes with him."

"She has a house and a baby to take care of. And now you," he rather pointedly reminded me.

Like I *asked* to be in that situation. If it weren't for the damn stairs that led to my apartment over the garage, I could take care of myself. It wouldn't be easy, but I'd taken care of myself for eighteen years before I'd been bonked on the head by a baseball bat and had to once again depend on Richard.

I decided not to press it. I'd wait for a better time to push my own agenda.

As we approached the cemetery, Richard asked. "So, how are you going to play this? As a human Geiger counter?"

"It's worked before."

He nodded. "Say you get some insight on a dead person who needs an intervention; what do you intend to do?"

"I've made a few contacts with cops since I've been back in Buffalo—"

"You mean Detectives Hayden and Wilder?"

"Yeah. They vouched for me with Detective Baldwin down in Manhattan. If I ask nicely, they may be able to introduce me—us—to cops in other jurisdictions, depending on what I learn today. If I learn anything."

"Do you get the feeling this is a cold case?"

I thought about it. "Yeah. Pretty damn cold. Like multiple decades cold."

"I like the sound of that. I told Brenda we wouldn't look into current cases. She's concerned that we could put ourselves in harm's way. But if you're talking about a crime that happened closer to a century ago, then there can't be anyone alive who could come after us."

"One would think."

Richard frowned. "You think otherwise?"

"I don't know what to think. I don't even know if we'll come across anything of interest. Right now I just have a gut feeling. Unfortunately, I've been mistaken before," I reminded him. Yeah. When I'd thought I'd come across a couple of bodies buried in a yard, when in actuality it was cremains that had been scattered.

We approached the corner of Delaware and Delavan Avenues and Forest Lawn's southwest gate and Richard drove right in. "Do you want to go in the Main Office?"

I shook my head. "I don't want to get out of the car until I absolutely have to. But maybe they have a map of the place."

"I'll go inside and see." Richard pulled the car into a parking spot, killed the engine, and got out.

I sank back in my seat, closed my eyes, and tried to glom onto whatever feeling I might perceive. Almost instantly, the vision of the headstone came back to me, but it was only visible from the backside. No carvings marred the pristine rose-pink granite. Did the color of the stone indicate the gender of the person buried beneath the monument?

Yeah.

Okay, it was a woman who had died ... but how? And when?

Richard returned with a couple of brochures, one of which unfolded into a big four-color map of the vast cemetery. Although it was over a century and a half old, the graveyard was still accepting new eternal residents.

Richard studied the map, pointing out its legend. "A lot of famous people are buried here. There's Millard Fillmore, our thirteenth president; politician, Shirley Chisholm; Rick James, the punk rock star. There's that Blocher Memorial, and over there is the Darwin Martin grave."

The latter was well known for employing famed architect Frank Lloyd Wright to not only build the long-demolished headquarters for the Larkin Soap Company, but his own now-beautifully restored prairie home on Jewett Parkway, which Maggie and I had visited and I'd taken at least fifty or sixty photos of.

"We should steer there," I said. Yeah, that felt right.

"Okay." Richard started the car, backed out, and turned right.

We drove slowly down the dark ribbon of asphalt and soon came upon Frank Lloyd Wright's Blue Sky Mausoleum. "Wow," Richard said, and braked. "Do you mind if I get out to look?"

"Go ahead." I'd already seen it—and more than once.

He pulled the car off the road, killed the engine, and got out. While he used his phone to snap pictures of the beautiful memorial and the goose pond beyond, I traced my finger over Section H on the map. Things started coalescing in my brain. The tombstone I'd been seeing belonged to a woman. A wife? A daughter? Yes, at least one of them—but at that moment, I wasn't sure which. The more I considered the situation, the more convinced I was that I had to be alone to encounter whatever or whoever I was to connect with. Oh, yeah—Richard was going to love that. Not.

Richard came back to the car, all smiles. "Wow, that was an experience."

"You think that's cool, you should visit all the Frank Lloyd Wright stuff that's available locally. Once my leg heals, I'll babysit so you and Brenda can tour the homes and the boat house."

"I'll take you up on that." He started the car and we took off once again. "Do you want to visit Rick James's grave?"

"I already have," I admitted. "Do you?"

"Not today. Maybe I'll bring Brenda and Betsy here and we'll do the whole self-guided tour."

"Sounds like a plan," I said, distracted. I kept rubbing my fingers over a certain area of the map, which I was pretty sure would reveal pay dirt, although what that motherlode was to deliver was still beyond me.

Up hill and down dale we went until we approached Section H. "You need to slow down."

Richard braked until the Mercedes came to a halt.

"This is it," I said.

He looked around. "Are you sure?"

I nodded.

Richard consulted the map once more. "The Darwin Martin site is just up that branch of the road. Do you want to see it?"

"I already have, but I think I should get out of the car." I pointed across the way to a large white granite bench that doubled as a monument. "I could go sit over there."

Richard nodded, cut the engine, and got out of the car, crossing in front to extricate me from the passenger seat. He leaned me against the car and handed me the crutches. "Do you mind if I take a look at the grave?"

"Sure. Go ahead."

Richard went right, and I hobbled left.

The stone bench resembled a church pew. A greenish lichen had infiltrated any tiny crevice and had spread across the stone. The family's name had been chiseled with pride, although they'd evidently died out for the last burial had been in the nineteen fifties, but the cemetery's maintenance crew kept the grass from growing too high around the memorial.

I sat down on the cold stone, glad the ambient temperature hovered in the mid-seventies, and set my crutches against the armrest. I considered hoisting my broken leg up to rest on the bench, but decided against it. Would I regret that decision later? I wasn't sure. Gravity wasn't my friend and I knew it would ache later in the day if I had to leave it down for too long. The truth was, all of me would ache after this foray, but I knew I needed to be here. I just didn't know why.

My gaze traveled up the road and I watched Richard inspect the Martin gravesite and take a number of pictures with his cell phone before he headed back to join me.

"What happens now?"

"You need to go away for a while."

"No way."

"Yes, way."

"Why?"

"Because if you're here—she won't come."

"She who?"

"I don't know. I haven't met her yet."

"A ghost?"

"A restless spirit," I suggested.

"Who is it?"

"I won't know until I meet her. But I know she won't show up if you're here."

Richard looked around us. There wasn't a living soul in sight—and, as far as I could see, no dead ones, either. It was eerily quiet, too. We were acres and acres away from civilization.

"Are you sure this is a good idea?" Richard asked doubtfully. "I don't like the idea of leaving you alone and helpless."

"I'm not helpless."

"Well, there's no way you could run away if something happened."

"Nothing's going to happen."

He glowered at me. "How long do you think this is going to take?"

"I don't know. But I know nothing's going to happen if you don't leave."

"Where am I supposed to go?"

"Drive around—go back to the cemetery's Main Office. I'll call you when I'm ready to go."

He shook his head again. "I don't like this."

"It's broad daylight. Ghosts aren't supposed to have a lot of power—if they have any at all—then."

"Let's hope you're right." Richard looked back to the car, then to me. "It's against my better judgment, but I guess if we're going to go into business we have to trust each other's decisions."

"I'm not saying I won't listen to your objections in the future, it's just that we're going to have to establish some ground rules, and one of them is that I know how this psychic crap works better than you do."

He nodded. "Okay. I'll circle the cemetery and park just over that hill so I can get here fast if you need my help."

I nodded. "Don't worry. Everything will be fine."

"If you could only promise that," he muttered, turned, and got back in the car. I watched him slowly drive away, sure he was watching me in the rearview mirror. Then the car was out of sight.

The wind rustled the leaves on the large maple behind me. A sparrow hopped around one of the nearby tombstones, picking at the ground, looking for something to eat. I studied my surroundings. No sign of anybody.

The cemetery really was a serene place. I thought back to the morning of the accident and wished Dave and I hadn't had our day—and my life—disrupted. If I'd stopped my bike just twelve or eighteen inches to the left, the SUV wouldn't have hit me, and I wouldn't be stuck in "cast prison."

A wave of frustration—bitterness at my situation—passed through me and I closed my eyes and leaned against the back of the bench. Maybe I'd just sit and soak up my fifteen minutes of sunshine, get my daily requirement of Vitamin D, and then call Richard to come get me.

"Excuse me," a woman said, her voice soft. "Is this seat taken?"

I opened my eyes and turned to see an attractive brunette dressed in old-fashioned attire standing between me and the sun. I had to squint to take her in. She looked like a flapper from a bygone age. "No," I said, and scooched over to the right, glad I hadn't rested my legs across the bench.

She settled at the far end of the cold granite seat, her back to the arm of the stone memorial.

"I'm Alice."

"Hi. I'm Jeff." I didn't offer her my hand.

Her smile was shy and tentative. "I haven't seen you around here before."

"I haven't been here much," I admitted.

"Are you visiting anyone special?" she asked.

"Darwin Martin," I said, and nodded up the lane to where the relatively new craftsman-style obelisk stood. The man had been buried many decades before, and his original headstone had been replaced to commemorate his friendship with the late, great architect Frank Lloyd Wright. "How about you?"

"I'm here on a regular basis," she admitted. "It's so peaceful."

"Yes, it is," I agreed, taking in the nearly silent grounds.

"You broke your leg," she said, glancing down at the cast that poked out of the bottom of the leg of my baggy sweatpants.

"Yeah."

"Does it hurt?"

"Not as much as when it first happened—but I don't sleep well."

"How did you do it?"

"I fell off my bike." I didn't feel the need to go into the details.

"You have a bicycle?" she asked, delighted.

"*Had* a bicycle," I said. "It's pretty much toast."

"I had a bicycle," Alice said, and turned her face to the sun, closing her eyes in what seemed like rapture. "The wind raced through my hair. I pedaled with all my might, and I never felt happier."

"I wish I could say that. I got hit by a car. I'm pretty much done with riding as a sport." I looked over at the crutches that leaned against the side of that cold stone monument. Yeah, I was *really* done with that piece of metal.

Alice ducked her head and seemed to shrink within herself. "You're different than most people who come through here."

"Oh, yeah?" I asked, glancing askance at her.

She nodded. "Most people aren't so...friendly."

Friendly? I'm sure most who knew me wouldn't say I'd ever been particularly outgoing. "Do you talk to many people?"

Alice shook her head. "No, not many. In fact, not anybody for a long, long time."

I had a feeling why.

"Tell me about yourself," I said.

She shrugged. "There's not much to tell. I never had a lot of friends at school—but a few good ones. I didn't have any brothers and sisters. My parents wanted a boy. It was a big disappointment for them."

"I have a half-brother and a half-sister. They were cherished. Me? Not so much." It was what it was, but damn, there was no way I was ever going to reconcile that fact.

"Um," she began, her expression thoughtful. "I'm wondering ... do you know that I'm—"

I turned to look at the pretty face before me. "Do I know that you're dead?"

Alice looked infinitely sad. "Yes."

"Something drew me here. I kind of figured it might be you."

"What do you know about me?"

"Nothing."

"Would you like to know more?" She almost seemed afraid to hear the answer—that I might dismiss her.

"Yes." It was an honest answer.

A grateful smile quirked the corners of her mouth. She stood. "Follow me."

I grabbed my crutches and painfully got to my feet,

then hobbled along behind her.

Alice walked up the road a ways and then turned and ascended a hillock. I sized up the landscape, and the muscles around my chest constricted. Without crutches, the rise wouldn't have been a problem; now, I wasn't so sure. I took a breath to steel myself and made my first tentative steps. It was easier to move, crablike—left foot first and then steadying myself with the right crutch. But the uneven ground conspired against me and after only a few steps, I lost my balance and toppled, slamming against one of the stone monuments before falling hard on my left side. Stars seemed to explode before my eyes as an incredible shock of pain thundered through me, leaving me breathless.

Suddenly Alice was there, kneeling beside me. "Are you all right?"

"Not really," I managed through gritted teeth.

"I'm so sorry," she cried. "I never wanted—I mean, I didn't think—"

"It's okay," I assured her, still trying to catch my breath. I quickly assessed the situation. This was not going to be easy, but it was probably doable. "I think I can scooch up on my—" I was about to say ass, but had a feeling innocent Alice would be offended by such nomenclature. "—butt. I'll have to go up backwards. You'll have to guide me."

"I can do that," she said earnestly.

I wasn't sure if she could hand me the crutches, so I struggled to retrieve them and then sat and thought about my next move for a few moments. "Okay; let's do this."

Alice stood, wringing her hands, and watched as I dug the heel of my left foot into the ground, tried to keep my broken leg—which suddenly seemed to weigh as much as a cement truck—in the air and inched my way up the rise.

Dig in—scooch up. Dig in—scooch up. It became monotonous. My T-shirt was soon drenched in sweat and I felt like I might puke when Alice finally said, "We're there."

Panting, I craned my neck and saw the rose granite already so familiar to me. I had to move a few more feet before I could see the front of the monument. Big bold letters proclaimed NEWCOMB.

"This is your family's plot?"

Alice nodded. She pointed down at her feet. "I'm here. Well, what's left of me."

"And you're not at rest?"

She shook her head. "Not really."

"Can you tell me why?"

Her bottom lip trembled, and her words came out a whisper. "Somebody killed me."

"I'm sorry."

She nodded, and looked embarrassed, as though maybe I might think she'd been careless with her life.

"You don't know who did it?"

She shook her head, her expression infinitely sad.

Was she telling the truth?

"What do you want me to do?"

Alice's gaze met mine. "I'm not sure."

"You've been here a long time—alone. Are you ready to move on?"

"I don't know. But before I can make a decision like that, I have to know what happened to me."

"What was your last conscious thought?"

A smile brightened her features. "All I remember is a feeling of happiness."

"Do you remember if you were alone, and if not, who you were with?"

Her expression darkened. "No. I was alive; I was happy; and then …."

I looked down at the ground. Embedded in the earth

was a rectangular piece of pink granite that proclaimed

DAUGHTER

ALICE

1909-1932

It wasn't much of a testament to the twenty-three years she'd existed on the planet. She'd been dead far longer.

"I need a little more to go on. Can you tell me the date you died?"

Again, she seemed to draw in on herself. "I don't remember."

"Do you remember your birthday?"

"June fourteenth," she said without hesitation.

A shiver rippled through me. "That's today. Happy birthday, Alice."

She looked pleased. "Is today really June fourteenth?"

I nodded.

"Then you must be my birthday present. That is, if you'll help me."

I let out an exhausted breath. "I'd like to try."

"A girl couldn't ask for more." Her eyes were bright—filled with hope. How could a dead woman hope?

"Where did you live?"

"With my parents on Humboldt Parkway. It was a beautiful house. I loved my room. It overlooked our big backyard. Honeysuckle grew up a long white trellis outside my window. It smelled like heaven. My papa was lucky in business—he ran several of them. Times were hard, but for some reason we always seemed to have money. Mama and I had beautiful clothes. Do you like this dress? It was one of my favorites. I'm glad they buried me in it."

The dress was beige, kind of baggy, and didn't seem to have a waist, or if it did, it hung low on her narrow hips. I guess that was the style at the time. Maggie had an array of pastel spaghetti-strap sundresses that were far prettier.

Maybe I'd ask her to wear one the next time she came to visit—and I hoped that would be soon.

"Do you have a girlfriend?" Alice asked, as though she'd been reading my thoughts.

"Yeah."

"Oh." She looked disappointed. "What's her name?"

"Maggie."

"Is she pretty?"

"She is to me. Did you have a boyfriend?"

"I have a beau," she said wistfully. "His name is Joseph Campbell."

"Really? He wasn't into mythology, was he?" I asked, hoping she didn't detect the amusement in my voice.

"What? No, no. He works in a butcher shop."

"And your parents' names?"

"Hiram and Cora Newcomb." She indicated another stone embedded in the ground. There was one for her mother, but a stone for her father was conspicuously absent. I noted the years of birth and death. That would be the starting point of my—and Richard's—investigation.

"Mama went not long after me. I thought we might be reunited, but I never saw her or papa again. Do you think he's still alive?"

She didn't seem to have a clue that she'd died a multitude of decades before.

I shook my head. "No. But maybe you haven't been reunited because you're still earthbound."

"Maybe," Alice agreed. She studied my face. "You don't look well."

Yeah, after taking that tumble, I felt decidedly *unwell*.

"You should probably go home to rest. Will the man who dropped you off come back soon?"

I nodded. "I just have to call him."

She giggled. "How can you do that? There're no drugstores around here."

I leaned back, reached into my pocket, and pulled out

my smart phone. "All I have to do is press this little icon and I can call him."

Alice frowned. "What about the operator?"

"Nobody calls the operator anymore. And I can take photos with this, too."

"Oh! Take mine," Alice cried excited, and smoothed her short brown bob.

I moved the phone to eye level to center on her, but when I looked at the viewfinder, there was nothing but the grass, the sky, and a sea of tombstones. "I'm sorry. The camera doesn't seem to be working today."

"Oh." She shrugged, as though used to being disappointed.

"I'll play with it. Maybe it will work the next time I come to visit you."

Her eyes lit up. "When? When will you come back?"

"In a few days. I have to do some research."

"Do you think you can find out who killed me that fast?"

"I'm sorry, but no. How will I find you when I return?"

Her smile was wistful. "Don't worry. I'll find you." With that, she pressed her fingers to her lips and blew me a kiss, then seemed to dissolve right before my eyes.

I sat there for long seconds, marveling at what had transpired during the previous ten or fifteen minutes until it registered that I felt cold, no doubt from sitting on the damp ground for so long. I looked down at the phone in my hand and pressed the icon to call Richard. He picked up on the first ring.

"Jeff?"

"I've fallen and I can't get up."

"I'll be right there."

FIVE

Richard's Mercedes appeared over the crest of the hill no more than ten seconds after we'd ended the call, but I knew I'd have to call again so he could find me, because I'd used up that day's allotment of energy during the trek to Alice's grave and wasn't up to trying to move under just my own power.

Richard stopped the car in front of the stone bench and my phone trilled. "Go down the road another ten or so feet. I'm up on the hill to the left."

He didn't reply, but the car crept forward.

"Stop!"

The car came to an abrupt halt. "I can't see you."

"But I can see you. I'll talk you through it."

Less than a minute later, Richard stood towering above me. "What the hell happened?"

"I'll tell all once we're in the car, if you'll please help me up."

That was easier said than done. Richard had a good thirty or forty pounds on me, but it was still a struggle for him to pull my dead weight upright, and even with the crutches I had to lean on him far more than I wanted to get back to level ground and the car. By that time, I was sweating yet again, but a cold chill also ran through me.

"You look a mess," he said once he'd climbed behind the wheel of the car.

Yeah, I was grass- and dirt-stained and damp. "I don't feel great, either. I hurt all over. When am I ever going to feel good again, Dr. Alpert?"

"My guess is August—maybe September."

My stomach did a little flip. "You're not kidding, are you?"

He shook his head. "Sorry, no." He started the car and took off slowly, letting me digest that somber piece of news for a minute or so before speaking again. "So, you met the woman?"

"She showed up only a minute or so after you left. My guess is she's been pretty lonely. I don't think ghosts do much socializing."

"So what's she like?" Richard asked, and I wasn't sure if he was curious or creeped out.

"Very nice. Pretty. Her name is Alice. She was twenty-three when she died. She thinks she was murdered, but she didn't give me a lot to go on. Just her birthday—which is today, by the way."

"Are you kidding?"

"Nope. I guess it was destined that we meet on the anniversary of her birth. She told me my arrival was her birthday present."

"That's just weird."

"We need to start keeping paper and pens in our cars to jot down notes. I don't want to forget what I've learned, and once I take that next pain pill—which will be the minute we walk in the door—I'm liable to do just that."

"Check the glove box; there might be something in there."

There was no way I was going to be able to do that while strapped in the reclined passenger seat. "No can do. Have you got a good memory for names and dates?"

"Yeah. Tell me."

So I did, as well as the address of Alice's former home.

"That's not a lot to go on," Richard said.

"If we stop at the cemetery's Main Office, they might be able to better refine those dates. If Alice was murdered, we might find a newspaper account of it and figure out the jurisdiction to see if they'll allow us to view their files—but we've got to know more than just the year of her death before we can do that."

"Right."

It didn't take long for us to reach the cemetery's Main Office once again, and Richard cut the engine. "I won't be long—I hope."

"I got nothin' but time."

I watched him enter the building, then tried to relax. My eyelids felt like they were attached to lead weights and despite the pain in my broken leg—and just about everywhere else—I must have dozed off. The car door slamming jarred me awake. "Sorry."

"Did you find out when Alice died?"

Richard shook his head. "It turns out the cemetery's website has a search feature. Everyone planted here—more than a hundred and sixty thousand souls—is searchable by name, with any information they acquired on the deceased. As soon as we get home, I'll have a look. But I did bum a piece of paper and a pencil off the lady behind the reception counter and wrote down the stuff you told me—just in case my memory becomes as faulty as yours," he said wryly.

I managed a smile, but even that seemed to tire me out. "Do you mind if I zone out for a while?"

"Go ahead. I've got lots to think about."

I'll bet.

I shut my eyes and didn't exactly doze, but wasn't exactly all there, either. All too soon, Richard nudged my shoulder. I opened my eyes and realized we'd arrived back at his house. Either Brenda was employing her own brand of ESP, or Richard had called to warn her we'd be arriving, because she was waiting to open the car door and fetch me.

"Jeffy Resnick, what have you done to yourself?" she asked testily, sizing me up.

"I did a Humpty Dumpty."

"I should say you did. I'm going to be doing laundry this afternoon. You may as well add those clothes to the pile."

"I need to crash."

"Not in those clothes."

"Yes, ma'am," I said contritely.

Once again, Brenda retrieved my crutches and helped me out of the car. I felt shaky with fatigue after my second venture out since the accident, and was glad when Richard showed up and they both helped me into the house.

"Do you want to crash on the recliner in the living room or your bed?"

"The bed's closer," I said.

"Do you need more help?" Richard asked, more to Brenda than to me.

"We've got it," Brenda said, but I noted her hand bunched around the back of my sweats to keep me upright as I shambled forward.

Brenda's craft room wasn't big, but it seemed like a half mile trek to make it to the bed. Brenda turned me around and tugged at my sweatpants before grabbing my arm to help ease me down on the bed, then we did a repeat of the night before. It was when I stripped off my grubby sweat-stained T-shirt that she gasped.

"What did you do to yourself?"

"I kind of fell over a tombstone."

"You do that again and you'll be *under* a tombstone." She examined the skin around my ribs. "Oh, hon, you could have broken a rib or two. You might need an x-ray. Does it hurt to breathe?"

"No. I'm good, I promise," I lied. "But I would like a pain pill." I was only about an hour early for one.

She shook her head, but turned for the dresser where my personal pharmacy had taken up residence, doled out a pill, and got me a glass of water from the bathroom. "Want me to bring you something to eat?"

"I'll have something later."

"Did you meet the ghost?"

I nodded. "Can I tell you about her later, too?"

"Okay."

"Why were you in the driveway when we got home?"

"I was on my way back from feeding your cat."

It was past noon. Herschel was used to eating in the morning—with a few snacks mid-day—and again at night.

"His name is Herschel."

"Yes it is," Brenda agreed.

"Why won't Richard let me bring him over here?"

She sighed. Was I about to get a sanitized version, or would she tell me the truth?

"Cats appear to be a lot of work."

"Is that you talking or Richard?"

"I've got a baby in diapers," she admitted.

Was she just parroting what he'd said? "I can take care of him."

"Hon, you can't take care of yourself."

A bubble of anger and humiliation rolled through me. I figured they'd get sick of taking care of me yet again; I just didn't know it would happen this fast.

I debated refuting her previous statement, but decided discretion was the better part of valor and all that horse shit.

Brenda handed me a clean T-Shirt and I donned it. It was too soon for the pill to have kicked in, but exhaustion pulled at me. I struggled to pull my legs up onto the bed and Brenda snapped to and gave me a hand.

"Thanks."

"You're welcome. Holler if you need anything."

"I will."

I wouldn't.

"Have a good nap."

"Thanks."

She gave me a half-hearted smile and pulled the door shut behind her.

The clock on the wall ticked way too loud. I hated the fucking thing. I hated the cute, pastel pictures on the rosy pink walls. I was so tired I wanted nothing more than to sink into sleep's oblivion, but I was angry. Too angry to relax. It was an old familiar anger. A stupid anger. But I only had one option open to me. Somehow I had to learn to take care of myself—free of the Alpert influence. It hadn't worked all that well years before, and probably wouldn't work at all now, but I had to at least try.

As I lay there, waiting for sleep to come, I formulated the first step in Plan A.

Unfortunately, there didn't seem to be a viable Plan B.

Forest Lawn Cemetery's extensive website held all sorts of fascinating pages and links, and Richard decided that apart from looking into Alice Newcomb's death, he'd have to spend some time reading through every page. But that could wait, he realized, as he looked up to see that Brenda stood in the doorway of his study. "What's up?"

"I've got tomato soup on low on the stove, and everything ready to make grilled cheese sandwiches. Are you hungry?"

He pushed his chair away from the computer. "I guess."

She didn't wait and took off for the kitchen. Once there, he took his usual seat. "Is Betsy down for her nap already?"

Brenda had her back to him, but nodded.

"Are you okay?"

Again she nodded.

"Then what's up?"

She shrugged. "Jeffy said he was too tired to tell me what happened at the cemetery, but I assume he was successful."

"He told me he met the ghost of a young woman in her twenties. The cemetery has an amazing data base. I've already found her and her mother. I printed out the pages for Jeff to read later."

Brenda didn't comment. She checked the soup, then went back to assembling the sandwiches without comment.

Richard continued. "Although this encounter isn't likely to enhance our professional portfolio, it should prove that we can navigate the murky waters of solving a cold case."

"I wouldn't be so sure."

Over the years, Richard had learned when it was important to listen hard to what Brenda had to say. He had a feeling this might be one of those times. "What do you mean?"

"When I was talking to Jeffy not ten minutes ago, I got a shiver of déjà vu. It wasn't something I understood, but I think you might."

"How so?"

"That's it. I don't know. But something in him changed in a heartbeat. It was an old hurt that never healed."

Richard didn't like the sound of that. Was he in for a bout of emotional blackmail? But from whom: Brenda or Jeff? And over what?

"I don't get it."

"Neither do I. Well, maybe I shouldn't have said—"

"What?"

She shook her head. "I'm probably imagining things." She plopped one of the sandwiches into the hot cast-iron skillet on the stove, then turned to work on the other.

Three minutes later, they ate their lunch in silence and then Richard went back to his study to try to find out more about Alice Newcomb. Lots of dead ends there.

Hours passed. He gave up his online searches and played with various words to try to define his vision of the company he and Jeff would run. Alpert-Resnick Insights? Resnick-Alpert Insights? R&A Insights? A&R Insights? J&R Insights? He liked the idea of "insights" in the title. Like a double entendre that paid homage to Richard's research capabilities and Jeff's unique psychic abilities. Yes, they'd be equal partners in this little endeavor. Little, because they'd start out small, but once they'd garnered a reputation....

His thoughts were interrupted when Brenda called him to dinner. How had the day gotten away from him?

Richard entered the kitchen and headed for the Scotch bottle in the cabinet near the stove, intending to celebrate. Betsy sat in her highchair, a bowl of peas and a cut-up banana before her, happily feeding herself. The table was only set for two. "Where's Jeff?"

"I had to wake him. He said he wasn't hungry and went back to sleep."

"He had a rough morning."

"So it seems," Brenda said coolly.

Richard grabbed a glass and some ice, then poured the Scotch—neat. "Is something wrong?"

"I hope not."

"What does that mean?"

She shrugged, retrieved two baked potatoes from the microwave, setting them on the plates and putting them on the table, before she turned back for the stove, grabbing a bowl of peas and a platter of baked chicken. They both took their seats at the table, and Brenda helped herself to the entrée before pushing the plate toward Richard, who'd suddenly lost his appetite.

"Something's not right," he said.

Brenda doled out a tiny portion of peas. "I'm glad I'm not the only one who feels it."

"What are we supposed to do about it?"

"Bend."

"What does that mean?"

Again she shrugged. "I'm not sure."

Betsy seemed to be having a jolly time rolling peas around her highchair's tray and dipping into her pile of sliced bananas while her parents picked at yet another meal in virtual silence.

SIX

The days were bad enough, but the nights could be absolute torture. Maybe I should have let Richard bring the TV down from the guest room upstairs, but there was no cable hookup so it would have been DVDs only, and jumping up and down every couple of hours didn't seem all that appealing at the time. And now the whole thing was moot.

My stomach growled loudly. It had been sixteen hours since I'd eaten a couple of slices of toast, but sustenance could wait. I struggled to sit up and every muscle in my body seemed to scream, thanks to my encounter with the tombstone earlier that day. I ground my teeth together and turned on the bedside lamp, then made sure the baby monitor was switched off before allowing myself a painful groan. I had to wait long moments for things to settle down before I could grab my crutches and get up. Next on the agenda: pants—or at least shorts. If I fell I didn't want to be caught in my skivvies. It wasn't easy, but I got them on, found my left shoe, grabbed my keys from the top of the dresser and, with no hand to hold them, bit the leather strap attached to the ring to hang onto them, and headed for the butler's pantry and the back door.

The night air felt damp and chilly as I shuffle-hopped across the expanse of driveway toward the garage. Once there, I leaned against the siding, retrieved my keys and sorted through them, thankful the light over the garage came on at dusk. I unlocked the door, reached around to turn on the light, and looked up the steps. Fourteen steps. I swallowed. A stairway to heaven—or at least freedom.

Again, I bit the leather tab and, with crutches held with my right hand, pivoted and fumbled for the bannister. *One, two, three,* and with a bent left knee, dropped back, juggling the crutches and awkwardly swinging from the bar until my ass hit the second step. My broken leg did not like being jarred, but since the rest of me didn't either, I tried not to pay attention to the pain that radiated through it.

I sat there for a couple of minutes to get used to the idea of what was yet to come: those other twelve steps. The plan was essentially the same as what I'd done to get to Alice's monument. Keeping the bad leg elevated, I dug in with the good leg and pushed up. I was glad there was no one around taking video, because traversing those steps were not my most dignified moments.

I was two steps from the top when I lost my grip on the crutches. They slid down the steps, making a terrible racket. Feeling heartsick, I sat there, sweating from exertion and had yet another decision to make. Go after them, or carry on.

I carried on.

Once my bony ass hit the landing, I let go of the keys, thankful I hadn't dropped them, too, and unlocked the door. The scant light coming in through the big living room window cast the room in shadows.

"*Mrrow?*"

"Herschel? Stay back." The last thing I needed was for my cat to escape; after all, I hadn't been able to shut the door at the bottom of the stairs. The keys went back in my mouth and I turned onto my belly and began to crawl. I managed to get inside and close the door, then turned over, grabbing the handle on the closet door to help pull me up into a sitting position. I reached over and locked the door. I couldn't reach the bolt, but at least I was inside and safe in what I'd come to think of as home. But for how much longer?

It seemed like all I'd done most of the day was sweat, and I felt pretty ripe about then, but it didn't seem to bother Herschel, who walked onto my lap, head butting my chin, and purring like a well-oiled machine. "Hey, buddy; I missed you, too."

I sat there for a few minutes, petting him, until Herschel looked like he might want to plop down for an extended visit, but I had too much to accomplish before I could allow myself to enjoy his company. First up were lights. I needed to see any obstacles in my way. I'd left the apartment before eight on the morning of the accident, with dishes in the sink and the bed unmade. There were probably clothes lying on the bathroom floor, too. I wrinkled my nose. Brenda had been feeding Herschel, but so far hadn't changed the litter box. As I recalled, the twenty-five pound bag I bought once a month had one change left in it, but I wasn't sure I was up to changing it then. And how was I going to get my trash down to the tote in time for garbage day?

I shook myself. First things first. I needed something to eat. The light switches were out of my reach and I had nothing at hand to use to flip them. If I could maneuver to the kitchen, I could open the fridge and that would give me some light—then I could make my next decision. So I crawled on my belly across the carpeted floor to the breakfast bar and into the kitchen. I pried the fridge door open and blessed the light that spilled out.

"Let there be light; and there was light; and it was good!" I told Herschel, who had no problem seeing in the dark. He seemed to think it was well-past time for a kitty snack, but I ignored his strident hints. Hopefully Brenda had fed him, whereas I'd missed two meals that day.

The fridge didn't have much in it, but a bottle of beer was within reach and I grabbed it. "Liquid bread," I told Herschel, who seemed skeptical. I twisted the screw cap, tossed it in the direction of the sink, and took a long gurgling swig of that beautiful Labatt Blue. Since I'd left my pain pills back in Brenda's craft room, those fine bottles of fermented malted barley might be the only thing between me and misery for the next few hours. I knew I should probably try to eat something, but most of my staples were located in the higher cupboards. I rummaged around and came up with a box of Ritz crackers with an unopened sleeve and tore into it. If only I had some cheese....

Okay, I had food and drink, now what should I do? Watch TV? It didn't appeal to me. I could check my email on my phone, but hadn't thought to do that earlier in the day. The computer desk sat against the living room's west wall. I found a tray in one of the cupboards, placed the opened beer—and another unopened one—on it, along with the crackers and flipped onto my stomach once again. I moved a couple of inches, dragged the tray along, and crawled yet again. It took me three or four minutes to reach my destination before I realized I probably wasn't going to be able to climb into my computer chair.

Screw that! I yanked the keyboard and mouse cables, glad I'd never gone wireless, and hit the PC's ON switch. While it booted up, I drank half the bottle of beer and ate a handful of crackers. I admit, it wasn't exactly convenient to try to read the screen way up above me, but the light it shed helped illuminate the room. Still munching crackers, I logged into my email account to catch up on stuff. There were way-too-many Facebook announcements, which I quickly deleted, and an email from Bison Bank. Probably an advertisement for yet another of their services. Still, I clicked to open it and read with growing puzzlement that my checking account was overdrawn. No way! I had overdraft protection from my savings account, which had a little more than two grand in it. I'd been saving a big chunk of my tips from the bar for ... well, I didn't really know what. Maybe a better car, or a vacation with Maggie—or maybe just a rainy day.

I typed the bank's URL into the search box, and when the screen came up added my log-in and password, then waited for the single-use code to arrive in my email. Once logged in, I wasted no time in checking my balances: zero and zero.

What the fuck?

Both had been emptied before I'd left the hospital— the same day my credit card had been compromised.

I stared at the zero balances once again and felt my throat constrict. I'd been hit by hackers—*and* a honking big SUV—while those I held near and dear felt used and abused because I wasn't in a position to take care of myself. And why had Maggie made herself so damned scarce?

I grabbed the beer bottle and drank the rest of its contents down in mere seconds, but as soon as the last swallow had gone down, I wondered if it all might come right back up. I tossed the empty bottle aside as the reality of all that had happened started to sink in. If I thought I could escape the Alpert penitentiary with the little I'd managed to save during the previous two years, those hopes had been unequivocally obliterated.

What the fuck was I going to do? How in hell could I survive? At that moment, I had no one to depend on and nothing to fall back on.

Nothing in my past—not even being mugged—prepared me for the overwhelming sense of futility and finality that swamped me.

"Brrrpt!" Herschel said, and sashayed past me, rubbing his head and marking my cast as his personal property

before heading into the bedroom.

I wasn't sure what I should do next. I could struggle to get up on the couch and crash there, or crawl into the bedroom and try to make it to the bed. Maybe I'd fall asleep and when I woke up everything that had happened during the past week would prove to be nothing but a bad dream. I'd dress, drink a cup of coffee, and wait for Dave to arrive and go on a ride—but this time I'd change the destination. And like a scared kid, I'd ride my bike on the sidewalk—not the mean streets of Buffalo.

I considered opening the other bottle of beer, but decided against it. I didn't bother shutting down the computer and rolled onto my belly to begin the long crawl to my bed, but when I got there found I didn't have the energy to try to climb my way onto it. Instead, I nearly popped my arm out of its socket yanking the bedspread off, grappled to snag a pillow, and billeted myself on the floor beside it. Herschel appeared from somewhere out of the darkness and nestled his warm body against my chest, purring happily. I envied the little guy. At that precise moment, I was sure I'd never be happy again.

Richard was often the first one up in the Alpert household. Okay, maybe he should amend that to say the first *adult* up in the household. He got up, showered, dressed, and found his baby daughter awake in her crib, telling herself some far-fetched story in a language he didn't understand. He picked her up, kissed her dimpled cheek, and changed her diaper before taking her down to the kitchen, settling her in her highchair with a cup of Cheerios before he started the coffeemaker. He liked to let Brenda sleep in, since she'd taken on more than her fair share of the household and childcare chores, as well as being Jeff's primary caregiver.

He took a couple of mugs from the cupboard, as well

as a bowl and the box of rice cereal for Betsy's breakfast, then puttered around getting everything ready. He'd feed the baby, and then take a cup of coffee into Jeff. Well, that is if Brenda came down fairly soon. He didn't want to leave the baby alone in her chair for even a moment, even though she was strapped in.

But then he looked out the kitchen window and his heart skipped a beat. The side door to the garage—and also Jeff's apartment—was open, and it hadn't been the night before.

"Da-Da," Betsy called. She was such a happy little girl that she never failed to make him smile...at least until that moment. He made sure she was securely strapped in before he headed for the butler's pantry. He didn't need to go farther, since he could see the door to Brenda's craft room was open and the day bed was empty. Was Jeff in the bathroom?

Richard practically ran the short distance. The bedside light was lit, and the tiny bathroom was empty.

"Holy Christ," he muttered and reached for the cell phone in his pocket. He called the landline as he made his way back to the kitchen. It rang five times before a sleepy Brenda picked it up. "'ello."

"Brenda, get up—now!"

"What?"

"Jeff's gone—and the door to his apartment is open. I can't leave Betsy to—"

"Where are you?"

"In the kitchen."

"I'll be right down." She hung up.

The coffeemaker continued to chug.

Betsy tossed a handful of Cheerios on the floor, laughing with delight.

Richard's gaze darted to the window and then to the hall beyond—back and forth—until a sleepy Brenda finally appeared, tying the belt of her pink chenille robe around her middle.

"I'll be right back," Richard said, although he expected it was an empty promise and flew toward the back door, exploded from it, and jogged across the driveway, trying to decide if it was worry or anger he felt.

Not only was the door open, but Jeff's crutches blocked the first couple of steps. He grabbed them, setting them aside and hit the stairs two at a time. The apartment door was locked, and he fumbled for his keys, thrust the proper one into the lock, and wrenched it open.

The apartment was deathly quiet. A beer bottle lay strewn on the floor, with another tipped over on a tray on the floor with a nearly empty packet of crackers next to the computer's keyboard and mouse.

"Jeff?"

No answer. He walked inside, checked the kitchen and the bath—found no one—and headed for the bedroom.

A huddled form lay on the floor wrapped in the bedspread. The black cat sat next to him, practically up his nostrils—reaffirming the urban legend Jeff had scoffed at—purring its brains out.

"Jeff!" Richard called sharply.

The form started, disturbing the cat, which jumped to its feet, whipped around, and then disappeared under the bed. "What the hell are you doing on the floor?"

His sleep-fogged brother blinked up at him. "Sleeping. What the hell do you think?"

"Why are you here?" Richard demanded.

Jeff groped to find a handhold to pull himself into a sitting position. "I live here. Or at least I used to."

Richard held out a hand. "Come on; I'll help you up."

"And then what?"

"We'll go back to the house."

"No, thanks. I'm fine where I am."

"I don't think so."

"Well, I do," he said belligerently.

"You can't even get off the floor on your own."

"If I had my crutches, I might be able to do so. Maybe you'll bring them up to me before you go home," he said pointedly.

"You can't do laundry. You can't cook for yourself."

"I've got a full bottle of ketchup and a twenty-gallon tank of hot water," Jeff grated.

Richard's fists clenched as his memory flashed back twenty-two years when he'd found out Jeff had been starving himself after Richard's grandmother had humiliated him by telling others he stole food.

He had to take a couple of breaths to quell his anger. "I'm not going back without you."

"And I'm not going without Herschel. It's a deal breaker."

"What do you need a stupid cat for anyway?"

"He doesn't get pissed off and let me know I'm a burden, and he'll never cheat on me, either."

The first insult was aimed at him—the latter at Maggie.

"You cannot take care of yourself!" Richard yelled as the unreasonable anger he felt reached new heights.

"Look, I love you guys; I love Maggie; and I love Herschel. Everyone gets the same amount—and I'm sorry you don't get it.

"Is that your final word?" Richard asked, fearing he might explode.

"Yes."

Richard stared at his brother for long seconds, before he pivoted, and stalked out of the room, heading across the carpet for the door, and slamming it behind him. At the bottom of the stairs, he bypassed the crutches still standing against the door to the garage, and slammed the one that led to the driveway.

He walked halfway into the driveway and stopped, angry with himself for losing his temper, and angry at Jeff for being so damned stubborn. He stood there, staring at his feet for a long time before the back door opened.

"What are you doing?" Brenda hollered.

Richard let out a breath and started for the house.

He met his wife at the door. "I lost my temper with Jeff. I was trying to calm down before I came back inside and took it out on you or Betsy."

"Richard Alpert, you have never taken your anger out on anybody. What happened that got you so upset?"

"He won't come back without the cat. It's a deal breaker."

Brenda sighed. "Is that all?" She turned back for the counter and claimed one of the cups that was only half filled with coffee. She poured another cup, handing it to him.

"I don't want that cat here."

"What's the big deal?"

"I don't like cats."

"No one says you *have* to like them."

"No, I mean it. I *really* don't like cats."

Brenda studied his face for long seconds, and then her eyes widened. "Oh. You mean, you're kitty phobic?"

He let out an anxious breath. "The clinical term is ailurophobic."

Brenda leaned against the counter. "But you've been over to his apartment hundreds of times and seen his cat."

"It usually hides from me."

"As Jeff keeps reminding us, Herschel is a *him*, not an it."

Richard's hand was shaking as he took a sip of his coffee, slopping it onto the tile floor. "I can't have that *thing* in my house."

Brenda reached for the paper towel rack, tore off a

sheet, and stooped to mop up the spill. "Where did all this come from?"

Richard shook his head. "I have no idea."

"Dogs don't bother you. I mean, you seemed to enjoy Maggie's dog, Holly, when she stayed with us that week."

"Maybe it's the pack mentality. But cats ...." He shuddered involuntarily.

Brenda tossed the soiled towel in the trash and moved to take her usual seat at the table. Betsy banged her empty bowl on the tray before her and Richard set his cup down, took the bowl from her, and refilled it with dry cereal.

Brenda sipped her coffee, looking thoughtful. "Jeffy can't stay there on his own."

"I know that. He slept on the floor because he couldn't get into bed. He'd been on his computer. The keyboard and mouse were on the floor."

"Is he okay?"

Richard shrugged. "I guess." Then he thought better of it. "Oh, shit. He asked me to bring him his crutches, and I was so angry I forgot. They're standing at the bottom of the stairs."

"As soon as I get dressed, I'll go over there. He needs to have those road rash wounds tended to. Maybe while I'm there I can broker a peaceful compromise."

"I don't see how. He says we've let him know he's a burden."

Brenda frowned. "That was my fault—yesterday—trying to cover for you about the damn cat."

"What did you say?"

"I let him know that I had a baby in diapers and didn't need any more work."

"That was when you said something about him changed. An old hurt that had never really healed?"

She nodded.

And that crack Jeff made about the ketchup had been just the tip of the iceberg. As a teen, he'd lived in the

Alpert home for more than three years. He hadn't been wanted—he'd barely been tolerated. He'd been verbally abused not only by Richard's grandmother, but some of the help, too. And Richard had been too wrapped up in his career to bother with the kid. Neglect, Jeff's high school principal had hinted, and suggested a visit from a social worker might be in the offing. He'd managed to avoid that—but the solution to the problem had been anything but satisfying.

"You're thinking about the past," Brenda said.

Richard nodded and felt the heat of a blush rise up his neck.

"How much do you want this little business enterprise you've proposed?"

He swallowed. "I think it could be good for both of us."

"Then bend. You don't have to bow to breaking—but you may have to compromise."

I can't let this beat me. It's just a stupid phobia. And yet, the negative feelings within him felt powerful and threatening—and yes, very, very stupid.

"Maybe ... maybe if he kept the thing in his room. But it can't wander the house. I don't want it anywhere near Betsy," he said adamantly.

"So, you'd like *her* to be afraid—and just as phobic—about the cat?" Brenda asked, her tone reasonable.

"No. It's just...." Richard looked over at his daughter whose chubby fingers attempted to stack the cereal—with little success. "That's as far as I'm willing to go."

Brenda nodded. "It's a start—and a good one."

Richard nodded, but he found it hard to meet her gaze.

"If you don't mind looking after Betsy, I'll get dressed and go over there and see if I can straighten things out with Jeffy."

Richard nodded, feeling foolish.

Brenda got up from her seat, stepped over to stand before him, and hugged him. "It'll be okay. Not great, but it'll be okay."

He wrapped his arms around her. Maybe okay was all he could expect—and tolerate.

SEVEN

Richard had been angry with me before, but never like what I'd experienced early that June morning. It was unreasonable to think someone that pissed off would bring me my crutches, so I was stuck on the floor until I could figure out my next move.

My next move was to get to the bathroom, but I couldn't get up, so there was only one thing to do; I had to pee in my shower. Only I couldn't reach the faucet and turn on the water. Great. Now my place smelled like a cat box *and* the men's room at the bus station.

I couldn't afford to dwell on either. I needed to contact my bank and find out what the hell I needed to do get my money back—*if* I could get it back.

My computer was only sleeping, and I got online once again. By then it was just after nine, and I got someone on a live chat who walked me through the things I needed to do to report the loss—the biggie being to get to the local police station to file a complaint. Oh, yeah, I could just hop in the car and bop right over there.

Somebody had my social security number. Were they opening accounts right, left, and center—scamming their way across the globe at my expense?

I called the local cop shop, explained my situation, but was told I'd have to come in—they didn't have the personnel to make house calls. I listened, kept swallowing to keep from choking, and wondered what the hell I was going to do, when I heard the sound of the door handle behind me rattle.

"Thank you," I said, and hung up the phone.

The door opened and Brenda poked her head inside. "I'm sorry, hon. I should have knocked first."

"You're always welcome," I said, but I'm afraid my voice was anything but welcoming.

She was weighed down with a big shopping bag in one hand and my crutches in the other. "I thought you might need these."

"Need; yeah. Want? Not a chance."

She wandered into the living room and set the bag down. "I haven't had breakfast. How about you?"

I shook my head.

"I brought over some bread. Oh, rapture! Dry white toast."

"I've got peanut butter, ya know. It's a life-sustaining necessity."

"That'll do for me," she said. "Want some coffee?"

"Yes, thank you," I said without enthusiasm.

"Oh, buck up, will you? I'm not here to yell at you … unlike *somebody* we know."

"Yeah."

"Of course you know why he's upset."

"Because he thought I'd get hurt climbing the steps and being here on my own. Yada, yada, yada."

Brenda nodded. "It really wasn't a smart move. But you know what? If it was me, I'da done the same thing." She sobered. "I'm so sorry I made you feel unwelcome in our home."

I shrugged. I didn't really want to have this conversation.

"Let's get you on your feet, and then we can talk."

Unfortunately, that was inevitable.

I had to scooch across the rug on my butt to the couch and between the two of us, I managed to stand on my good leg. Brenda handed me the crutches then shook her head, studying said leg. "What in God's name did you do to yourself?"

It was then I realized that just about every inch of the skin on the front of my good leg was covered in rug burns.

"How bad does it hurt?"

"A lot less than the other leg, so I guess I didn't much notice it. But I could sure use a pain pill about now."

"How about half of one now, and half when we get you back across the driveway."

I shook my head. "I ain't goin'."

"Of course you are," Brenda said, and grabbed my arm, steering me toward one of the stools at my breakfast bar. She helped me get settled before she grabbed the bag and started emptying it on the counter. She did indeed have half a loaf of white bread, all the crap she needed to fix the sores on my face, and my bottle of pain pills. She'd already split one, so she must have been pretty confident she could change my mind about leaving my home sweet home to land back in a place where I'd inconvenienced the rest of my family.

She took a couple of cups out of the cabinet, turned the cold tap on for a splash, and then handed one to me with half a pill. "Half means you won't somersault down the steps when we leave. We can be out of here in about a half-hour and then you can have the other half."

"No," I said and downed the pill.

"Herschel can't come on the first trip, but I can come back and get him. We can use that litter box that's in the garage—the one you took to Maggie's last fall," she said and filled the coffeepot with water.

After his raging bull act, Richard's sudden change of heart was totally unexpected. "What kind of magic did you use to get Rich to change his mind about Herschel?"

She found the filters. "I got him to admit his problem."

"Which is?" I asked testily.

"It should have been obvious to both of us," she said, searching for the coffee.

"It's in the cupboard down below." She found it and started measuring. "Come on—spill it!" I implored.

She looked at me with infinite patience. "My dear husband—and your big brother—has a phobia concerning cats."

I raised an eyebrow. "You're kidding."

She shook her head. "Nope."

"He's, like, ninety-nine times bigger than Herschel—he can't possibly be afraid of him." As though he knew we were talking about him, my cat sauntered into the living room, sat down, and began to lick his stomach.

"There's no accounting for these things." Brenda grabbed the bread, and turned toward the toaster.

My cell phone's familiar ringtone chimed and I looked around me. Brenda turned again, dug into the shopping bag once more, and handed me my phone

I looked at the number and tapped the talk icon. "Hey, Dave. What's up?"

"I just wanted to see how you were doing."

My good leg was singed with rug burns; my broken leg throbbed with every beat of my heart, and the ribs along my left side still hadn't forgiven me for falling the day before.

"To be honest, not good. I've had a couple of bad days. I fell, and—"

"Aw, man—I'm so sorry," he said guiltily.

"Don't worry about it. I have it on good authority that I'll be as good as new by August—or September."

"I was hoping to come by and see you to talk about...." He hesitated. "Stuff."

"I'd love to—but I'm really not up to it today. Do you mind?"

"Oh. No. Sure." The words were right, but he sounded like he'd been taken aback by my non-invitation. And since I knew he felt responsible for my predicament, he wasn't likely to push it.

"Okay," he said. "I'll call in a few days. And when I come, I'll bring beer."

"Sounds good," I agreed.

"Okay. Sure. Yeah. Bye."

The call ended.

"What's with your friend?" Brenda grabbed the coffeepot and emptied what had already dripped into it into a cup. She dumped some milk in, stirred, and then handed it to me.

"I think he wants to apologize again for me getting hurt. He doesn't have to do that."

"You should let him visit...let him off the hook."

"But I don't blame him for what happened."

"You said it yourself; he blames himself." She placed two slices of bread into the toaster and, with some direction from me, found the peanut butter. Of course, Brenda was right. Old soul that she was, she was nearly *always* right.

The toast popped up and she spread both slices with that wonderful golden goop, handing one to me and taking the other for herself.

"I feel better about things," I said, took a bite, chewed, and swallowed.

"You do now—but we haven't yet fixed your face, and you know it's going to hurt."

Yeah, it would. But Brenda had a gentle touch. Already the road rash was beginning to heal. I still had a pizza face, but the scabs were growing smaller, leaving healthy pink skin around the edges.

"Eat up," she said. "I have a feeling this is going to be one long and painful day—and I'm not just talking about your injuries."

She had that right.

It was nearly noon by the time Brenda had shuttled me, my cat, and all Herschel's supplies across the driveway. Herschel didn't quite know what to make of his much smaller territory, but when I collapsed on the bed from sheer exhaustion, he was right there beside me, letting me know he had my back. Richard, on the other hand, was conspicuous by his absence.

Hours later, a sound woke me—like something rattling around on the floor. I wasn't sure what was going on until a black projectile came flying through the air and jumped on the bed, did a one-eighty, then flew back down to the floor.

"Herschel," I chided, feeling crappy. But when I looked at the clock, I saw the day had slipped away. It was four-thirty; time to get up. Time to face my brother.

A roll of curly ribbon went flying by on the floor, with Herschel in hot pursuit. "You're not supposed to touch Brenda's stuff." But as I looked around the room, it now looked like a curious cat's paradise filled with boxes and baskets to get into, and half-finished projects to attempt to dismantle. I was going to have to have a conversation with Brenda about that PDQ.

After following nature's call, I realized keeping Herschel locked in Brenda's craft room wasn't going to be as easy as planned. No sooner had I headed for the door than he was at my heels, threatening to trip me. Maybe bringing him across the driveway wasn't going to be as easy a transition as I thought. I had to back out of the room using one of my crutches to block his escape. As soon as I closed the door, I heard the sound of furious scratching. It kinda broke my heart to abandon the little guy once again.

No one was in the kitchen and the crutches dug into

my armpits once again as I hobbled toward the living room. Nobody there, either. That only left one more place to check: Richard's study.

I tried to be quiet, but the old parquet floor creaked and the thump of the crutches had to be heard by half the neighbors. Still, when I made it to the doorway of the study, my brother's back was still turned as he consulted his computer. I waited for more than a minute, but still he didn't acknowledge my presence.

Finally I cleared my throat. "Hi."

He swiveled part way around. "Hi."

"Is Brenda upstairs changing CP?"

"Probably. Do you need something?" His voice was devoid of emotion. Devoid of everything.

I let out a breath. "Yeah. A shot of bourbon."

"I could probably help you with that." He got up, heading for his dry bar across the way.

I made a beeline for the couch so that I could put my bad leg up. Bad leg. It sounded like I blamed the poor battered appendage for what had happened to it. Screw that. I blamed the friggin' SUV driver. It occurred to me that no one had mentioned if they'd ever tracked down the bastard responsible. Most likely it would never happen. Another fact to make me grumpy.

I settled the crutches on the floor and Richard turned to hand me my drink, neat. He had poured a glass for himself as well. He took the wing chair adjacent to me. I raised my glass. *"Na zdrowie!"*

"Cheers," he replied, but his voice held no merriment. He also didn't seem to want to look me in the eye. This wasn't the time to talk about his problem with Herschel, so I decided to take the conversation in a different direction.

"I never got to search the cemetery's website to look up Alice Newcomb."

"I did." He got up again, walked over to his desk, and

picked up a manila file folder. He returned and handed it to me.

Inside were several printed sheets. One for Alice; one for her mother, and one with a list of possible names for our proposed business. I bypassed that to concentrate on Alice's information, which I quickly read through.

Alice Elizabeth Newcomb had indeed been born on June 14, 1909 to parents Hiram and Cora Newcomb. She'd died on April 2, 1932. Included was an obituary that ran in Buffalo's *Courier Express.*

Miss Alice Newcomb, daughter of Mr. Hiram Newcomb and Mrs. Cora Newcomb, went to be with the Lord on April 2nd. A memorial service will be held at Blessed Trinity Catholic Church, April 5, at 10 am. Afterward, Miss Newcomb will be laid to rest at Forest Lawn Cemetery.

I skimmed through the information on her parents, but nothing jumped out at me.

Richard hadn't found a news story explaining how Alice died. Was it because the cops never solved the crime, or had her well-to-do father suppressed the unsavory manner of his daughter's death? Or was it just that the story was too old to warrant it being scanned for the Internet?

Alice's mother had died less than two years after her only child, and old Hiram had gone on to wed a second Mrs. Newcomb. He'd been buried in the Williamsville Cemetery along with said new wife some twenty-five years after Alice's death, which accounted for the empty grave in Forest Lawn.

"This doesn't tell us a lot," I commented.

"No, but we haven't scratched the surface when it comes to researching her life. A trip to the library will definitely be in order to check their microfilmed or CD records."

"I'm surprised you haven't already done that."

Richard hesitated before answering. "I wasn't sure if I

should bother."

"Are you giving up on this idea of yours so easily?"

"I wasn't sure you'd want to pursue it."

"I kind of made a commitment to Alice. I'd be a real piece of shit if I didn't follow through with it. We're talking about the fate of her eternal soul."

"I thought you didn't believe in that."

"I don't. But she does."

Richard shook his head ruefully. "Far be it from me to try to stop you."

He said no more, but I got the feeling he was pleased I hadn't shut down the whole concept of us working together.

We sat in companionable silence, or at least that's what it looked like. For several minutes, I sipped my bourbon and wrestled with telling him about my banking woes, but it was too late in the day to do anything about it anyway. I knew he had the computer skills to hack into data bases that had mega security, but I wasn't yet sure I wanted to rope him into my petty problems. Last I'd heard, he had more than fifty million bucks behind him. My paltry two grand was chump change. I suspected he'd just offer to write me a check to replace the loss, but that wasn't what I wanted. Yeah, I'd keep this little bump in my financial road to myself—at least for another day or so. We had other things to think about.

Footsteps forewarned Brenda's arrival. A smiling CP was attached to her left hip. "Oh, there you two are." They entered the room. "Scooch over, Jeffy, so that Betsy and I have a spot to sit."

Oh yeah, that was *so* easy to do, but I managed it nonetheless.

Brenda sat down, crossed her legs and settled Betsy— my little Cherry Pie—on her foot, bouncing her up and down, which delighted the baby no end.

"I've got a surprise for you, Jeffy."

"Oh?"

"Maggie's coming for supper."

My spirits instantly rose. "Really?"

"Yup. We're going to have a picnic. Hot dogs, potato salad, and baked beans."

The word 'picnic' instantly made me tense. "Are we eating outside?"

"I hadn't planned on it, but we can if you want."

The thought of traversing the driveway, to the deck, and then up the steps—and having to repeat the process on the way back—was enough to raise my hackles. I'd traveled far enough that day. "Maybe we could go outside in August," I suggested.

"It's not all that far away," she said optimistically.

Yes. I had to keep reminding myself that a broken leg wasn't forever. It was a damned inconvenience, but I would heal in a matter of months and my life would go on pretty much as it had. Okay, I might not have a job, and with an empty bank account I'd be flat broke, but at least I'd be able to walk on my own two feet again—something those who'd lost limbs couldn't say and do.

I wondered again if I should mention my new financial crisis to Richard and Brenda but decided against it. It could wait. And yet, the whole thing bothered me. I was such a small fish in the grand scheme of things. If someone hacked Richard's bank accounts—and he banked at the same branch as me—they could have fleeced him for millions. Why steal my paltry two grand? Somehow it didn't seem worth a hacker's time and effort.

"You look pensive," Richard observed.

"Just thinking."

"About?"

"Our futures. But then my brain is so scattered, the crap I have to take to stay ahead of this leg," I said sourly, "makes me feel foggy."

"You're not taking all that much," Brenda piped up.

"Believe me, it's more than I want."

"Don't miss taking the anti-inflammatories," Richard said.

I almost laughed. "I won't—if someone reminds me."

"I'm on it," Brenda said, still bouncing a giggling CP. "But if we're going to eat before midnight, I'd better open that can of Grandma Brown's beans, doctor them up, and put them in the oven to bake."

"Go for it," Richard encouraged her.

Brenda snagged the baby and got up. "You can sit here by yourselves, or you can come and keep me company in the kitchen."

I was game, but Richard's eyes widened and he seemed to blanch. Was it because Herschel was just a short walk through the butler's pantry, ensconced in Brenda's craft room? The whole idea that my ten-times-smarter-than-me brother had some kind of phobia was still pretty startling.

"I'm not sure I can raise my sorry ass," I said, hoping to cover for me and Richard.

"That's okay," Brenda said. "Maggie probably won't be here until six. You've got an hour to cool your heels. And Betsy and I have lots to do to get ready, don't we baby girl?"

CP just giggled.

They left the room, leaving us guys alone.

I wondered if I dared have another drink. Probably not. Then again, if I could hold off on another pain pill for a couple of hours, why shouldn't I? I decided to wait to see if the doctor in front of me would offer a refill.

"What's our next step?"

Richard looked up from his drink. "Step?"

"Yeah, if we're going to go through with this business venture."

He exhaled a long breath. "I guess I go to the library tomorrow and try to find out more about Alice's death."

"I could come with you—"

He shook his head. "I don't need company, and you don't need to be on your feet more than necessary."

Thank you for that. Then again, it meant another boring day lying around doing nothing. Maybe I'd call Dave and see if he wanted to visit, after all.

Once again we heard footsteps on the parquet floor outside Richard's study, but it wasn't Brenda. "Hey, guys, how's it going?" Maggie asked.

"Hi, Maggie, Richard said.

I turned to see my smiling lady. "What are you doing here? Brenda told us not five minutes ago that you wouldn't be here for at least an hour."

She bent down to kiss me, but I could see she held something behind her back. "I got out of work early and I brought you a present." Her arm whipped around and she thrust a long, narrow plastic rod toward me.

"It's a gripper," Richard said.

"I call it a picky-uppy thing," Maggie said with a laugh. The gripper had a handhold with a trigger, while the bottom had pincers to grab stuff. "It was Lily's. She left it when she moved to Florida to live with Gary and Brian. I thought you might be able to use it."

"I sure can, thanks." I tried it out by reaching for a magazine on Richard's coffee table. Got it first try! "This is going to make life a lot easier."

"Sit down and stay awhile," Richard invited her.

"No, thanks. Brenda tells me there's a beer in the fridge with my name on it. I brought store-bought potato salad that needs some serious upgrades before its edible, too. Besides, I need some girlfriend time."

"Call us when supper's ready," Richard called as Maggie retreated.

I used the gripper to pick up another magazine, moving it from one end of the table to the other. "This really will come in handy," I said, and for the first time in a week felt hopeful.

"I'm sorry we didn't think to get you one before this."

They'd already done far too much for me. "I've got one now." I pulled the gripper's trigger a few times and smiled. What a great toy. I could see uses for it well after my leg healed and decided Maggie wasn't getting it back. When she got old and frail, I'd buy a new one for her. I set it down by my crutches.

Okay, now what could Richard and I talk about? He was hot that we should start a business venture. That could either be a safe or volatile subject. What I didn't want was for it to drive us apart. Maybe I should—and God I hated the term—leave my comfort zone and test the waters.

"What if we actually *could* pull off investigating cold cases. How am I supposed to live on what could be no income?"

"You don't want charity from me. You made that clear twenty-three years ago," he said neutrally, but still—I winced. "I don't need the money."

"Then you're saying the spoils all come to me?" He shrugged. "And how—and more importantly who—do we bill for what we do?"

Richard seemed to squirm. "I haven't exactly figured that out."

"Charging for our, or at least *my* time—and enough to make a living wage—would be expensive for the average Joe. That means we'd be cutting out a large portion of the populace when it comes to clients. And, let's face it; the majority of cold cases come from a part of the county where money is the scarcest."

"I've thought of that. And the more I think about it, the more I'm sure you're right. My whole idea to set something up was to make a difference. Not just to help survivors get closure, but to help restless spirits find the same kind of resolution." He looked me straight in the eye. "Would you honestly let pride stand in the way of that happening?"

"You're saying I should just give in and once and for all attach myself to the Alpert teat?"

"It's not like you wouldn't earn it—the same way I did: through misery."

I gave a mirthless laugh. "Were you miserable?"

"Not too long ago, you asked me if I'd ever had fun."

I sobered, remembering that conversation when we'd gone to New York to find my wife's killer. He'd admitted he didn't know how to have fun. Maybe I should have admitted to him then that I was just as clueless.

"I dunno, Rich. I've worked damn hard to try and make it on my own. It's still a bitter thing to have to accept as much as I do from you. But don't take that wrong," I hurriedly added. "I appreciate everything you've done for me—past *and* present. But an aversion to feeling indebted is ingrained in me. I'm not sure I can overcome it."

"Then, realistically, what do you think you *can*—and want—to do if your time at The Whole Nine Yards is over?"

"If I hadn't been hit by a Goddamn SUV I would have never had to contemplate the question."

"You can't change what happened."

No, I couldn't.

"Maybe you should look at my money in a different light."

"Oh, yeah?" I asked skeptically.

"My grandmother treated you abominably. Some of the money behind me came from an inheritance she got from her family, but the truth is the majority of it came from my grandfather. He worked hard to earn it. Like you, he came from nothing. And let's face it, being married to my grandmother—he earned every penny of what financial gain she brought to the marriage."

He had that right.

"And if it's any consolation, the old man liked you. He went to bat for you on more than one occasion. He had many regrets when it came to our mother, too."

"The poor guy was pussy whipped."

"I'll say. He married for better or for worse, and I don't think he ever had a happy day with my selfish, self-centered grandmother. And I'm positive he would have wanted you to benefit from his labors, because he was never able to help our mother. He felt tremendous guilt about it."

Old Mr. Alpert and I had never been friends, but I hadn't hated him the way I'd despised his malicious wife.

"He went to bat for me?"

Richard nodded. "The day you left for the Army, my grandmother had Gordy—" the Alpert's handyman "—take down our basketball hoop." He paused. "I had an apoplectic fit and—" He paused, and I got the feeling there was more to the story than he was likely to admit. "Grandfather was almost as angry as I was."

"You left only a week or two later," I recalled.

"Yeah. I only saw them a couple of times after that, but every time I spoke with Grandfather on the phone, he asked about you."

"He did?"

Richard nodded. "I'm pretty sure he'd be as proud of what you've accomplished as I am."

"You've got to be kidding."

"What do you mean?"

"I'm a fucking failure. I've never amounted to anything," I said, and the sting of it really hit me—like being doused in acid.

"Even before you had this psychic insight, you were good at what you did—solving crimes for your insurance company. What you did gave a lot of people closure. There were letters, you know."

"What do you mean?"

"I kind of ... looked into the files at the place you worked for before you were mugged."

"You hacked into my employer's files?" I asked, aghast.

"Only those that pertained to you. There were a bunch of thank you letters from grateful clients."

What the hell was he talking about?

"There must have been twenty of them—thanking the company for coming up with grounds for lawsuits; for successful resolutions—all tied to your investigations. They never shared them with you?"

If they did—I didn't remember.

"One of your managers wrote that you were the hardest-working investigator he ever supervised; that you always went the extra mile. And your performance appraisals were always top-notch. Until that last one," he added.

Yeah, until after my wife Shelley's death and I'd switched from the crime unit to fraud. Then I'd been thrown to the wolves and eaten alive.

I had to do a mental head shake. Maybe everything he said was true, but that still had no bearing on where I was at this point in my life. I could barely hack working part-time at a bar. True, the skull-pounding headaches I got had been coming with less frequency these past few months, but when they hit I was virtually incapacitated. How long would a conventional employer put up with the kind of absences I needed to take just to survive?

"I'm going to need some time to digest all this," I admitted.

"Like you said, we've got nothing but time."

That was for damn sure.

EIGHT

Brenda wasn't kidding when she said we'd have a picnic. I hadn't taken her literally, but between them, she and Maggie moved some of the furniture in the living room, and Brenda spread out a blanket. Richard grilled the dogs, but was as unenthusiastic as I was about sitting on the floor—and we opted for comfortable chairs while the women sat on the blanket and called us party poopers. The adults juggled paper plates and CP thought it a hoot to have her Mom and Auntie Maggie down at her own level as she ate her chopped up hot dog.

Richard kept looking over his shoulder, as though Herschel was about to pounce at any minute, and nobody mentioned that miniature elephant in the room. I wondered if Brenda had mentioned Richard's problem to Maggie. I wasn't about to ask—in case she didn't know. No way did I want to embarrass my brother.

It was Brenda who called the picnic to an end when it was CP's bedtime. The furniture was pushed back into place and Richard and I shared an after-dinner drink and some innocuous conversation while the ladies cleared up. When they reappeared, Brenda urged Richard to retire to his study, and while he moved to comply, I saw the girlfriends share a knowing look, although I wasn't exactly sure what to make of it. Maggie seemed self-assured, while Brenda's expression seemed less than enthusiastic.

Once Richard and Brenda were gone, Maggie sat beside me on the couch. "That was fun." She reached for my hand. At her touch, I was bombarded with a myriad of sensations. She definitely had something on her mind, and whatever it was, she was enthused and optimistic about it. Meanwhile, my hackles rose.

"How's your leg doing?"

I shrugged. "Yesterday was not good. I fell."

"So Brenda said."

"And it's been a long, tiring day. I went back to my apartment last night and—"

"Yeah; Brenda told me all about it. I'll bet you're glad to have Herschel for company, though."

I'd slept for hours that afternoon, and the poor cat had been cooped up alone in the craft room for hours, so it was Herschel who desperately needed company—not me.

"I'll be glad to get rid of this cast and get my life back," I admitted.

"I'll bet. You know, I was kind of thinking along those lines, too."

Here it comes, I thought with dread.

"I was thinking ..." Maggie began, sounding wistful. "It might be a good time for me to relocate."

"Oh, yeah?" I asked. Maybe I was wrong.

"Yeah. My job is in Tonawanda. It's a pain in the ass to drive all that way in winter."

"I thought you were happy in Clarence."

"I was, but now that Lily has moved to Florida, I'm not sure I want to deal with being a landlady. This is the time to go, too. Property values are skyrocketing. I could make a killing."

That made sense, but I had a feeling there was more to her decision.

She snuggled closer to me. "Maybe it's time for us to make a bigger commitment."

Uh-oh.

"What are you saying?" I asked, hoping she didn't catch the concern I felt.

"We've known each other for over two years. Maybe it's time we moved in together."

"Now?" I asked, looking down at the brace encasing my upper leg and the cast below it on my lower leg.

"Well, obviously not right now, but once I sell my house it would be something to think about."

I didn't reply. The idea scared me shitless.

"What do you think?" she pushed.

I let out a breath. "As you say, it's something to think about."

"But?" she asked.

Oh, yeah. She'd caught my lack of enthusiasm. But it wasn't about being with her. It was a much more fundamental concern.

"Lily paying monthly rent was what helped you pay your mortgage, right?"

"Yeah."

"How much did she pay?"

"Six hundred."

I'd paid more than three times that for a bedroom, tiny bath, and galley kitchen back in Manhattan. But Richard charged me chump change for my digs over his garage. He wouldn't have charged me a nickel if I hadn't insisted on paying *something*. As a part-time bartender, I lived on tips—which were never a given, and I was pretty sure that job was now history.

"Maggs, look at me. I can't even live in my own home right now. There's no way I can even think about moving."

"Oh, sure—I didn't mean this week. But I figure it will take at least two or three months to sell my place and then find another. And, of course, I want you along to help choose my next home."

I nodded—but the truth was, I wasn't ready to move

to the next level in our relationship, and the reason was pretty damn clear. I didn't want to be a financial burden to Maggie. I absolutely loathed the fact that I was far too dependent on Richard's generosity, but he was a multi-millionaire. He could well afford to take care of his ne'er-do-well kin. Maggie wasn't in that position. But I also had a feeling that no matter what I said, I was going to end up on Maggie's shit list. There was only one thing I could do.

"Maggs, can we talk about this after I get out of this stinking cast?"

She let out a loud—and obviously exasperated—breath. "I've gone over the numbers and ... I can carry my house for a couple of months, and then I'm going to be in the red."

She'd lived in the duplex for almost twelve years. She'd been collecting rent from her ex-mother-in-law for nearly as long."

"But—?"

"As part of the divorce, I bought out Gary's equity. That meant the mortgage went from reasonable to more than double. Even though Lily was paying me rent, I still had to take out a home equity loan when I lost my job at Bison Bank and was unemployed for so long. And now I make less at my new job. I'm sinking fast," she admitted.

"Taking in a tenant would help."

"I told you—I don't want to do that."

"I know, but it *would* help."

"I guess," she grudgingly admitted.

"You could still put the house up for sale. The tenant's rental agreement would have to be honored by the next owner, but it would help you out in the short run."

She frowned. "Is there a reason you don't want to live with me?"

She was determined to pin me to the wall.

"Maggs, I'm broke."

"Still?" Her question sounded like an accusation.

There was no way I was going to bring up the latest development on my financial horizon.

"Yeah. By the time I pay my utilities, car insurance, and my rent—I have next to nothing left."

"Couldn't you ask Richard—?"

I held up a hand to cut off that line of discussion. "Don't go there."

"But—?"

"I mean it, Maggs—don't go there."

Her eyes filled with tears. "So, you don't want to help me?"

I heaved a sigh. "I can't work for at least another six or eight weeks. Tom's already hired a substitute bartender. What if he doesn't want me back?"

"Oh, come on. Bartender jobs are a dime a dozen. You're better than that."

"Yeah, but there are some weeks I can barely cut doing even that."

Her lips pursed. I could tell—feel—she wanted to say so much more, but thankfully she opted not to. Unfortunately, she didn't have to actually say anything out loud for me to know exactly what she felt.

"Please, Maggs. This isn't the time to talk about the future simply because...." I didn't finish the sentence.

"Maybe you're right," she said, and a wave of arctic cold passed over me. Her heart had just hardened. It was time for me to give her an easy out—or rather, a fast escape.

"It's been a really long—painful—day," I said and rubbed the top of my brace. "I'm going to need to crash pretty soon."

She stood. "Sure. I understand."

She didn't.

Still, she bent down to kiss me, but there was a distinct lack of passion in the gesture. She straightened. "We can talk about this some other time."

"Thanks."

She reached for my hand and squeezed it. "I'm sorry. This was a lot to spring on you when you're still recovering from your accident."

"Thanks for understanding," I said, but knew that was far from the truth. She loved me, but she hoped I could rescue her from her financial situation and that just was not in the cards.

"I can see myself out," she said rather tartly, turned, and headed out of the living room. It was too much effort for me to turn to watch her go, so I listened to her footfalls fade and the back door slam.

The clock on the mantel ticked way too loudly, but couldn't blot the sound of the tires burning the asphalt as she took off.

"Oh, Maggs," I lamented in that oh-so-quiet living room. I'd left the gripper in Richard's study, but I didn't want to watch TV, so the remote was safe from me. I just sat there, staring out of the leaded, beveled glass windows and tried not to think for a long, long time.

The sun had set by the time the hall light winked on and Brenda emerged. "Jeffy?"

"I'm here."

"Where's Maggie?"

"Long gone."

Brenda swooped in and turned on the lamp on the side table to my left. She settled herself on the coffee table. "Did Maggie drop her bombshell?"

"Oh, yeah," I said, wishing I had a nice glass of Maker's Mark to sip.

She sighed. "I tried to warn her that this might not be a good time to broach the subject."

"I appreciate that. Unfortunately, she's panicking. She doesn't want to deal with a tenant, and I can't say I blame her. But until she can sell the house, it's really her only option."

"What if your accident never happened? Would you have considered moving in with Maggie?"

I didn't even have to think it over. "No. I can't pull my weight, and even if she said she accepted that fact, it would always be a source of contention." I shrugged. "I'm fucked no matter how I look at it. And it looks like I'm always going to be a burden to you and Richard and I hate it."

Brenda reached for my hand. "You are *not* a burden."

Oh, yes I was, and she knew it, too. And now that Herschel had arrived on their doorstep, I would prove to be even more work for Brenda, because now Richard wouldn't alternate helping me get up in the morning or to help me go to bed at night.

"I'm sorry, Brenda. I'm really, *really* sorry to have dumped so much shit on you." I had to swallow a few times so I wouldn't cry.

"Don't be so melodramatic," she said reasonably. "I like to think of this little interlude as keeping my nursing skills sharp. You're doing me a favor."

"And you're a liar."

She shrugged. "I'm betting after the day you've had that you're more than ready to down a pain pill and hit the sack."

"You've got that right."

She reached for my crutches and handed them to me. "Then let's do it, because I'm just about ready to call it a night, too."

"It's still early. What about Rich?"

"He won't admit it, but he's pretty freaked about a cat being on the premises. I seriously doubt he's going to get more than thirty seconds of sleep tonight."

The shit was piling higher and higher. "Okay then, if you'll help me capture him, and you don't mind trucking all his stuff back across the driveway, he can go back to my apartment tonight."

"The hell he will," Brenda said adamantly. "There's no way I'm going to let Richard teach our girl to be afraid of a cat. The thing is, he doesn't even know—or remember—*why* he's afraid of cats. He's a grown man. He needs to face and get over this phobia—even if he has to consult a professional to do so."

Somehow, I managed a smile. "You wanted to say shrink, didn't you?"

Brenda smiled, too. "Yeah, but he wouldn't like me to use that term."

I nodded. "Is there a way we can make this easier on him?"

"Maybe. I'll Google it—and if I don't find what I'm looking for, I know a few doctors I can ask. But if you're going to spend even more time in my workroom because of Herschel, maybe you'd like us to bring your computer over. What do you think?"

"God, yes."

"We'll make it happen tomorrow." She smiled. "Being stuck in that cast and brace only seems like forever because you're living it hour by hour, but I promise you— you'll be back on your feet and home before you know it. Come on."

Brenda helped me to my feet and we started across the house to my temporary home, stopping in the kitchen to grab a can of cat food. As anticipated, Herschel was waiting behind the door in the darkened room.

Brenda reached in and turned on the overhead light. I preceded her and plopped down on the bed, then I doled out the cat food in a clean plastic one-use bowl she provided. Brenda put it down in the bathroom near the litter box, then changed the water bowl.

"Poor cat. Imagine having to eat your food next to your own toilet."

I could see that Herschel had already kicked an inordinate amount of litter out of his box. Brenda would have to sweep it up. Yet another chore for her. The woman had already earned her wings; the halo couldn't be far behind.

Once again Brenda helped me get ready for bed. It's amazing how fast you lose your modesty under such circumstances. As her last duty, she doled out a pill and handed me a glass half filled with water. "You're due for a shower."

I dreaded it, but she was right. "Maybe tomorrow...or the next day."

"Then start using deodorant a little more liberally," she suggested, not bothering to hide a smile.

I would. I let out a weary breath and looked at the little white pill in my palm. God, I hated taking the damn pain meds. They made me feel off-kilter during the day and, though they allowed me to sleep at night, I often woke feeling disoriented. Not taking them wasn't much better, but I resolved to try making it on over-the-counter stuff—at least during the day. I downed it anyway and set the glass aside.

"Good night." She kissed my cheek, turned off the overhead light, and left Herschel and me on our own.

While my cat enthusiastically chowed down, I turned off the bedside lamp and lay back against the pillow. What a crappy day. The highlights? CP's giggles and our picnic dinner. The lows? Richard and Maggie and the problems they had to struggle with because of me, and all the extra work Brenda had taken on to care for me.

I shut my eyes, wishing for sleep to come, knowing tomorrow promised to be yet another shitty day.

NINE

Richard brought my computer over the next morning. Brenda cornered Herschel and shut him in the small bathroom. I watched poor Richard sweat bullets as he set up the system while an indignant Herschel scratched on the bathroom door, howling with displeasure.

Richard made sure I could get on the Internet, but then escaped, heading for the main library downtown to try to find more information on Alice.

"We won't see him until suppertime," Brenda predicted sourly.

She left me alone to play on my computer, but needing to keep my leg elevated made for an awkward arrangement. After about an hour, my leg ached so bad that I put the computer to sleep and grabbed my crutches. My recliner was calling me, and since Herschel was curled up in CP's stroller, it seemed like a good time to make my escape.

I felt bad always dragging Brenda away from whatever she was doing, but she plunked CP in her little play "yard"—the politically correct name for what used to be called a play pen—settled me with my leg propped up on pillows, leaving the remote, my cell phone, and the gripper at the ready before she left CP and me to do some laundry.

CP was happily playing with old-fashioned wooden blocks and I was flipping channels when the ringtone on my phone sounded. I glanced at the number and hit the talk icon.

"Hey, Dave. I was going to give you a call later today."

"Saved you the trouble," he said with a hollow laugh. "How're things?"

"Getting better," I lied.

"I'm glad to hear that." He did sound relieved.

"What's up?"

"Well, things at the bar aren't so good."

"I guess that depends on your point of view. Richard took me there a couple of nights ago and Tom seemed as happy as a pig in shit that the joint was jammed. But I agree with you; the vibe felt all wrong."

"Funny you should put it that way. Tom always used to say that he trusted your vibes. I wasn't quite sure what he meant, but that's sort of what I wanted your opinion on."

"I'm not sure I'm up to going back there any time soon," I hedged.

"I don't blame you. But I'd like to talk to you about it more—but not on the phone. Can I come and see you after my shift—around five-thirty?"

"I'll be here."

He laughed. "I figured as much. See you then?"

"Sure."

The connection broke.

Dave was like Richard; we didn't connect on a psychic or emotional level, which was fine with me. But the concern in his voice had raised my hackles. What kind of shit would he lay on me later in the day?

Richard switched off the cranky old microfilm machine and looked over the notes he'd taken. Expansive notes. Later, he'd type them up before he offered to let Jeff read him. He'd been told that he didn't suffer from the dreaded phenomenon of physician's penmanship, but he used his own brand of shorthand that no one but he could decipher.

His search for information would have been faster if the older records had been saved to a data base—but that might not happen for years. There were probably too many other expenses that came first on the library's list of things to do. Perhaps he'd donate a million or two to make it happen.

Stacking his yellow pad, torn pages written on both sides, and copies of various decades-old news articles, he shoved them into his briefcase, rewound the roll of crinkled acetate, and got up from his seat. He returned the roll to the reference librarian and bid her a good afternoon.

As he left the area, he noticed a clock on the wall and winced. It was nearly three-thirty and he'd missed lunch. Funny, until that moment, he hadn't even noticed the hollow feeling in his gut. Still, if he stopped for something to eat before he went home, it would probably ruin his supper and he didn't want to disappoint Brenda, who already had more than her share of work to shoulder. And he had one more stop to make before he went back to ... well, knowing there was a cat inside the house made it feel like his home had been invaded by a creepy alien.

The funny thing was, he couldn't remember ever having had a bad experience with a cat. Somehow, he associated that feeling of dread and revulsion with other not-so pleasant memories of his long-dead grandmother. Could she have drilled a loathing for felines into him at an early age?

Maybe Brenda was right; perhaps he should consult a psychiatrist or psychologist about his phobia. Still, after Jeff's horrific experience the year before, he found himself as reluctant to trust in that kind of doctor-patient relationship as Jeff did. Would a self-help book suffice? He doubted it, but he was willing to give it a try. And since he was already at the library, he decided to check out a couple of tomes on the subject. If nothing else, reading them would help pass the time while he hid out in his study.

The briefcase felt heavy as he made his way back to the ramp garage across the street from the library. He found the Mercedes, drove to the pay station, and headed north toward home. But the house on LeBrun Road was not his current destination.

Once back on Main Street, he turned east to Bailey Avenue and hung a left and then a right a ways down to Millersport Highway to the Amherst PD. Perhaps he should have called first and made an appointment to see the only cop he was familiar with in that jurisdiction.

He parked the car and strode into the station, stopping at the reception desk.

"Can I help you?" asked the woman behind the counter.

"Yes. Is Detective Wilder in? I'd like to speak to her, if I may."

"And you are?"

"Richard Alpert. Hopefully she'll remember me."

The woman made a call. "She'll be right out. You can take a seat." She indicated the chairs across the way.

"Thank you." But Richard was too antsy to sit. He wandered across the room to gaze out the window at the park-like lawn and landscaping.

"Dr. Alpert?"

Richard turned. Bonnie Wilder didn't look much different than she had almost two years before when Richard had first met her. Middle-aged, with streaks of silver in her brown hair, she'd been the officer in charge during the investigation into the trouble at the Williamsville Women's Clinic ... at least before the FBI came storming in.

Wilder reached to shake his hand. "It's good to see you again. You're lucky to catch me here on a Saturday— I try to keep halfway decent hours to placate my family. What can I do for you?"

"It's not so much what you can do for me, but what my brother and I might do for you—or at least local law enforcement in general."

Wilder's expression was skeptical. "Oh, yeah?"

"Is there somewhere we can talk?" Richard asked, noting the woman at the counter was eavesdropping.

"Sure." Detective Wilder led Richard back to a conference room he was already familiar with. They took their seats. "So, what's on your mind?"

"I'm sure you remember that my brother, Jeff, has a unique sensitivity."

"Oh, yes." Her expression was more grim than upbeat.

"We're in the first stages of starting a business. We'd like to take on cold cases. Really cold cases."

"And you want me to supply you with a few?"

"Not necessarily, although we'd be open to looking at any files you'd care to share."

Again, her expression was skeptical.

"My brother recently encountered a restless spirit."

"A ghost?" Her skepticism reached even greater heights.

Richard continued. "This spirit indicated she may have been murdered. Sure enough, I spent the day at the library downtown looking into her death. She died of strangulation. From what I gather, no one was ever arrested for the crime."

"When was this?"

"April second, nineteen thirty-two."

Wilder had gone from looking skeptical to downright uncomfortable. "Did the crime happen in Amherst?"

Richard shook his head. "The body was found behind a speakeasy on Asbury Alley in downtown Buffalo."

"Then I don't see how I can help you."

"If the victim's case is indeed still open, we'd like to try to figure out what happened to her."

"And why would you do that?"

"She asked my brother for help."

"Why didn't Mr. Resnick come with you to ask for my help?"

It was Richard's turn to look uncomfortable. "My brother was involved in a rather nasty traffic accident last Friday. He was on his bike, at a stoplight. A hit and run."

"Oh my God. Is he okay?"

"He's pretty banged up. Multiple fractures and a nasty case of road rash, but he's on the mend. We haven't heard from the Buffalo PD since the day of the accident."

"If you'd like me to look into it, I'd be more than happy to do so."

"Yes, thank you. It's going to be a long and painful healing process, and I believe it would be good for Jeff to have something to distract him during that time. And then there's Alice."

"Who?"

"Alice Newcomb. She's the restless spirit who reached out to Jeff."

Wilder's gaze seemed fixed on the faux wood surface of the steel-and-Formica table before them. "You know, if I hadn't seen what your brother came up with when he touched the assassin's rifle shells, I would not have believed such insight was possible."

"You wouldn't be the first."

"What happened in Manhattan in March? A Detective Baldwin contacted me asking my opinion on your brother. I told him I thought he was the genuine article."

"Thank you for that. Jeff was able to identify the man who killed his wife."

"Oh my God! Are you serious?"

Richard nodded. "Deadly serious."

Wilder shook her head. "How can I help?"

"We'd like to look at whatever files the Buffalo PD has on Alice's case. We'd like to help her find whatever peace the news would give her. We thought if you could give us a recommendation, we could go on from there."

Wilder bit her lip. "I'm not at all sure my brother officers from other jurisdictions would be as open to trusting your brother's intuition as I was."

"And why did you give him a chance?"

She shrugged, and her wisp of a smile was ironic. "Because I could see how much he cared for your wife—and for you. He was no bullshit artist, and believe me, I've seen more than my fair share of that kind of personality."

"So you'll help us?"

Wilder hesitated. "I'll make some discrete inquiries. Just one question; why are you doing this?"

"Me, personally, or Jeff?"

"One or both."

It was Richard's turn to hesitate. If he was honest, he'd say it was to chase away a profound boredom that continued to haunt him, but Jeff was into helping Alice heart and soul. As for the future ... that was open for debate.

"We'd like it to eventually morph into a business, but neither of us sees it as a real paying proposition."

"Then why pursue it?"

"Because ... because people—alive *and* dead—need resolution. Jeff became a different person after he identified his wife's killer."

"And has that person been brought to justice?"

"Well, sort of. He was murdered by the survivor of someone else he'd killed."

Wilder's mouth dropped open in alarm. "What did your brother think about that?"

Richard shrugged. "Karma."

Wilder nodded, but it was more than a minute before she spoke again. "Okay, I'll check in with the Buffalo PD about your brother's hit and run and try to find out what I can on this restless spirit. Do you have any documentation?"

"Yes, and I'm more than happy to show or tell you about it."

Again Wilder nodded, then looked at him askance. "And would the two of you be willing to look at some of the Amherst PD's cold case files?"

"Absolutely; and the older the better."

"Why?

Richard's lips quirked into a smile. "Because we're cowards. We'd prefer not to stir up a hornet's nest."

"It doesn't matter how old the case. In my experience, there's always someone who wants to suppress the truth and thwart justice. What you're proposing could be extremely dangerous, and I hope you realize that."

"We do," Richard said gravely. Before that moment, he'd never thought of himself as a thrill seeker, but that had been a big part of the appeal of working for the think tank in Pasadena. Sure, he and Brenda did a lot of mundane research and testing, but from time to time they'd experience a heart-pounding adventure. The truth was they'd—or at least he'd—loved that aspect of the job. Now they led very quiet lives—a little bit too quiet. Jeff had been the catalyst that brought Richard back into a world that sometimes held the same kind of intrigue.

He hadn't lied to Brenda. He would avoid danger whenever it presented itself. But avoid intrigue?

Never.

TEN

Brenda had been right—or at least close in her prediction that Richard wouldn't arrive home until late in the day. It was after five, and since I'd been running on OTC pain relievers, I was more than ready to drown my aches, pains, and sorrows with a couple of generous shots of happy hour Maker's Mark. But no sooner had Richard arrived, than so did my co-worker, Dave. As he'd promised, he brought a cold two-four of Labatt Blue. Damn. To be polite, I was gonna have to drink a couple of bottles, but no way was it gonna deliver the level of buzz I craved.

Dave sat on the couch adjacent to my recliner. We hadn't seen each other since the hospital, and he'd winced upon seeing my face covered in a plethora of nasty scabs. They were a mess, and as long as I didn't smile, they didn't hurt half as much as the shattered bones in my leg.

"So you're on the mend," he said, handing me one of the beers.

"It's gonna be a couple of months before I'm out of this cast, but—yeah. Every day is a little better." Little being the operative word; miniscule would have been a much better descriptor. I cracked the cap on the bottle. "So, what have you got to tell me about what's going on at the bar?"

"Maria is a bitch."

"That was my impression, too, but there's no arguing she's brought in more business."

"Yeah, and scared all our regulars away. Guys who'd been coming to the bar for more than a decade. They kept Tom in business through a lot of lean years."

"Scared them away?" I asked, playing devil's advocate.

"A couple of the guys told me she glared at them with that evil eye of hers, then told them to leave and not come back."

"Why would she do that?" Despite my own misgivings about the woman, it made no sense to tell long-time *paying* customers to vamoose.

"She's got some kind of convoluted reason—although not one that I can figure out."

"I got the distinct feeling I wasn't going to be asked back to work there."

"Yeah, and now she's got *my* shift. I'm really hurting financially—and it's only been a week."

How ironic that he'd discovered the reality of my situation. He'd worked the more lucrative shifts, leaving me with the hours that held no promise of any kind of financial freedom.

"So what are you saying?" I asked, not sure I even cared enough to hear the answer.

"I was hoping you could look into the bitch's background. You *were* a trained investigator." It sounded like he'd thrown my former job title in my face as though in challenge.

"*Was,*" I echoed.

"You figured out who killed Walt." The man who'd held my job before me—and who'd also been our boss's cousin. I had never taken credit for that discovery—at least not aloud. Had Tom mentioned it to Dave?

Dave reached into the breast pocket of his golf shirt. "I waited until Tom went to the bank this morning to make a copy of this." He handed me a folded piece of paper.

I looked it over. "Maria's job application?"

Dave nodded. "It's got what you need to look into her background, right?"

Yeah; her name, address, and added later in Tom's hand, her Social Security number.

"I added the make, model, and license plate number of her car, too."

So he had.

"Just what do you think I can do? Do I need to remind you I'm pretty much housebound?"

"You said you went to the bar the other night."

Yeah, and I'd been paying for it—at least physically—ever since. Of course, traversing the driveway and scooting up the steps to my apartment and back down again hadn't helped, either.

"You've got contacts, right?" Dave went on.

"Not as many as you'd think."

"I just have a feeling this bitch is bad—*really* bad," Dave said grimly. "And she's been sucking up to Tom. Flirting with him. She's got to be thirty years younger than him—if not more. It just feels like she's got some kind of scam working and I'd hate to see her pull shit on the poor guy. He's such a sucker for a pretty face."

Yeah; I'd seen that for myself.

"Okay. I know a couple of people I can call—and there's always the Internet. I'll see what I can dig up."

"Thanks, Jeff. It might just save both our jobs."

I gave him what I hoped was a reasonable facsimile of a smile, but I already knew I'd never again work at the Whole Nine Yards. "I'll do what I can."

Dave smiled, once again looking relieved. Sure, he expected me to solve all his problems and then he could go back to the life he'd known and enjoyed—but I wasn't sure that was likely to happen, either.

"How're you doing with that beer?"

"I'm good," I said as he cracked open another. But how I wanted those shots of Maker's Mark—and the promise of not only dulled pain, but a dull mind—even more.

"Cheers," Dave said.

I hoisted my bottle of beer, but felt anything but cheerful.

Dave stayed another twenty minutes, and he gave me a hand to get to my feet before me and my crutches followed him to the back door. Brenda bid him a cheerful good-bye, too, and I used my right crutch to close the pantry door to the drive before I hobbled back to the kitchen. The maple table in front of the window was not set for supper, and CP's highchair was also missing.

I gave Brenda a quizzical look. "What's going on?"

"We're eating in the dining room tonight."

"Why?"

"Richard thought you'd have more room to keep your leg elevated."

"Bullshit."

"I couldn't have said it better. Why don't you go in and sit down."

"I can help you. I mean, I'm not completely useless. I can still chop onions and toss a salad."

"Too bad we don't need those skills tonight." She nodded toward the seldom-used dining room. "Go on and sit down. Maybe you can get something sensible out of Richard."

She hadn't meant to guilt me—but I felt that way nonetheless.

I wasn't exactly able to perform a three-point turn, but I did manage to turn around and head for the dining room.

As she'd indicated, Richard sat at his usual seat at the

head of the table with CP in her highchair at his right side.

"Hey, Rich."

Richard looked up from the papers that were strewn before him. "How are you feeling?"

"Okay." Well, it was mostly true. I leaned against the table and struggled to yank out one of the heavy cherry chairs when Richard leapt to his feet to help me.

"Want the hassock from the living room or some pillows to prop up that leg?"

"I hate to put you to so much trouble."

"It's no trouble," he said, settled me in the chair, and then disappeared. CP had a number of pastel-colored plastic blocks on the tray of her highchair. She inched one of them to the edge of the tray, stole a look at me, then pushed it over.

"Uh-oh!" I said. She giggled and started pushing another block toward the edge.

Richard returned with the footstool and the pillows from my recliner, setting them under the table and getting my leg situated.

"I hate all this," I muttered.

"I know you do." He resumed his seat. "I got a lot done today—learned a lot. Are you up to hearing about it?"

"Of course." Well, maybe.

CP pushed a second block off her tray.

"Uh-oh!" I said.

She giggled.

Richard collected the scattered pages and handed them to me. "Would you like to read them now, or should I give you an overview?"

I hated to admit it, but.... "I'm a little frazzled after my conversation with Dave. Could you give me the highlights and then maybe tomorrow I could read them and give them my full attention?"

Richard nodded. "There's the *Courier Express* short piece on Alice's death, and the official obit, but that's not the interesting stuff."

"Oh?"

"It turns out Alice's body was found in the proximity of three speakeasies."

I noticed that Richard had a glass of what would have then been classed as hooch. Me? No such luck. "When did Prohibition end?"

"Nineteen thirty-three."

"Just a year after Alice died." I thought about it for a few moments. "She told me her last memory was of being happy. I wonder if she remembers where she was just prior to her death."

"That's a question you'll have to ask her the next time you see her. It's a pity the cops can't interview murder victims. What an opportunity you have to potentially solve hundreds of crimes."

Maybe, but did he realize how creepy that ability was? I remembered seeing the movie *Sixth Sense* and the horror the poor little kid who saw dead people experienced. True, my encounters with the dearly-departed hadn't necessarily been ghastly, but the knowledge that restless spirits really did roam the earth, and apparently in droves here in Buffalo, was something I didn't want to contemplate too often.

"I don't want to only associate with the dead."

Richard shrugged. "Then you'll have to do more to cultivate friendships with the living."

If he was trying to be funny, he'd missed the mark. After all, he and Brenda rarely socialized with friends and colleagues, either. More often than not, it was Maggie and me that filled their social calendar.

"Did I say something wrong?" Richard asked.

"Why ask?"

"Because you look … sad."

"I was just thinking that my only real social outlet, besides you and Brenda and Maggie, is my job. Or, was my job. But if we go into business together, it's likely I'll be even more isolated."

Richard frowned. "I guess I never considered it from that angle."

I shrugged. "Then again, I lived in Manhattan for fourteen years and never had a best friend. I played racquetball with the same guy for years—and now, thanks to the mugging, I can't even remember his name. But we were never friends. I went to a shooting range on a regular basis, but I always went alone. It turns out you're the best friend I've ever had."

"Thank you."

He didn't say more. I guess that meant he didn't consider me his best buddy. It was probably his friend back at the think tank in Pasadena. If Richard ever had a problem, he called his friend, Michael. He'd called the guy on my behalf more than once, so I guess I shouldn't have felt bad about it, but somehow I did.

Well, so what. So fucking what!

CP pushed the last block off her tray.

"Uh-oh!"

Richard absently bent down to pick up all the blocks so the game could begin again.

Brenda appeared at the doorway. "We won't be eating for at least half an hour. Would you guys like some cheese and crackers to stave off hunger?"

"I could use a double shot of bourbon."

"Is that wise?" Brenda asked. "Wouldn't you be better off with a beer?"

A beer was a lot more volume and a hell of a lot less alcohol than a couple of shots.

"I'm hurting, and I don't want to take a pain pill until I hit the sack. If I drink another beer, I'll have to get up and pee in the night, and I don't want to have to do that, either."

Brenda's gaze shifted to Richard, as though asking permission to fulfill my request. I glanced in his direction to see him give a curt nod.

"Okay," she said reluctantly, but I'm not sure she approved.

"I'll have a refill, too, if you wouldn't mind," Richard said.

Brenda nodded. "Coming right up." She grabbed his empty glass and disappeared around the corner.

CP watched me as her little fingers pushed a pink block toward the edge of the tray once more.

It was time to turn the conversation back to business—since that seemed to be what Richard wanted to talk about. "What else did you learn today?"

"I spoke with Bonnie Wilder of the Amherst PD."

"Oh?"

Richard nodded. "I think she could be a valuable ally."

"How so?"

"She's going to speak to the Buffalo PD about the status of your accident, and ask if we can view the files on Alice's death."

"Oh, you with the glib tongue."

"We need an 'in' with someone in law enforcement. I figured she'd be more receptive than Detective Hayden."

He had that right.

The block went sailing over the edge of CP's tray.

"Uh-oh!"

CP's eyes were bright as her little fingers picked up a block and she examined it closely.

"Anything else?" I asked Richard.

"Just what's on these pages."

I nodded.

"You said your conversation with Dave left you frazzled."

"Only because it involved Maria Spodina. He wants me to look into her background. He gave me all the info I need."

"Maybe we could use this as another trial run for our business."

"Maybe." My gaze shifted to the table top and suddenly I felt as though I wanted to cry. But I wouldn't do it in front of Richard. No way.

"What's wrong?" He asked, his voice kind.

It took a few moments before I could answer. "I'm feeling really overwhelmed."

"Uh-oh!" CP called out and giggled.

"Well, who wouldn't be?" Richard said, ignoring his baby girl. "You've been through a hell of a lot in a short time. You're in constant pain, and both Maggie and I are pushing for you to make decisions that require a clear head."

At least he was aware he'd been trying to force me into a corner. I chose to respond to the other topic.

"I assume Brenda told you about Maggie's bright idea."

"Yeah. This is not a good time for such a proposition."

"No," I said, feeling shaky. "I've lost my job at the Whole Nine Yards—"

"Uh-oh!" CP called again.

"You don't know that for sure," Richard said.

"Oh, yes I do. You're proposing I take a job without a chance of making a living—because you don't need to; Maggie wants a roommate who can pay half the freight, and nobody has asked me what the hell I want to do."

CP pushed the last of her blocks on the floor and Richard bent down to retrieve them again. He set them before the baby, his expression pensive. "I guess we need to talk about that, and I realize it's a powder keg subject."

Too many emotions vied for prominence within me:

pride overwhelming all else. But was pride just an emotional indulgence?

Luckily, Brenda chose that moment to reenter the dining room, which gave me time to think about what I wanted to say next. She set a tray on the table, then handed me a glass, another to Richard, and set a plate of cheese and crackers between us. "Eat hearty," she said before heading back to the kitchen.

"Uh-oh!" CP said again, since she must have figured out I wasn't up to playing the game anymore.

I reached for a piece of cheddar and popped it into my mouth. Extra sharp. Nice.

"So," Richard said, taking off where we'd left off. "What do you want to do?"

That was a hard question to answer. Part of me wanted to go back in time to when my now-dead wife and I had been so happy. Before she'd become a coke head. Before she'd been murdered. Before I'd had my head caved in. Part of me was ecstatic to have reconnected with Richard, and to have found Maggie, but part of me was resentful of both of them, too. They wanted to pull me in far too many directions.

"I'm in a world of pain and misery," I answered honestly. "Right now I'm not capable of making a rational decision."

Richard's smile was ironic. "I think you just made one."

"Uh-oh!" CP said, and I noted only two blocks remained on her tray.

Richard expected me to clarify my thoughts. I took a breath and plunged on. "I would love to please both you and Maggie, but … I'm not sure that's possible. Who do I choose to disappoint more? You or her?"

"We've had the disappointment conversation before, and you know where I stand."

Yeah, I did. Still…. "Maggie and I haven't had that

conversation."

"You guys are good together," he said neutrally.

"Connected? Yeah. Financially? No way."

"I can always—"

"No!" We'd been down that road before. I hated the fact that he'd had to rescue me financially far too many times. There was no way I was going to ask him to be responsible for Maggie, too. He'd never said so aloud, but I knew he hadn't forgiven her for cheating on me, which was weird, because I had. But there were times I could see it in his eyes and by the things he didn't say. He was always too polite to vent steam, to make anyone uncomfortable, and I knew it was more for my sake than hers.

"Uh-oh!" CP said as the last block sailed over the edge of her tray.

I sipped my bourbon and glanced at my watch. It was only a quarter to seven. We weren't going to eat for at least another twenty-five minutes and I was so wiped I wondered if I'd be able to stay awake long enough to get through dinner.

Poor Herschel had been on his own for hours, which made me feel shitty for abandoning the little guy. Well, we'd probably have a minimum of twelve hours to share. Of course, if I was lucky, I'd be asleep for most of that time, but then so would he.

I took another sip of bourbon and noticed a pile of what were obviously library books on the sideboard. Titles like *Managing Your Phobia, Overcoming Anxiety, and Stop Stressing Forever.* Had Richard borrowed books that might help him overcome his fear of my cat?

"Uh-oh! Uh-oh!" CP pounded her highchair's now-empty tray with her flat palms.

"Okay, okay," Richard placated, ripping his attention away from the pages that sat in front of him. He picked up all the blocks, setting them in front of his daughter once again.

"That girl has you wrapped around her little finger."

"Excuse me, but I believe she's got you pinned, too," Richard said.

Yeah, she did.

"What's on tap for tomorrow?" I asked.

Richard's eyes lit up. "First—you read all my notes. We can't make any decisions until you do."

"And then?"

"We go to work."

Work? I was in almost constant pain; I could barely move—I felt utterly exhausted … and in my heart, I knew I would somehow be ready.

"You've got a deal."

ELEVEN

Unlike the promise of the book's title, Richard stared at the text before him and felt anything but angst free. Just reading the last few paragraphs had caused his hackles to rise. He wanted not just a glass, but a tumbler of Scotch. He resisted that temptation—but just barely.

Footsteps on the parquet floor heralded Brenda's arrival. She entered the study, aimed for the couch, and flopped down.

"Everybody tucked in for the night?" Richard asked.

"Betsy and Jeffy—but I'm not far from crashing, either."

He could hear the fatigue in her voice; could see the unhappy set of her mouth; noticed how her gaze seemed riveted on the floor.

"What's up?" he asked, and tried to prepare himself for an onslaught.

"It's too much. It's just too much," she said and there was a bit of a tremor in her voice.

"Tell me," he said.

"This is a big house."

"The cleaners come every week."

"But Betsy creates a lot of laundry. She has a lot of toys that you don't like to see covering the floor."

That was true. But he knew what the real problem was.

"You know I love Jeffy—" she began.

Here it came.

"But he's virtually helpless."

"I know having him here is a lot of work for you."

"It is. I haven't worked as a floor nurse for a very long time. I'm not used to it anymore."

"The solution is obvious; we can hire someone to come in and—"

"That is *not* going to happen," Brenda said adamantly. "You bring in a stranger to take care of Jeffy and he'll be crawling back across the driveway dragging his cat carrier with him."

"Then what are you suggesting?" he asked, dreading the answer.

"You need to get your shit together and help out more." She didn't sound angry, but she was resolute.

"I can take care of Betsy while—"

"No. You need to attend to your brother. A: he's your family. B: he's skinny, and he's kind of frail, but you're bigger than me and better able to haul him around. And C: he's embarrassed as hell to have me take care of his personal needs. So for God's sake, cut the poor guy some slack and give him a hand."

Yeah, he'd done some of that when Jeff had been released from the hospital, but that was before the cat came into the picture.

"You're asking me to—"

"Grow up," Brenda said firmly, her level gaze cutting straight through him.

"Couldn't we board the cat until Jeff recovers?"

"No." Her voice was icy.

Richard proffered the book he'd been reading. "I'm only on chapter four."

"Then you'd better take up speed reading. What do you think an eight-pound cat is going to do to you, anyway?"

"It could scratch me—or Betsy."

"Not likely. Jeffy's father had the cat declawed. I'm sure it wouldn't be something Jeffy would have done—but there's no chance of the cat harming anyone."

"It's still got teeth."

"Which *he* won't use unless you pull his tail or do something else to annoy him."

"Now you're calling it him."

"Because that's his gender. And every time you call Herschel an it you hurt Jeffy's feelings. He loves that cat."

"And I can't imagine why."

"It doesn't matter. You just need to get over it—*and* the cat."

"You just can't turn off feelings like—"

"I know that. But we don't have time for you to contemplate your navel for a few weeks, months, or years while you figure out what's behind your problem."

"You're not at all sympathetic," he began.

"None of us asked to be in this situation—least of all Jeffy or his cat, but we are where we are. That means me *and* you have to do our share. You know if your positions were reversed that Jeffy would do anything he could for you."

"Yeah," he admitted.

"No one says you have to like Herschel, and I really get that he makes you feel uncomfortable, but we can't go on like we have the past couple of days."

Brenda was unnerved by bugs—ANY bugs. She always yelped when encountering one. She didn't seem to understand that Richard felt the same way about cats, only he wasn't prone to terrified outbursts. Luckily, he hadn't had to deal with them much. When Jeff had brought the cat home it hadn't bothered him, but Richard never thought he'd have to deal with the animal. It had usually hidden when he'd visited Jeff's apartment. Was it possible the cat was as wary of him as he was of it? Had Jeff acquired a cat who could read people in the same way

Jeff could, or was that a trait inherent to the species?

"What do you want me to do?"

"If you could get Jeffy up in the morning and put him to bed at night, it sure would be a big help. That way I can focus on the baby, the laundry, and feeding the four of us three meals a day."

"But we could hire—" he began.

"I am not your grandma. I don't care how much money we have—that's not the kind of life I want to live."

"Have you even considered that outsourcing those kinds of tasks would give someone else meaningful work?"

"Are you trying to pull a guilt trip on me?" she accused.

"Of course not."

"You may have grown up never making your bed or having to load a dishwasher or cut the grass, but that's not the life I want for our daughter."

Though Richard *had* lived a life of privilege, he hadn't turned out all that bad. He'd been a good student, had gone to college and med school, and earned his MD. He'd gravitated to the same kind of work ethic Brenda was advocating.

"It's just that we don't have to struggle with this kind of stuff. It can be so much easier on all of us if we just make a few calls and—"

Brenda practically jumped to her feet. "Time for me to go to bed." She turned and headed out the room with no good-night kiss—no anything.

"Wait!" Richard called, and she stopped at the open doorway, her back still to him. "I don't understand why you feel the way you do—but I trust everything you've said."

Brenda turned around to face him, her expression guarded.

"You're right," Richard conceded. "I never made my bed. I never performed any chores, and I was never as happy as Betsy is playing with a stupid set of blocks. I never want her to feel as miserable as I—and Jeff—ever did. We're a family, and we need to act like one."

"No matter how painful and inconvenient it is?" she asked.

"Yeah," he said wearily.

Brenda reentered the room, strode across the expanse of floor to his desk and walked around it. She bent down and gave him a loving kiss. "This is what it means to be a family. It isn't always pleasant, but it's always good."

Richard reached for her hand and squeezed it. "Then I'm willing to pull my weight and do what I have to do."

"Even if you're freaked out?"

"Nobody said it was going to be easy."

"Nothing worthwhile ever is," Brenda said, and bent down to kiss him again. This time, there was real passion in her kiss, and he reveled in it.

They broke apart.

"I think I might just join you in turning in for the night."

Brenda's smile was inviting, and she pulled him out of his chair. "Yes, you definitely need to come to bed, and right now."

Richard made no effort to stifle a smile. He turned out the light over his desk and willingly followed his wife.

I took Richard's typed notes with me when I retired that evening, but my mind was toast. I took a pain pill and was in bed and asleep before eight-thirty.

Herschel woke me about six the next morning. He was hungry, but all I had to offer was a half-empty packet of treats to dump into his food bowl until someone came to get me. Of course, Hershel didn't mind an additional portion of his favorite snack.

I managed to get to the john and return to perch on the day bed to read Richard's notes and was not cheered by his sparse prose.

Alice had been strangled. Her boyfriend had been found nearby beaten and suffering from a fractured skull. I could identify with the poor guy. And yet ... somehow I felt like there should be a big question mark left after his name, and I had no idea why. And I had no idea how to pursue such an insubstantial lead, either.

The notes weren't as informative as I'd hoped, though I bet Richard had spent many hours pouring through old records to acquire the material. What we really needed was to read the police reports. I had a funny feeling that they might not be as illuminating as I hoped, either. Had Alice been seen as just a frivolous girl who'd been caught up in an at-the-time illicit activity of visiting a speakeasy with her beau and died as the result of a simple robbery?

I didn't know all that much about the Prohibition era. Maybe that was a starting point. I hobbled to my computer and brought it back to life. I did a Google search and found that Ken Burns had done a documentary for PBS on the subject, which might be a lot easier to digest than a ponderous tome. It could at least be a starting point. Richard would probably be willing to spring for the DVD and I was sure he wouldn't be adverse to researching local records, either.

Still, something in the back of my mind said we needed to delve into Alice's father's past—or at least his life after the death of his first daughter—and I wasn't sure why.

Alice wasn't my only concern. Dave wanted me to look into the life and times of our mutual nemesis, Maria Spodina. That might actually be a much bigger challenge. I did a preliminary Google search on her and only found her address listed online. It matched what Dave had given me. She'd listed only one reference on the application she'd filled out for Tom, but that was a starting point. Unfortunately, it probably meant a field trip to the bar where she used to work.

I was going to have to suck it up and force myself to go out and about. I was sure Richard would be more than happy to play chauffeur. After all, he wanted to establish this new working relationship more than I did. But anything that required moving and strength drained not only my energy but my will, as well.

There were a plethora of avenues Richard and I could pursue, but I had a strong feeling that I needed to connect with Alice again before we could move forward. Then again, I wasn't sure that she would be able to give me the kind of information I—we—needed to solve her problem. I got the feeling she was stuck at a certain point in time and might not be all that helpful when it came to talking about the circumstances of her death.

I sat in front of my computer contemplating my—our—next move when a knock sounded on my door. Herschel looked up, instantly alert. There was an eagerness in his eyes—a strong desire to escape.

"I'm decent," I called, and the door opened.

Richard poked his head inside. "Is it safe for me to enter?"

I was surprised to see him and not Brenda. "That depends on what you call safe. Will you be charged by a raging rhino? No. But if you're afraid of the ferocious panther across the room from me, then—yeah, you'd better run for your life."

"Not funny," he deadpanned. He entered the room and offered me a can of cat food. "It's for your—"

"Herschel. His name is Herschel," I reminded him.

"Yes. Feed him so we can get you up and out of here. We've got a busy day ahead of us."

Yeah, we did.

Richard had also arrived with a clean disposable plastic bowl and he backed off as I doled out Herschel's food. Back at my apartment, I'd have chopped up the turkey and giblets pâté with a knife, but had to use the can to hack it into chunks, while Herschel danced all around me in joyful anticipation. I held the bowl out to Richard.

"What do you expect me to do with it?"

"Put it on the floor in the bathroom."

"*Rah!*" Herschel howled. The poor little guy was hungry.

Richard looked panicked. "You do it."

I pointed to my leg. "Do you really think I can stand on two feet to do it with this hunk of fiberglass and a brace on my leg?"

Richard grimaced and took the bowl from me. He walked the five steps to the bathroom. Herschel rushed alongside him and for a moment I thought Richard might just throw the bowl onto the floor and bolt. Instead, he calmly set the new bowl on the floor and picked up the old one, quickly backing away—his spine unnaturally straight. He seemed to be swallowing a lot, and sweat had broken out on his brow.

"You done good, Rich."

He didn't acknowledge my praise and instead, looked pretty damned freaked. He seemed to shake himself. "Where do you think we should start today?"

"I'd like to reconnect with Alice, although I'm not sure she's going to be of much help, but I feel like I need to reassure her that we're looking into her problem."

"Did you read my notes?"

"Yes. And I have a strong feeling that we need to research Alice's father. I have a feeling that he—" I wasn't sure how to put what I felt into words.

"Do you think he had something to do with her death?"

I shook my head. "No. But ... I have this idea that her

violent death wasn't exactly a surprise to him."

"You're kidding."

I shook my head. "No." I studied Richard's face. He'd only been a father for eight months, but if the situation warranted it, I knew without a doubt that he'd throw himself under a bus to save his baby girl. Alice had already told me that her parents had been disappointed that their only child was a girl. Had Hiram Newcomb in some abstract way been responsible for his daughter's death? That idea was repugnant to me—but somehow not entirely unbelievable.

Richard changed the subject. "Brenda wants you to take a shower."

"We've got to make some choices. A sponge bath and I can function for most of the day, or take a shower and I'm wasted for a good part of the day."

"It's up to you," he said.

"Then I vote for the sponge bath and slathering myself in deodorant. Because I'm damn tired of being exhausted by what's supposed to be simple shit."

"We can hire—"

"No! I don't want that. I've had way too many people touching me these last couple of years. If I didn't connect with others the way I do, I could probably handle it. But you have no idea how creeped out and violated I feel by another's touch." Whoa—that came out way more vehemently than I'd intended, but he seemed to get the message.

Richard's gaze slid across the floor toward the bathroom floor. Herschel had finished his breakfast and was now licking his front paws. "I think I can identify with you on that."

Yeah? Maybe in some ways we were both on the same wavelength.

"Okay. So, after washing and breakfast, what's our plan?" he asked.

"A trip to the cemetery. If I can again find Alice."

"And then?" Richard asked, his gaze once again straying to where Herschel sat.

"We punt."

He looked back to me and seemed unhappy with that answer. "Which means?"

"We sit and talk and decide our next move."

He nodded. "That seems reasonable."

We looked at each other for long seconds. It seemed like it was me who needed to address the new normal. "So, are you now my designated caregiver?"

Richard found the floor to be infinitely interesting—sort of. "Brenda is rather overwhelmed by things."

I'd known that, but I didn't blame her for feeling that way.

"I'm sorry to be such a burden." This was an old—very old—hurt. "I can't tell you how grateful—"

"Shut up." He didn't say more.

I couldn't, either.

"So, what's the sponge bath process?" Richard asked.

I had to stifle a laugh. As a physician, he'd probably never had to do any basic patient care. Well, it couldn't hurt for him to be made aware of all the one-on-one attention a nurse had to supply his or her patients. "It all starts with soap and water. And don't worry, I'm perfectly capable of handling that part on my own."

To say he looked relieved, was putting it mildly.

TWELVE

By the time I got washed, changed, and had breakfast, it was after ten. Everything took so Goddamn much time. But finally Richard got me into his car and mentioned how they were contemplating buying a minivan to replace Brenda's sedan. The thought was, that it would be easier to transport baby Betsy in the years to come. Yeah, I believed in that and the tooth fairy.

Richard drove down Main Street and I looked out the passenger window, taking in the sights. During the past two years, I'd pretty much become a homebody. I loved tending the garden in Richard's yard. I went to work. Maggie and I had good times barbecuing and spending quiet time together. But knowing I was stuck in a room inside Richard's house for the foreseeable future made me feel claustrophobic. Now that I was confined, I felt the need for wide open spaces.

No doubt about it, Forest Lawn Cemetery was nothing but wide open spaces, since its denizens were buried beneath the ground.

We'd been to the cemetery on weekdays, when not many people were around, but on that Sunday there seemed to be a lot of people enjoying the quiet, visiting the graves of their loved ones, and using the place as their running and biking routes—not unlike Dave and me. Richard drove along the asphalt path until we again reached Section H, and I was glad it was as deserted as usual. He stopped the car and cut the engine in front of the bench monument where I'd last encountered Alice.

"Is there a chance I could meet your friend?" he asked.

"I don't know."

"Could you ask?"

He'd met my psychic mentor, Sophie Levin, but only once. It was because she'd decided to connect with him—not vice versa.

"I will," I told him, "but don't expect much. It may be that she has no choice in the matter."

Richard nodded. "I'll do the same as last time; drive around the cemetery and wait over the hill until you call. But please, don't go traipsing around and fall again."

"That's the last thing I want to do."

Again he nodded, got out of the car, looked all around the area, then came around to the passenger side and helped me out, handing me my crutches. "Be careful."

"I've got your cell phone on speed dial," I reminded him and wondered if he really thought there were thugs hanging out in the cemetery, ready to pounce.

He watched me hobble over to the bench before he got in the car and took off. I watched him disappear.

Once again, I noticed the near total absence of sound. All I heard were the leaves gently rustling in the trees, while all around me were the graves of more than one hundred and sixty thousand souls. It was a little disquieting. Not so much being surrounded by so many of the dead, but that the only restless spirit I'd encountered was Alice.

"You're back."

Alice's soft voice startled me. I turned to my left. "You can give a guy a heart attack by just showing up like that, and I'm not eager to leave this earthly plane."

"Neither was I," she said ironically. She sat down on the bench opposite me, feet flat on the ground, legs pressed together looking prim and proper. "Your face is healing."

"Slowly."

Her smile was tentative. "I missed you."

"Me? Or just the opportunity to have someone to talk to?"

She shrugged. "A little of both, I guess. Did you find out who killed me?"

I shook my head. "Sorry. It's only been a few days. My partner and I have done some research, but all we've come up with are a lot more questions."

"You've got a partner?" she asked, intrigued. "Are you a gumshoe?"

I was tempted to answer in my best Bogie slur, but decided against it since I was pretty sure the guy didn't become a known actor until Alice had been dead at least a decade. "Sort of."

She waited for more of an explanation.

"My brother and I are talking about starting a business to help people like you."

"Restless spirits?"

"Cold cases." I had to explain what that meant.

"You mean, nobody's been looking into what happened to me?" she asked, distressed.

"Not for a long time," I admitted.

Poor Alice looked crestfallen. Everyone she'd ever loved—and probably even knew—was dead. It seemed that I was the only one who knew, cared, or remembered her. It was a sobering thought.

"Tell me about your partner," Alice said at last.

"He's a doctor. He's married. He has a little girl who's just eight months old—"

"Ohhh," she cooed.

"And he'd like to meet you."

Alice drew back. "Oh, I don't think so."

"You don't want to meet him?"

"I—I don't think it's allowed."

"Who says?"

She seemed to squirm.

"Never mind."

"What did you find out about me?" Alice asked.

"Are you sure you want to hear?"

She nodded. "Yes."

So I gave her a quick rundown on all that we'd learned. Her frown deepened as she listened. "Is that all?"

"That's what we've learned so far from public records. Not everything is on the Internet."

"The what?"

"It's complicated," I explained. "We haven't tracked down what happened to your beau yet. He was badly hurt, probably by the person or people who killed you."

"Oh, poor Joseph. Did he recover?"

"I don't know. We're hoping to get a look at the police records, but at this point, we don't even know if they still exist."

Her eyes seemed to grow moist and her lower lip trembled.

"We're not giving up. In fact, we've hardly even started. It could take us a long time—and maybe never—to figure out what happened to you and why. I was hoping you could answer some questions for me."

"I'll try," she said sincerely.

"Okay. First of all, what were you doing at a speakeasy the night you died?"

Alice's eyes widened, and her mouth dropped open. "Nice girls don't go to speakeasies," she said, her voice hushed.

"But you did."

"I am a *nice* girl," she reiterated.

"I'm sure plenty of nice girls went to places like that—just looking for a little fun, right?"

"My father would not have approved."

"There's not much he can do about it now. And speaking of your father, you said he ran a number of businesses. Can you tell me the names of them?"

Alice frowned. "Papa didn't talk about them much. He said a girl like me didn't need to worry about such things. He told me I needed to concentrate on learning what it took to be a good wife."

I had to remind myself that Alice had been born a hundred plus years before. I knew neither Brenda nor Richard would ever want CP to settle for only that. Brenda had put her career on hold while CP was young, but she had plans to return to the workforce at some point. Not that she would ever need the money, but because she found being a nurse and helping people to be a worthy endeavor.

"Can you tell me anything about his businesses? The names or about what industries they involved?"

"Papa sometimes talked about imports, but never to Mama and me. Sometimes I would hear him on the telephone talking to the people who worked for him."

"Do you remember any of their names?"

Alice giggled. "One of his foremen was named Shifty Hartz. I always thought that was a funny name. Papa used to mention him a lot, but I don't know what his job was."

The more I heard, the more I began to believe that Alice's father was involved in something that wasn't on the up and up. Since she'd died during Prohibition, I kind of got the feeling her father might have been involved in the illicit liquor trade, especially if he was into importing goods. Buffalo was across the river from Canada where alcohol had been totally legal during the thirteen years of Prohibition in the US.

I was no walking encyclopedia on the era, but I did know that it was the reason organized crime gained a stranglehold on the country that lasted for decades. But if all Alice knew about her father's business dealings was that it allowed her to buy pretty clothes and shoes when many more had nothing, then she wasn't going to be able to help Richard and me find her killer.

It suddenly occurred to me that Alice's death might have been collateral damage. What if her father had crossed someone? Perhaps not only did he import illegal liquor, but what if he'd owned one of the speakeasies around Pearl Street? Alice's death might have been a simple hit by Hiram Newcomb's enemies or competitors.

I tried another tack. "Did your folks ever serve liquor in their home during Prohibition?"

"Oh, no. Mama was a member of the Women's Christian Temperance League. She wouldn't allow wine or beer in the house. Not ever!"

"How did you feel about that?"

Alice looked embarrassed.

I tried again. "Why did you patronize a speakeasy?"

"I loved my Mama, but I didn't want to *be* her. I wanted to have *fun.*"

And who could blame her?

"Tell me more about your beau."

Alice's smile was radiant. "He's so wonderful."

She spoke about him in the present tense, and I didn't correct her.

"He's got brown hair, brown eyes—like yours—and is so kind and gallant. He always held the door open for me. He always protected me. He—" She stopped.

"Did he try to protect you the night you died?"

Alice frowned. "I'm rather confused about that night. I may have had a little too much to drink. There were glasses of gin and...." She didn't elaborate farther.

"Do you remember leaving the club?"

Again, Alice's expression darkened. "Maybe."

"You said you remembered being happy. You enjoyed yourself that night?"

Her smile returned. "Oh, yes! We danced—we drank. We sat with friends and shared wonderful things to eat."

"Friends? Do you remember their names?"

Alice's smile grew bigger. "Bessie Armitage and her beau Francis Ogilvy. Sophie Stanley and her gentleman Andrew Cambridge were there."

"Where did you met these friends?"

"I went to school with Bessie and Sophie at Miss Farthingate's School for Young Ladies—although I'm sure Miss Farthingate would have been scandalized to learn that three of her charges ever darkened The Blue Moon's door."

"That was the name of the speakeasy?"

Alice nodded. "It was the best of the best here in Buffalo. Although sometimes our gang of six would cross the river and go to Fort Erie. We didn't have to feel guilty for the booze we drank in Canada." She looked at me. "Did Prohibition ever end?"

"Not long after you died," I assured her.

"That's good. What do you drink?"

"I'm a bourbon man."

"I don't think I ever had that. I wish I could try it."

"So do I."

We lapsed into a long interlude of silence. I looked over the acres and acres of tombstones, while Alice seemed more introspective. She was the first to speak again. "Have I told you enough to help you find out who killed me?"

"I don't know," I answered honestly. "What if I learn things you won't want to hear?"

"Such as?"

I thought carefully about what I was about to say. "There's a reason I can see and talk with you."

"I wondered about that."

"I have what is called an empathic ability."

"I don't know what that means."

"It means I can feel—understand—what others are going through. Something drew me here to you."

"I can't think what. I didn't know—or see you—until you were here one day, and I hoped you could help me. I'm so thankful that you arrived."

Her words did not comfort me. I had assumed she'd drawn me here to Forest Lawn. That she didn't think she had made it all the more confusing. Something else had to be going on—but what that was, I had no clue.

"Can you tell me anything else about the circumstances of your death?"

Again Alice seemed to shrink into herself. "No. But I will think about it and perhaps when you return I'll be able to tell you more."

"That would be helpful."

Alice stood. "I should probably let you go for now. When will you return?"

"In a few days." I looked down at my cast. "Right now it's hard for me to get around." Or concentrate.

Alice nodded. "You need to take care of yourself. Do you have anyone to help you?"

I wish I could say that Maggie was there for me, but the truth was it was Brenda and Richard twenty-four/seven.

"I'm good," I told Alice, but there were levels of good and they seemed to shift on any given day.

She nodded. "Until we meet again." Alice grew more and more transparent until there was nothing left but the soft rustle of the leaves and just me sitting there.

I looked around me and suddenly felt terribly alone. Alice had been by herself for decades with no one to talk to, no one to connect with—isolated. I'd always thought of death as the absence of everything. My Catholic upbringing surfaced and I realized Alice's predicament; she had landed in purgatory—stuck somewhere between the living and the dead.

I didn't want to think about it.

I pulled out my cell phone and hit Richard's number. "Please come and get me."

Seconds later, the Mercedes bounded over the hill and came to a halt in front of me. Richard cut the engine once again and got out of the car. "So—success?" He sounded hopeful.

"That's debatable." I reached for my crutches and wobbled to my feet. "Can we go somewhere for lunch to talk, or do we have to go home?"

"You don't want to go back to the house?"

I shook my head. "I need to hear voices other than the ones in my head. Will Brenda be pissed if we go out without her?"

"I don't think so," he answered quickly. Was it possible he wasn't yet ready to go home because he didn't want to face Herschel? "What did you have in mind?"

"Nothing fancy. Just a chance to get out among people. I'm starting to feel stir crazy."

"You're not the only one." He helped me back into the car, then crossed to the driver's side and got in. "There's a pad and pen in the glove box if you want to write anything down."

"Good idea."

By the time we reached the restaurant, I'd finished my notes, but I wasn't sure what any of it was worth or what it could mean.

Brentano's parking lot was nearly full when Richard pulled up in front of the popular Italian restaurant. All the handicapped parking spots were full. "Do you want to try somewhere else?"

Jeff shook his head. "I'll just have to hobble along as best I can." He sounded depressed.

The closest spot was too narrow to open the passenger side door wide enough to extricate his brother, so Richard took one at the far end of the lot. Two minutes later, they entered the eatery.

After being seated, and Jeff's broken leg was accommodated, Richard ordered drinks, while his brother read over the notes he'd made on the way. "Well?"

Jeff looked up. "I got the names of some of Alice's friends, but they've probably been dead for decades. They might have children, but it's not likely they would have known about Alice. She didn't seem to know just what her father's business dealings were, but the more I learn, the more I think he may have been a rumrunner."

"That's interesting," Richard said, just as their drinks arrived.

"Ready to order?" asked the thin waitress with the bleached blonde ponytail. At least it was blonde on top. The underside was a vivid shade of purple.

"We'd like to enjoy our drinks," Richard said.

"Sure thing. Give me a wave when you're ready." She headed to the next table to check on her other customers.

"Rumrunners," Richard repeated.

Jeff nodded. "Alice said he dealt in imports and that her mother was a staunch teetotaler. Meanwhile, she liked to go drinking with her friends and have fun."

"Sounds like any normal twenty-three year old."

Jeff shrugged, his gaze focused on the drink he hadn't yet taken a sip of.

"What's wrong?"

"According to Alice, she had no idea that she and I were destined to meet. She says I just showed up."

Richard frowned. "But you said you'd been getting flashes of her tombstone for a couple of weeks before you ended up meeting her."

"That's right." Jeff finally picked up his glass and took a minute sip. "Something feels very odd about that."

"How so?"

He shrugged. "That's it. I don't have a clue. I asked if it would be all right for you to meet her, and she said she didn't think that would be possible."

Richard thought about it for a few moments. "Do you think talking it over with your psychic mentor, Sophie, would do any good?"

"I usually walk to the bakery to see her."

"That isn't going happen anytime soon."

"No. And I doubt if you showed up that she'd be there to greet either of us." Jeff took a big gulp of his drink. "I think I'll go crazy before this damn cast on my foot comes off. I feel so friggin' helpless. Everything takes so Goddamn long. Everything has to be planned—even simple stuff like taking a leak."

"Yeah, but you *are* healing. All you have to do is look in the mirror to see it."

"Alice agrees with you."

Something else was bothering Jeff, and Richard had a feeling he knew what it was, too. "What else is going on with you?"

Jeff hesitated, but then he moved the glass to his mouth and sucked back the rest of his drink before setting the glass back down on the table. "Maggie."

Of course. Richard chose his words carefully. "She's got a lot going on; that is, if she's serious about moving."

"I think it's a given. She's out there all alone in Clarence. Why wouldn't she want to be closer to her family ... and us?"

It sounded like the latter part of that sentence might have been an afterthought.

Jeff shook his head. "You know, the two of us can't seem to catch a break. Every time it seems like things are about to get good, some kind of shit hits the fan."

Richard nodded and sipped his scotch, but didn't comment.

Jeff picked up his empty glass. "You aren't going to let me have another, are you?"

Richard shook his head.

Jeff seemed to mull over what he wanted to say next. "It's not just the leg that's keeping me from moving in with Maggie."

Richard raised an eyebrow.

"I'm ... broke."

"No, you're not."

"Yeah, I am. Remember I told you my credit card had been compromised? Well, it turns out the bad guys hacked my bank accounts, too. Everything I had is gone. I can't even buy Herschel a can of cat food."

"When did this happen? Why didn't you tell me?" Richard asked, feeling a little betrayed.

"We weren't exactly speaking on when I found out."

"After we leave here, we'll go straight to the bank and I—"

Jeff shook his head. "It's Sunday. Besides, I'm already running on empty. In fact, I'm worried today's little expedition might put me back to square one."

"Then how about this; I can call my lawyer and set up a financial power of attorney—just until you're back on your feet. That way I can look into your banking problems and try to straighten them out."

If anything, that suggestion seemed to make the poor guy deflate even more. "It's something to consider. Just one less brick on your shoulder while you recover."

Jeff said nothing. He didn't have to. The color on his cheeks was from embarrassment.

Richard decided to change the subject. "What do you want to do next?"

Jeff seemed to shake himself, his expression changing from defeated to contemplative. He straightened and transformed into the skilled investigator he'd been before he'd been mugged. "I need to address Dave's concerns about Maria. I meant to do a Google drive-by of the address he gave me, but just didn't get around to it. Since all I have to do is sit on my ass while you drive, maybe we could take a spin down her street on the way home and have a look."

"Fine by me. Where is it?"

"Brownstone Crescent—right in Amherst."

"Are you sure?" Richard asked, frowning.

"Yeah, why?"

"That's a pretty pricey neighborhood."

"Really?"

"Yeah. A couple of doctors from the hospital foundation live there."

"Maybe she's got the worst house on a good street."

"That can happen," Richard conceded, but somehow he didn't think so.

"Of course, Maria could simply be living with a parent—or maybe a sugar daddy," Jeff offered.

"I'm pretty sure we can look up who owns it online."

"Yeah. But I'd still like to drive past."

"Not a problem."

Jeff nodded and turned his attention to the menu. "Do you think a guy could get a ham sandwich here?"

Richard glanced over the items on offer. Thankfully, the place did offer a deli sandwich section. Good. He didn't think his kid brother could handle one more disappointment—small as it was.

Jeff picked up his empty glass, shook the ice, then sipped the watery liquid within it, looking bereft.

"I guess one more round wouldn't hurt," Richard said.

The barest hint of a smile crinkled Jeff's lips. "You're on."

THIRTEEN

Food doesn't interest me all that much, but there's something to be said about a ham sandwich on good seeded rye with Swiss cheese, iceberg lettuce, tomato, and mayo. I have to admit, the sandwich and scoop of mighty-fine mac salad that arrived as my lunch actually made me feel almost human again. And instead of gulping my second drink, I savored it, because being a guest in the home of a doctor and a nurse, I never knew when I'd get to imbibe once again.

Getting back into Richard's car was just as big a pain in the ass as getting out of it had been, but soon we were heading for Maria's neighborhood. I looked forward to putting all this physical activity behind me and figured by the time we returned to Richard's house, I'd probably fall into the recliner and conk out for the rest of the day.

Richard pulled off Sheridan Drive and onto Brown-stone Crescent, a street of newer builds, and we searched for Maria's house. Richard braked and we rolled slowly by number sixty-six. I found it hard to swallow as I took in the huge house with its many peaks. A three-car garage was tucked into the north side of the stone-clad, two-story McMansion. The yard was nicely landscaped and I guessed there had to be four or more bedrooms within. Perhaps there was an in-ground pool out back as well. A Google satellite view might tell me for sure.

"Wow," Richard said, his voice subdued.

"Yeah," I had to agree.

He drove down the street, turned around, and drove us past the bitch's house once more. A black BMW sat in the driveway, as did a Ford Focus. I bet it was the Focus Maria drove to her job at The Whole Nine Yards."

"What do you think?" Richard asked.

"That something very fishy is going on. Bartenders—even popular ones—don't make the kind of money to afford a place like this, and I've got a feeling she owns it."

"I'll look it up on the county site as soon as we get home. I'll also look up the address on Zillow to get an idea of its worth."

"Thanks."

We drove the rest of the way home in silence. I was preoccupied with thoughts of how my dire financial state compared to Maria's apparent good fortune. A low-cut blouse could not be the only secret for her success.

Richard pulled into the driveway, but this time we had no welcoming committee. He helped me from the car and into the house. Brenda was nowhere to be seen—probably off grocery shopping. I had two choices on where to crash; my room or the recliner. I felt like a traitor for choosing the recliner, but I wanted to cut Richard some slack by not forcing him to face Herschel so soon. I settled onto the chair and zoned out before I knew what hit me.

The shadows were long by the time I awoke. In the distance I heard the murmur of voices coming from the direction of the kitchen. I fumbled for my crutches, managed to haul myself upright and made a side trip to the tiny powder room I'd previously avoided before joining them.

"Welcome back to the land of the living," Maggie said, and rose to meet me, planting a pleasant kiss on my lips. It was a better greeting than I could have hoped for considering how things had been the last time we spoke.

She helped me get settled at the table. The three of them had drinks before them on the table, but I guessed that CP, who was strapped in her highchair, and I were going to have to go without as nobody offered me—us—a libation.

I glanced at the clock, surprised to see it was almost seven. "Wow. I feel like Rip Van Winkle."

"You must have been tired," Maggie said in almost her usual voice. Almost.

"It's been a long day," I agreed, wondering what—if anything—Richard had shared with her about our adventures. "To what do we owe the pleasure?"

Maggie looked across the table at my brother. "Richard called and invited me to dinner."

So, it hadn't been a spontaneous visit on her part. Still, she was there and I wasn't about to complain—at least, unless the subject of my moving in with her came up again.

"I'm glad you accepted."

"It's absolute chaos at my house right now, so I was happy to leave it behind for a few hours. I've had three Realtors come by to give me advice and tell me what my place is worth. My apartment is fine, but I've got to put a little TLC into the bottom unit. Paint, pull up the old carpets, and cross my fingers that someone will love it as much as I once did."

"I wish I could give you a hand," I said wistfully.

"I know," Maggie said rather flatly, and left it at that.

The three of them sipped their drinks.

My leg hurt, but I wasn't going to go for that pain pill until bedtime. I didn't really need a drink. I just wanted to be sociable I told myself.

Yeah, right.

"Is anyone going to offer me a drink, or do I have to get up and make one myself?"

Richard and Brenda exchanged glances. Had he tattled that I'd had two drinks at lunch?

I turned to grab my crutches when Richard finally stood. "I'll get you one. *One,*" he emphasized.

Crawling across the driveway with my crutches and cat carrier in hand was beginning to look pretty good about then.

Less than a minute later I, too, had a glass in front of me. "Thanks. What are we having for supper?"

"We didn't know when you'd wake up, so we decided to go for pizza. Is that okay?" Brenda asked.

"Fine with me. What about CP?"

"She's already had her dinner," Richard said. "Some horrible brown glop."

"I beg your pardon," Brenda said, giving him a scowl. "It was homemade chicken with veggies and gravy, and she enjoyed every bite."

CP banged a pink plastic donut on her highchair tray as though in agreement.

The four of us looked at each other. We all plastered fake smiles across our lips. It didn't feel particularly good to be sitting in that kitchen with not much to say. I figured I better break the ice.

"So, have you ordered the pizza?"

"Not yet," Brenda said.

"What do we want on it?" I asked.

"Lots of good stuff," Maggie suggested.

"Anything but anchovies, and I'm good," I agreed.

We spent the next couple of minutes negotiating, coming up with double cheese, sausage, pepperoni, sweet and banana peppers, mushrooms, and onions—the same as we always ordered."

Richard made the call to the pizzeria.

"The veggies cancel out the calories from the meat," Maggie said with confidence.

"But only if we stand on one foot while we eat it," Brenda piped up.

"That leaves me out," I said.

"I don't think crutches count," Maggie pointed out, but her frivolity seemed forced. She sipped what looked like a gin and tonic. "Richard says things might be kind of hinky at The Whole Nine Yards."

Hinky? I looked at my brother, who shrugged. "Something's definitely weird there," I agreed.

"He said you guys were looking into it—sort of as a hobby." Again I looked toward my brother. He obviously hadn't told her about his proposed business venture, and I wasn't about to, either.

"I can't do a lot right now but it's something to keep me—us," I amended, "busy."

"What *do* you suspect is going on?" Maggie asked.

"I'm not sure."

"I looked up Maria's address on the county site and she *is* listed as the owner," Richard said.

"And it's worth?" I asked.

"Eight-hundred grand."

"On a bartender's tips?" I asked, aghast.

"You must be doing something really wrong, Jeff," Maggie said. She meant the words to be funny, but nobody—least of all me—laughed.

"Maria took my job," I said succinctly. "I won't be invited back."

"Which makes this a great opportunity," Maggie said cheerfully.

"That's right. You have a chance to explore many other options," Richard said.

Oh yeah? Then why did I feel like a complete failure who was going to have to start from square one—once I could walk on my own again?

"How long did the pizzeria say it would be until the delivery guy shows up?" Brenda asked, obviously trying to change the subject.

"Twenty-five minutes," Richard said.

I gave Brenda a look that I hoped conveyed my thanks.

"I'd better get Betsy ready for bed. Want to help me, Maggie?"

"Sure thing."

Brenda got up from her seat and released CP from the highchair's restraints, then the women went off in the direction of the stairs to the second floor. We listened until we couldn't hear them anymore.

"I'm sorry," Richard apologized. "I guess I shouldn't have invited Maggie to supper."

"No. It's okay. I wanted to see her. I just wish things weren't so tense."

"I'm sure Brenda will try to smooth things over."

"Yeah," I agreed. Good old Brenda. "Sorry I pooped out on you this afternoon."

"Hey, you're doing way better than I would have expected."

"No shit?" I asked, disbelieving.

"No shit," he said with what sounded like honesty.

I nodded, but the tense feeling in my gut didn't seem about to give way. "I'm not at all happy to hear that Maria owns that house. Why would someone that successful—someone with what looks like ample assets—apply for a job as a bartender in a place that was only doing marginal business?"

"Business wasn't marginal the night we went there."

No, it wasn't.

"Dave mentioned that Maria was coming on to Tom. What if that's her modus operandi? What if she lulls some unsuspecting bar owner into...." But that's where my divine inspiration gave out.

"Are you saying you think Maria dupes the owners of failing bars to turn things over to her?"

"I'm not sure. But we ought to look to see how many times she's been married and if she's set up some kind of shell company. It could be she acquires struggling enter-prises and hooks them up with a national franchise."

"I still don't get how she'd make out in the plus col-umn with all that back-street dealing."

"Me, either. I'm just tossing out scenarios. But I trust my gut, and I have a feeling what I just suggested is pretty much the truth."

"What can we do to stop her?"

"Virtually nothing. If we had proof, real proof, I could warn Tom—and probably make an enemy of him at the same time."

"It does seem inevitable," Richard agreed. "He would-n't be the first older guy duped by a pretty, younger woman. What will you tell Dave?"

"Nothing yet. We don't have anything concrete on Maria."

"We know virtually nothing about her," Richard said. "Was her social security number on that job application Dave gave you?"

"Yeah."

Richard's mustache quirked. "Then we've got every-thing we need to look into her financial past and pres-ent."

I squinted at my law-abiding brother. "You never told me how you gained so much IT knowledge; how you're able to infiltrate computer networks."

"And leave no trace," he added, with just the hint of smugness.

"So?"

"That think tank I used to work for in Pasadena did a lot more than just judge medical procedures and equip-ment. They're one of the foremost authorities on artificial intelligence."

"And?"

"I told you about my friend, Artie, right?"

"Just in passing."

"Artie isn't a person. It's a super computer. Artie is short for artificial intelligence."

We were moving into the creepy zone. "No shit?"

He nodded.

"What was Brenda doing while you messed with all that?"

"Artie was developed and tested before she came on-board. But I kept up with all that. I no longer work for the foundation, but my friend Michael, and Artie, keep me up to date. I still do the occasional freelance job for them."

"So what you're saying is that you can hack computer databases with impunity?"

Richard shrugged. "Pretty much—but only in a good cause."

"And who judges what constitutes a good cause?"

He didn't even blink. "Me."

It was a good thing I trusted Richard with my life, because that kind of knowledge could be used for God only knew what.

I sipped the last of my bourbon and looked at the clock. We still had another ten or more minutes before the pizza was to be delivered. I wondered how much longer Richard and I had before the ladies joined us once again. I plunged ahead with my questions, because I might be too wiped in another half hour to be able voice them.

"Being able to hack into computer files and leave no trace could be an enormous asset to a fledgling business like you propose."

"You got that right. Unfortunately for us, what we need to learn about Alice isn't available to us via that route."

"No, but it could come in handy for other investigations."

"You almost sound like you're interested."

"I admit, I'm intrigued. I'm just not sure I can reconcile myself from living off that tainted Alpert fortune. You know I've fought against it for most of my life."

"Yeah," he said miserably. "I figure those who can afford to pay us should do so. But what about people—or entities—like Alice? Doesn't she deserve to find resolution? You can't bill a dead woman. But what if it's your destiny to get vibes from those who've passed on—to help them move on—to find justice? More importantly, to help them find peace."

"So, you think we'll find paying—and non-paying—clients for this proposed business?"

"Who knows?" he said, and though I can't read my brother's emotions, I could hear a sense of optimism in his voice. And for the first time, I had to acknowledge that I felt the same way. How cool would it be to solve crimes—like Batman and other super heroes—and yet remain virtually anonymous?

Yeah … definitely cool.

And yet … the whole idea was also troubling.

"Whenever people delve into what they think are righteous crusades, they often lose their moral compass. I don't want that to happen to us. Ever."

"I have a suggestion."

"Which is?"

"We bring in a third party to act in that capacity."

"Oh, yeah? And who would that be?"

"Brenda," he said succinctly.

I nodded. Richard and I trusted one other person on the planet implicitly: his wife—and my friend.

"Would she want to be involved?" I asked.

"She's a great wife—a terrific Mom—and she's bored stiff without a job." I doubted that last part.

"We wouldn't be offering her real employment."

"No, but she'd have an opportunity to give back and, honestly, that's all she really wants."

I nodded. "The three of us would need to sit down and talk about it in minute detail."

"Is tomorrow too soon?"

I shrugged. "Have you run this by her?"

"Not in great detail. But I know her as well as I know myself. She's the smartest, most articulate, and most grounded person I've ever met in my life."

"You don't have to sing her praises to me. But would she be willing to help us?"

Brenda was suddenly standing in the doorway. "Do you even have to ask?"

Maggie was just a step behind her. "What do you mean? Did I miss something?"

Brenda looked at both Richard and me, then Richard looked at me with an expression that seemed to convey an "I told you so" message.

"We're good then," I asked. Richard and Brenda both nodded.

"Good for what?" Maggie asked, confused.

"Pizza," I said.

And as if on cue, the doorbell rang.

"Ah, dinner has arrived," Brenda said, sounding cheerful. "Richard, go pay the guy while Maggie and I set the table."

"Will do." He got up from his seat.

Brenda went to the cabinet that held the dinner plates. She took out four of them and handed them to Maggie, who set them on the table. I snuck a glance at Brenda. Her smile mirrored the anticipation that seemed to be building inside me.

Richard reentered the kitchen, pizza box in hand. He set it in the middle of the table, and the three of them took their seats. Brenda opened the box and started doling out pieces. After my big lunch, I wasn't sure I'd even be able to eat an entire slice. Besides, I had way too many possibilities whirling through my brain.

Maggie started talking about packing up the contents of her home. The rest of us sat there, eating, and looking at each other, trying to suppress smiles.

FOURTEEN

Despite the almost three-hour nap I'd had after my experiences that day, I'd been right in thinking that I'd still begin to sink fast—unable to eat even an entire slice of that wonderful pizza before I began to droop.

"I'm sorry, but if I don't hit the sack soon, someone is going to have to hire a crane to haul me back to my bed."

Brenda shot a look in Richard's direction. He pushed his chair back, but before he could stand, Maggie piped up. "I'll do it."

"Are you sure?" Brenda asked.

"Of course." Maggie rose, grabbed my crutches and handed them to me. "Come on, big boy. Time for beddie-bye."

The exertions of the day left me feeling drained. I wasn't even sure I could haul myself to my feet. It was on my third try when Maggie finally grabbed my right elbow and hauled me to my feet.

"Thanks." I looked in Richard's and Brenda's direction. "See you in the morning."

"Good night," they chorused.

I stumped my way toward the bedroom and was surprised when Maggie shut the door from the kitchen to the butler's pantry behind us.

"What's going on?" I asked as we made our way to my temporary digs.

"Apparently while you and Richard were out today,

Brenda went to your room with an armload of clean laundry and Herschel escaped. It took her more than an hour chasing him around the house before she could capture him and bring him back here."

Aw, shit.

"He's got to be lonely," Maggie went on as I opened the door. Sure enough, Herschel shot out of the room as through blasted from a canon—only with the door to the kitchen shut, he couldn't go far.

"Herschel!" I called, but the cat ignored me.

"I'll make sure he's locked down before I leave," Maggie said and reached into the room to flick on the overhead light. She knew the spare room almost as well as I did. After she'd nearly died when my car had been forced off the road in Vermont almost two years before, she'd been injured and sentenced to use crutches. She'd stayed a week with Richard and Brenda until she was able to navigate stairs and could return to the second-floor apartment in her duplex.

I hobbled over to the day bed, which had already been turned down—by Brenda's hand, no doubt—and sat. Maggie stood over me. "Now what happens?"

"I peel off the day's clothes and put on a sleep shirt. But I can sleep in this one. I just need to get rid of the sweats. They make it too hard to pee in the night."

"Oh?"

"Brenda always makes sure my little buddy—the urinal—is close by."

Maggie's eyes widened with what looked like dread. "Who empties it?"

"Whoever gets me up in the morning."

"They take turns?" she asked, and didn't sound exactly thrilled.

"Yup."

"Oh. Well … I guess as medical professionals they're used to that."

"I can't exactly use the crutches and carry the thing to the can to empty it myself."

"I guess not."

She towered over me, just looking at me.

I scooched until I could pull the sweatpants off my ass, but couldn't do much more. "Can you yank them off?"

"Oh, sure." And she did, but I was pretty sure she wasn't enjoying the procedure. "Now what?"

"The hamper," I suggested and pointed.

Maggie's smile looked forced. She'd never had to take care of an infirmed someone. When her ex-mother in law had had a stroke, her ex-husband paid for in-home care after the old lady had left the rehab facility and until he could make arrangements for her to move to Florida to join him and his husband. Maggie had held the old lady's hand during her stay in the hospital and rehab, but she'd never had to actively take care of the old lady and seemed ill-equipped to take care of me, too.

"Now what?" Maggie asked.

"I either go to the bathroom or pee in the urinal."

"Oh. Can you make it to the bathroom?" she asked, sounding a little desperate.

It was my turn to force a smile. "Sure."

Again, she helped me to my feet, handed me my crutches, and stood away from the open bathroom door while I took care of business.

"You didn't wash your hands," she told me as I hobbled back to the day bed.

"It's kind of hard to do when you can't really stand at the sink." Had she forgotten the drill from her much shorter stint on crutches or was it because her injury—while painful—had healed a lot faster than I was likely to do? As I recalled, she was on crutches for maybe ten days before she moved on to use a cane. I would have to rely on them for six to eight weeks.

"I'll bring you some hand sanitizer the next time I

come."

"I'll bet Brenda has a bottle socked away. I'll ask."

"Or I can before I leave." Maggie sounded like her escape might be imminent. I was a little disappointed, but I couldn't say I blamed her.

"Herschel needs to be fed."

"Oh." Was that her new favorite expression? "Where's his food?"

"The kitchen. Usually Brenda brings it when she puts me to bed."

"Oh." She stood there for long seconds. "I guess I can go get it. I'll be right back."

She left the room and I heard Herschel make a quite vocal protest before I heard the door to the kitchen shut firmly.

"Herschel! Come here, boy!"

My cat did not obey my call, and I heard him paw the door to the kitchen. Richard would have a shit fit if Maggie opened the door and the cat made another escape. An almost-empty packet of cat treats sat on the two-drawer file cabinet that acted as a nightstand next to the day bed. I shook it and, sure enough, Herschel came running. I fed him treats one by one until Maggie reappeared. Not only did she have a can of cat food and a clean plastic bowl in hand, but a pint-sized bottle of sanitizer.

"Hold out your hands," she told me, and squirted a dollop onto my palm. I rubbed my hands and then Maggie grabbed a tissue from the box on the dresser, squirted the clear goop on it, then slathered the handholds of my crutches with the stuff. "All nice and clean," she said and forced yet another smile.

I can read Maggie like a map—and the vibes I was getting were pretty confused. She cared about me—I knew that—but delivering the kind of personal attention I needed right then was definitely not her thing. We were great together, but I wasn't sure that we'd ever be good actually *living* together. What a bitter pill. I'd harbored the idea—the desire—that one day we'd cohabitate, but I was also sure that now—or even some time in the near future—was not the time for that to happen.

I peeled off the cat food lid, dumped it into the bowl, used the lid to chop it up, and handed it back to Maggie. "He eats in the bathroom."

"So I gathered."

Herschel was dancing around her legs as she moved to the bathroom, put the food down, tossed the old bowl into the wastebasket, and changed his water. She joined me once again. "Now what? Should I tuck you in?"

I shook my head. "That won't be necessary." What I really wanted was for her to lie down next to me. I wanted to wrap my arms around her and fall asleep, spooning. That wasn't likely to happen in a single bed.

I patted the mattress. "I'm pooped, but could you just sit with me for a few minutes?"

"Sure." She sat beside me all right: stiffly.

I put my arm around her shoulder and pulled her closer. As I'd hoped, Maggie melted into me, wrapping her arms around me and leaned in to give me a kiss. That's when her cheek rubbed against mine—and the road rash I'd nearly forgotten about, screamed in protest. I recoiled, hitching in a breath.

"Oh, God, I'm sorry!" Maggie wailed.

"No, No—it's my fault I—" But I wasn't sure what to say. I was getting damned tired of apologizing.

Maggie pulled away from my embrace. "It sure looks like our love life is going to be put on hold—yet again."

"I'm sorry." I winced at having to make yet another apology.

She patted my good knee. "It's not your fault. None of this is your fault. But damn—are we what's known as star-crossed lovers? Nothing ever seems to go right for us."

"The same thought has crossed my mind. But that

doesn't change the way I feel about you."

Again she patted my bare knee. "Me, too." She leaned forward to place a gentle kiss on my lips, then retreated once more. "I might not be around much in the next couple of weeks. Now that I've made the decision to move, I want to get it done as soon as possible."

"I wish I could help."

"I know. I spoke to Brenda about it. If Richard agrees to take care of Betsy—and I don't think he'll object—she's going to go with me to look at open houses on Sunday."

"What's your criteria?"

"A two- or three-bedroom bungalow in Tonawanda with a fenced yard for Holly, and a place that's pretty much turnkey." She paused. "I sure wish it was you helping me pick out a place."

"Me, too. But moving around is really hard right now. I had to force myself to go out today. I'm going to try to do more of it, but it's pretty exhausting."

"It'll get better," she assured me and patted my knee once again. She gave me one of her most affectionate smiles. "You look tired."

"I am."

"What else do you need before you go to sleep?"

"A pain pill and some water."

Maggie stood, found the yellow pill container on top of the dresser, doled one out, and then got me a glass of water from the bathroom. I took it and handed back the glass.

"Do you need help getting that leg up on the bed?"

"I can do it myself—but I wouldn't say no to a helping hand."

Between the two of us, I got settled on the bed.

"You never sleep on your back," she commented.

"I don't have a lot of choice right now. I hurt no matter what position I'm in."

"It won't last forever," she said, echoing what both Richard and Brenda had told me.

"Believe me, I'm counting the days."

Maggie pulled the sheet up, covering me, then leaned down and gave me a sweet good-night kiss. "I love you."

"I love you, too, Maggs. I'm sorry I'm not in a position to show you just how much."

"You will," she said, and it felt like a promise. "I'd better scoot before Herschel tries to make another great escape. We'll talk again tomorrow."

"Good night."

She headed for the door, switched off the overhead light, and left me alone with just the glow of the nightlight on the far wall.

I leaned back against the pillow and focused my gaze on the darkened ceiling above. Okay, for the time being the two of us were in limbo ... or perhaps in stasis. She was too tied up in her desire to move, and I had at least two months to heal. Our times together were going to be hit or miss for a while, but maybe I could talk her into coming to stay with me across the driveway for the occasional weekend. Richard actually *liked* Maggie's dog, Holly, so maybe he and Brenda would be willing to take care of her and let me go back to my own place for a short respite. God, how I missed my own bed—my home.

Herschel suddenly levitated to land beside me—without a sound and without jostling the bed. I couldn't wait for morning to come so that Richard, Brenda, and I could discuss the future. I just wasn't sure Maggie would be happy about whatever we came up with. Our relationship too often teetered on shaky ground.

Maybe it was wishful thinking, but it seemed like the pain pill kicked in and I pulled the sheet up to my neck and finally slept. But then I dreamed of a murky sky, a hooded figure, hollow footfalls, and the shock of a terrified scream...

And I wondered who it was that was destined to die.

FIFTEEN

Brenda was my designated caregiver the next morning, and like Maggie, she closed the pantry door to the kitchen so that Herschel couldn't escape. "You're going to take a shower today," she commanded, and produced an aluminum and hard plastic stool that barely fit the three-quarter shower stall in the tiny bathroom that adjoined the craft room.

"I don't want to do this. I don't care if I stink."

"Yeah, well, I do." Brenda produced a large, heavy-duty black garbage bag, a roll of duct tape, and sat me down inside the shower to figure things out. Once I'd taped the loose ends of the bag over the top of my thigh, she came in to turn on the water, angling the spray away from me until she decided the temperature was within reasonable tolerance. She handed me a washcloth and a bar of soap.

"Go to it," she said, and retreated.

The hot water felt wonderful as it pounded against my skin. I worked up a satisfying lather and washed as much of my body as I could, and then rinsed. Then I sat back, with eyes closed and let that magnificent hot water pummel me for long minutes.

After a while, Brenda called out, "If you don't come out soon, you're going to disintegrate."

I'd dreaded the shower, but it felt so damn good, I didn't want it to end. "I'm done," I reluctantly called.

Brenda reappeared to help me towel off and then helped me dress. "Richard, Betsy, and I have already had breakfast. What would you like?"

"Just coffee and toast, please."

She nodded. "You can eat during our business meeting."

"Are you okay with all that?"

"If you guys will actually listen to me, yeah."

"Then let's get to it."

A minute later, Brenda and I managed to leave my digs without Herschel escaping, and entered the kitchen. Richard sat at the table with the morning newspaper spread out before him, while CP snoozed in her high-chair.

"Good morning," Richard said, after he'd made sure no feline had escaped.

"Same to you." I took my usual seat, chucked the crutches, and Brenda helped me settle my leg on the un-used chair.

"Do you want anything special for breakfast?"

I shook my head. "Brenda's already got my order."

A cup of coffee appeared before me, and then Brenda pushed two slices of white bread into the slots on the toaster.

"Brenda says we're going to have a business meeting."

"I'm not so sure of that, but we can at least discuss the things that need addressing."

"Such as?"

"I got a call from Bonnie Wilder of the Amherst PD. She's willing to help us."

"That's a good sign."

"I also told her we hadn't heard a damn thing since your accident, and she got us an appointment later this morning with the Buffalo PD to talk about it."

"What are we likely to learn?" I asked as Brenda slid a plate with two perfectly browned pieces of dry, white toast before me and took her usual seat.

"Apparently there's video of the accident."

I picked up a slice of toast, but my stomach had done a flip-flop at Richard's words and I wasn't sure I was going to be able to eat it. "And?"

"That's all she said."

Did I really want to see a video of me flying across an intersection and destroying multiple bones in my right leg?

No. But I knew I'd do it because that's what an investigator does. My specialty had once been crime scenes. I'd studied horrific photos—including those of my murdered wife—but I'd never had to look at photos or video of myself as victim.

"Do you think you'd be okay seeing that?" Brenda asked.

"Of course," I bluffed. I could be a stupendous bullshit artist if need be. "Anything else?"

"Yeah. Detective Wilder is still working on us getting to see the police reports on Alice's murder."

"That's encouraging," I said and forced myself to take a bite of my by-now cold toast.

"It might take a day or two for the Buffalo PD to find the case files. Stuff that old has never been scanned. Apparently they're in the bowels of some police station. But it's a start."

"That covers two of our three—what?—investigations."

"What do you want to do about Maria?" Richard asked, and we both turned to look at our moral compass.

"Just what is your impression of this woman?" she asked.

"Not good."

"Nothing specific?" she pressed.

I shook my head. "I only tuned into the vibes that were attached to the beer she poured for me. But whatever I glommed onto, it wasn't pleasant."

"You need to be more specific," Brenda said, her gaze intent.

I took another bite of toast and chewed while I thought about her request. "Acid," I said finally. "When I think of her, it feels like I'm being dipped in acid. It doesn't make sense—because obviously that never happened—but that's the impression I got from holding the glass she touched."

"You've been wrong before," Brenda said playing devil's advocate. "The fortune teller in Clarence. The chalice at the antique shop."

Brenda wasn't being cruel; she was pointing out past mistakes—or perhaps they were misinterpretations. Both incidents had happened during the first months after I'd been mugged with a baseball bat and acquired second sight. I'd been batting a thousand for more than a year, no pun intended. It was never pleasant, but I had learned to trust the funny feelings I experienced.

"I have faith in what I felt during that encounter."

"But it was a *fleeting* encounter," she persisted.

"Are you saying Jeff should give the woman a second chance?" Richard asked.

"If it was you, wouldn't you want the benefit of the doubt?" she asked.

Richard and I exchanged uncomfortable glances.

"I guess," I conceded. "But that means another nighttime trip to the bar, which is hard for me to do right now."

"Difficult, but not impossible," Brenda stressed.

Again, I looked at Richard. After all, he would have to take me there.

"We can do it in the next day or two," he agreed.

Brenda nodded. "Okay."

I sipped my cooling coffee and ate another couple of bites of toast before the conversation rekindled. Richard broke the quiet. "What do we do about making this little endeavor into a real enterprise?"

He was hot to make whatever we were doing into a bona fide business, but I was still iffy about wanting to make it official and I got the feeling Brenda felt the same way.

"Let's take this one day at a time," I suggested. "Right now, I *need* to take life one day at a time. I hate it, but I can't promise I'll feel up to being able to work—or even think clearly—on a daily basis, at least not right now."

"I get that," Richard said.

"I can't give you a more definite answer. Sorry, Rich. You're just going to have to be patient."

He let out a weary breath. "I'll try."

I ate another bite of toast while Richard and Brenda looked elsewhere. CP's little body jerked and she awoke with a start, scrunched up her eyes and began to cry.

"Oh, you're okay," Brenda chided, but she also extracted the baby from her imprisonment and plopped her onto Richard's empty lap. He bounced CP on his knee a few times and the tears and wails subsided. She really was a good baby.

"What time do we meet the Buffalo cops?"

"Eleven." Richard continued bouncing CP, who'd cheered considerably.

I looked at the clock. It was only an hour away. We'd probably have to leave in half an hour or so.

"What do I do about lunch?" Brenda asked.

"I don't know when we'll be home, so you and Betsy should go ahead and eat. I'll let you know if Jeff and I catch something on the road or will come home."

Brenda nodded. I could tell she wasn't exactly happy about that scenario. Richard and I had eaten out the day before. It had been a while since Richard had taken his wife out to lunch or dinner. Maggie was super busy, but maybe I could convince her to babysit so that my caretakers could get a night off from being parents and taking care of me, too. Then again, Maggie was up to her eyeballs in work to get her house ready to sell, and I couldn't lift a finger to help.

And yet, if Richard offered to take me out to lunch yet again, I knew I'd jump—only not literally—at the chance to be away from the house for an extra hour to two. I don't think I'd ever experienced such a profound sense of cabin fever as I'd had since breaking my leg. The mugger's had not only fractured my skull, but had broken my arm, though it hadn't hurt half as much as the leg injury, and though I'd had limited use of my left arm for a little over six weeks, I wasn't nearly as incapacitated as I was with this damn multi-fractured leg.

I finished the last of my toast, drained the tepid coffee from my cup, and looked at the clock. In just about an hour I'd have to face looking at the video of me being whacked by an SUV. I wasn't afraid, but I was bummed by the whole idea. But I also needed to get past the experience. And yet, I had a funny feeling that watching that video was going to give me a lot more questions than answers.

The Buffalo Police Department's B District headquarters was technically on Main Street downtown—just a couple of blocks from where Alice's body had been found, but Richard had no idea if the sleek looking, two-toned brick building that occupied that corner had been the local cop shop decades before.

He parked the car in the handicapped spot closest to the station's back entrance off Tupper Street, and then got out to help Jeff exit the Mercedes. Brenda's minivan was supposed to arrive the next day, which meant hours away from home spent getting the bank draft, acquiring the car, reinstalling Betsy's car seat—time not spent working on their fledgling hobby—hopefully future business—which had barely gotten off the ground and still had no name. He'd done research online and decided they ought to file as a limited liability company, with himself, Jeff, and Brenda as partners. He still had to draft the articles of organization, apply for a tax number, set up a bank account, and decide on graphics for the website, business cards, and everything else the company would need.

Richard wasn't about to voice the need to establish the structure for such an endeavor. He still wasn't sure Jeff—and especially Brenda—was fully on board, but someone needed to think about the legal aspects of such an alliance.

Jeff stood for long seconds, staring at the station's brick façade, his expression pensive.

"You okay?" Richard asked.

"Sure."

Richard didn't believe him for a second. He held the door and Jeff entered the building before him. They proceeded to the reception counter.

"Excuse me; we're here to see Detective Domkowski," Richard said.

"Take a seat; I'll let him know you're here."

Jeff looked at his brother and shook his head. "I'll just lean against the wall—it's too hard to sit and then have to stand in a short period of time."

The uniformed officer made a call and about a minute later a plainclothes detective arrived in the lobby. "Dr. Alpert; Mr. Resnick?" He offered his hand. Richard introduced them and shook, but Jeff just nodded, still gripping the handholds on his crutches.

The detective led them down a series of corridors and eventually they paused before an open doorway. The detective held out a hand, ushering them into yet another interrogation room. Richard had seen far too many of them during the past two years, but if their business was going to take off, it was likely they'd be seeing far more of them across the city—and possibly the region.

He got Jeff settled in a chair and elevated his broken leg before taking his own seat. "I'm a bit disappointed that we hadn't been given an update on Jeff's accident before Detective Wilder from the Amherst PD contacted you on our behalf," Richard said.

Domkowski nodded and addressed Jeff. "I'm sorry, Mr. Resnick. I'm a afraid your case fell through the cracks. The officer in charge of the investigation suffered a fatal heart attack and—"

"Oh, God—I'm sorry," Richard said, cutting him off.

"It was a shock. We've been trying to catch up on the cases he was juggling, but it's been—" The man said no more. Richard had no psychic insight, but from the detective's expression and tone, the man had obviously lost a friend.

No one spoke for long moments before Jeff broke the quiet. "I'm sorry for your loss, detective. I'm betting your friend would have worked his ass off on this case."

"You've got that right," Domkowski said.

"Do you have crime scene photos?"

The detective had arrived with a manila folder in hand, so Richard guessed his brother used the question to move things along.

Domkowski pushed the folder across the table, and Jeff opened it. From where he sat, Richard couldn't see the file's content. Jeff sported a poker face as he flipped through the photos before pushing the folder toward Richard.

His gaze settled on the first photo, which was of the racing bike twisted into multiple angles and felt his fists clench. Other shots showed blood on the asphalt, and an anguished Dave speaking with a uniformed officer on a sidewalk.

"My brother tells me there's video of the accident,"

Jeff said.

"Yes," Domkowski said, but didn't offer to show it. "Do you have any enemies, Mr. Resnick?"

"Not that I know of."

"Have you had any other troubles of late?"

Jeff didn't immediately answer, but Richard could see his brother instantly tense.

"I've got a problem with my bank, but thanks to the accident, I haven't had time to address it."

"Go on," Domkowski said.

Jeff let out a breath. "I appear to be a victim of identity theft. Someone compromised my credit card, checking, and savings accounts. Apparently, it happened the day before my accident. I found out about it when I got home from the hospital."

"Again I ask; are you sure you don't have any enemies?"

"No. Why?"

Domkowski got up and walked to a TV on a stand, which also held a DVD player. He picked up the remote, switched on both and hit play.

The video was black and white and not all that clear. Still, Richard found himself holding his breath as a couple of guys on bicycles approached the intersection. The camera had been situated behind them. It had to be Dave on the left, decked out in spandex riding gear that covered his arms down to the wrists and from his waist to his ankles. Jeff had worn shorts and a T-shirt. A sedan pulled up behind the two.

Time marched on. Dave spoke to Jeff, who reached up to tighten the strap on his helmet, then both men looked forward. The traffic light must have changed, because both riders prepared to take off again. It was then that a big dark SUV roared into the shot, but instead of staying in its lane, it veered to the left as though aiming straight for Jeff. The bike tilted, the handlebars seemed to get caught in the vehicle's wheel well, sending its rider into the intersection. The SUV sheered right and the bike and its occupant skittered across the asphalt, momentum sending both rolling and sliding across the tarmac until they crashed into the granite curb on the opposite side of the road.

The video froze. Jeff lay face-down on the road, his right leg tangled in the twisted metal of what had once been his sharp-looking racing bike.

The video started once more and the three of them watched the scenario unfold from a different angle— from the opposite side of the street. The bikers spoke to each other. Jeff tightened the strap on his helmet. The bikers prepared to take off. The SUV veered into the shot, took out the left-hand rider and his bike—sheered away, propelling the victim across the blacktop.

The video started once more, replaying the first version of the accident, and Richard at last tore his gaze away from the TV's screen to look at his brother. Jeff's gaze was focused on the TV, looking studious, but his eyes had a dark, dead look to them.

The footage played three times before Domkowski hit the stop button. His expression was hard. "After viewing the video, my colleagues and I agree on two points. One, that the driver of the vehicle acted with wanton depravity by deliberately veering to hit you, Mr. Resnick. Second, the possibility that you were specifically targeted."

Jeff's gaze shifted to the top of the table.

"I'll ask the question again; do you have any enemies, Mr. Resnick?"

Jeff shook his head. "Not that I'm aware of.

"Then perhaps you'd better think again—and long and hard—about it."

Jeff shook his head, looking thoughtful.

"What about those guys that got bounced out of the

bar last month?" Richard asked.

Jeff's expression darkened, and then his eyebrows shot up. "I'd forgotten all about that."

"About what?" Domkowski asked.

Jeff shrugged. "I'm a—" He paused, frowning. "I was a bartender at a place in Snyder called The Whole Nine Yards."

"Was?" Domkowski asked. "Did you get fired?"

Jeff shook his head. "Nothing like that. The bar was a three-man operation. The owner, my co-worker, Dave, who was riding with me the day of the accident, and me. My boss had to hire someone to take my place. She's brought a lot of business to the bar. I may not get asked back."

Domkowski nodded. "And the guys that got bounced?"

"I didn't escort them out myself; they were a lot bigger than me. My boss takes care of troublemakers. He's about six four and has at least sixty or seventy pounds on me."

"But *you* were responsible for the guys being tossed out?"

Jeff shrugged. "I guess."

"Were they drunk?"

"No, but they came in with 'tudes. Big-mouth college students. It wasn't their kind of bar, although I suppose now that Maria's there, it just might be."

"Maria?" Domkowski asked.

"My replacement."

"She's brought in a different clientele," Richard added.

"Yeah, and the till is full, too," Jeff put in.

"Do you think those guys could have held a grudge?"

"Over something that petty? I don't think so. And if they did, wouldn't they have retaliated a lot sooner than last week?" Jeff asked.

Domkowski didn't answer. Instead, he jotted down a few notes. "Tell me again the name of the bar and its owner?"

Jeff told him.

"I'll make a point of contacting him and asking about the situation," Domkowski promised.

"Is there anything else you can tell us?" Richard asked.

"We've contacted every collision shop in the Buffalo area, asking them to report driver's side panel damage on any black SUV that comes in for an estimate, but so far we haven't heard back from any of them."

Jeff nodded.

"We'll do our best to try to track down the person who hurt you, Mr. Resnick."

Again Jeff nodded. Richard could bet his brother was thinking the same as him: that they weren't likely to find the culprit or culprits any time soon.

"Can I answer any other questions for you?" Domkowski asked.

Jeff shook his head. "Thank you for taking time out to speak with us. I hope you'll keep in touch."

"Count on it."

Jeff looked toward Richard, who got up and retrieved the crutches and helped him to stand.

"I'll show you out," Domkowski said, and the brothers followed him back down the maze of corridors to the station's lobby.

"Thank you for seeing us," Richard said, and offered the detective his hand.

"Yes, thanks," Jeff said and leaned his full weight on his left crutch in order to shake hands with Domkowski.

The brothers left the station and headed for the Mercedes. Once inside, Richard started the engine and lowered the windows, but didn't immediately pull out of the lot. "So?"

"They've got no clue who did this to me. It's not a pri-ority and we'll likely never hear from Domkowski again."

"Is that a gut reaction, or did you get anything from shaking hands with the detective?"

"A little of both."

Silence fell between them.

"Are you okay after seeing that video?"

"I guess. The details were so blurred, it wasn't like I could even tell it was me being thrown across the inter-section. But I have a feeling the memory of that video is likely to bite me in the ass in the way of nightmares."

Richard couldn't think of anything to refute that statement. "What do you want to do next?"

"I suppose I should go to the bank to figure out my next step in reporting the identity theft, although I still haven't filed an official report with the Amherst cops."

Richard looked at the dashboard clock. "It's almost twelve. There might not be anyone available to help you until at least one. How about lunch?"

"Sounds good, but we need to do something for Brenda. She's been doing more than her fair share taking care of you, me, and CP, and she hasn't once complained to me. We—or at least I—need to somehow express my thanks for all she does. I think she'd love to have a date night with you. Unfortunately, I can't babysit CP the way I am now. Maggie's got a ton of bricks on her shoulders, but maybe I could convince her to take a night off from packing to be with me and CP. I was sort of hoping she might spend a weekend with me back at my place to give you guys a break. Maybe we could combine the two."

"Maybe," Richard agreed. He knew Brenda had been shouldering far too much of the household responsibili-ties, but his phobia regarding Jeff's damn cat kept him holed up in his office with the door shut. That closed door had also kept him from spending time with his wife and daughter, and it was unfair to all of them. He'd have to figure out a way to make it up to Brenda and Betsy.

The temperature gauge on the dash told him he could now engage the AC, so he switched it on and closed the windows. "Got a lunch preference?"

Jeff shook his head. "But we should stop to get Brenda some flowers and candy on the way home. She won't care if they come from the grocery store."

"I can do better than that," Richard said.

"Undoubtedly, but it's the gesture that counts."

"How did you get so good at figuring out women?"

"Don't forget, I can read Maggie and Brenda like books. They aren't into grandstand gestures. Give your wife a kiss or two during the day, and a few kind words, and your life will probably improve a thousand percent."

"And you do this for Maggie?"

Jeff looked away. "Not nearly enough."

SIXTEEN

We stopped at a diner, where Richard had his old standby Reuben and I ordered a bowl of Italian wedding soup. I could have done with a cup, because it was all I could do to get down half the serving. I wasn't eager to admit it aloud, but the video of the SUV actually aiming for me had been far more disturbing than I'd let on. Was I the target or would the psycho driving the vehicle have picked off Dave had he been in my position? I wasn't likely to ever find out the answer to that.

Considering it was a Monday afternoon, the Amherst branch of Bison Bank was pretty dead. We signed in at the reception counter and soon a woman of about fifty with bleached blonde hair, a long-sleeved blue dress—no doubt worn because of the bank's arctic temperature—and French manicured acrylic nails, came out of her cubicle to fetch us.

"Sarah Yarnell," she said, thrusting a hand in Richard's direction. Dressed in Dockers and a nice golf shirt, he looked a lot tidier than me in my sweatpants and crutches. "How can I help you?"

"It's me, actually," I said. "My accounts have been compromised."

She took in my attire, looked at me skeptically, and I could tell our trip there might be a complete waste of time. Sarah invited us to her cubicle and dutifully told me—in great detail—what the bank would do to try to recover my money, but the vibes I received when shaking her hand told me otherwise. Customers with compromised accounts were looked at as liars and cheats until proven otherwise.

Since we were already there, I shivered while Richard arranged for the bank check to pay for the minivan. That would save time the next morning.

We left the bank and got back into Richard's car. "So?" he asked.

"My money's gone. I know how these things work. The money was transferred to one account, and then to another, and another, and to another and another, and they'll follow the trail only so far and quit, especially since it's such a paltry sum."

"You know, with just a little computer sleight of hand, I could—"

"No," I told my brother. "Two grand isn't worth you hacking into the bank's accounts."

"I'm good," he said, and I knew it was no brag, but there was no way I wanted anything to sully his reputation—especially on my behalf.

"I may just become a curmudgeon who keeps his money in a sock in a drawer and never trust online anything again."

"It's an inconvenient way to live, especially since very few enterprises deal in cash these days."

Neither of us spoke for a long couple of minutes. I stared out the passenger side window while Richard drove. I thought back to a time when two grand didn't mean all that much to me—that was when my wife Shelley and I were saving to buy a house in New Jersey. It was expensive to live in Manhattan, but we'd decided we would bank as much of her income as we could and live on my salary. It had worked out well—until Shelley became a cocaine addict. She'd once thrown in my face the fact that our savings was basically money *she'd* earned and so what if she spent it on herself? Yeah, so what if spending that money on drugs brought her closer and closer to death?

No matter what happened with Tom and Maria at The Whole Nine Yards, I already knew that my time there was up. Did I want another penny-ante job that had me depending on tips to live, or did I cave and let Richard support me and Herschel—knowing the very thought of my cat made his skin crawl?

It was an uncomfortable place to be.

"What are you thinking?" Richard asked.

"About how far I'm wedged between a rock and a hard place."

"I know." His voice sounded weary. "I'm lucky to be in a position where I don't need to care about our new business making a profit. I wish you would accept—"

"Please, Rich, don't go there."

"We *need* to go there. You need to look at my money from a different perspective."

"Oh, yeah?"

"Don't laugh at what I'm going to say."

I let out a breath. "Okay."

"In the grand scheme of things, money is just numbers."

"What?" Where the hell was he coming from?

"You just hope that the numbers rise. But if the numbers behind you are higher than what you need to get by, then all is good."

Was he speaking in tongues? "What?" I repeated.

"It comes down to being family. Family takes care of one another—especially if they care, and you know Brenda and I care about you."

"I get that, but I have no idea what you're inferring."

"Okay, take the whole thing with trading in Brenda's car. She was prepared to buy the new minivan with her own money—but she shouldn't *have* to. Yeah, she's trading in *her* car, but she's doing so to better accommodate Betsy—*our* child. The minivan needs to be a *family* purchase. Her savings shouldn't have to take a hit."

"So what are you going to do? Split the difference?"

"Not on your life."

"How did you talk her into it?"

"I didn't need to. She accepted my offer—perhaps reluctantly—but she did accept my reasoning."

I didn't reply. Maybe I'd ask Brenda about it the next time we had a minute or two to ourselves. She wasn't all that fond of the Alpert's old money, either.

We stopped at a florist who also happened to sell boxes of Godiva chocolate, so we—or at least Richard—were good to go in expressing our appreciation to his wife for all she'd taken on to help me. And yet as he pulled into the driveway, I knew that something was wrong.

Richard held the storm door open for me and I went inside, crossing the butler's pantry and heading into the kitchen. Brenda and CP were nowhere in sight.

"We're home!" Richard called. We waited a few seconds. "She must be upstairs, maybe putting Betsy down for a nap."

But I knew that wasn't the case.

"Where do you want to plop?" Richard asked me, placing the bouquet of flowers and the box of candy on the kitchen table.

"The recliner." Somehow I knew that was the safer answer.

"Do you need to use the john or anything?"

I shook my head. "I'm good to crash for a while. It's been a long day." Sadly, I was already exhausted by the errands we'd run and the day was only a little more than half over. I hobbled off toward the living room.

Richard veered off for the foyer. "Brenda! Brenda!"

Still no answer.

I flopped into the welcoming recliner, setting my crutches on the floor. I pushed back until the chair had extended its full length.

"Coming," Brenda called, and I heard her footfalls on the stairs. I closed my eyes and tried to relax, but I already knew that sparks were about to ignite. I could hear the murmur of voices, and even from a distance could feel Brenda's tension rise.

"How could you let this happen?" Richard said sharply, obviously upset.

And then I knew the cause of his agitation.

Brenda spoke in hushed tones but nothing she said seemed to placate my older brother. He practically stomped down the hall and then I heard the door to his study slam shut.

I pushed myself forward until I was sitting. "Brenda?"

A few moments later, Brenda appeared before me. "Do you want a pillow under that leg?" she asked, her voice subdued.

"Yeah, thanks." Ever the good nurse, she settled one of the king-sized pillows under my leg before she sat on the couch. "Herschel's loose in the house somewhere, isn't he?"

She nodded wearily.

"How'd it happen?"

"The door to the craft room must not have caught. I was going to get something from the freezer for dinner and he was behind the butler's pantry door. He shot out of there at a gallop. By the time I got to the living room, he was nowhere in sight. I've spent the last hour looking under beds and couches. I can't find him."

I nodded. "He wants to be with me. I suspect if I hang out for a while, he'll come out to join me."

"Did you know he'd gone missing when you walked into the house?"

"I had a feeling. Rich is about to have a stroke, isn't

he?"

"He's not pleased," Brenda said quietly, which was an understatement. She shook her head. "This was bound to happen sooner or later."

"I know," I said guiltily.

She let out a breath. "This may actually be a good thing. It might be an opportunity for Richard to face his fears."

"I'm sure he's not looking at the situation in that light."

"I don't like spiders, but I deal with them," Brenda said firmly.

"Yeah, but how would you feel if there was a snake loose in the house?"

Brenda frowned. "I'd freak out, and much louder and crazier than Richard," she admitted.

"I guess we have to look at it from his perspective."

Movement caught my eye and as I'd predicted, Herschel strolled into the living room as though he owned the place. He jumped up on my lap and let me pet him. "You're a bad boy, Herschel."

"He sure is," Brenda said, annoyed. "I chased all over the house looking for you and you have the audacity to just saunter in here?"

Herschel turned his back to her and began to purr—loudly.

"I'm sorry. I'm—we're—" I corrected, but she didn't let me finish.

"You're both a pain in the ass," she agreed, "but if the situation were reversed, Richard and I know you'd be there for us—and Betsy."

Yeah. I would.

"I hate that Rich wants me to choose between him and Herschel. If push came to shove, you know I'd choose Rich. But this is just a temporary situation. I can't abandon Herschel, either. Do you think I should board him?" Not that I had any money, and my new credit card hadn't yet arrived, either.

Brenda shook her head. "Back in Pasadena, I had a friend—Sally Schmidt—who took a three-week cruise. She boarded her cat at her vet's office—a place she trusted. And yet that poor cat was so stressed out it died from missing her. She never forgave herself. You love Herschel. If that happened, you'd never forgive yourself, either."

Yeah, but I could go visit him. It would be time consuming and difficult—and I'd have to depend on Richard or Brenda to take me there, which would be extremely inconvenient—but it could be done.

I changed tacks. "Would you guys trust me on my own at night back across the driveway?"

Again, Brenda shook her head. "I wouldn't feel comfortable with that arrangement. The truth is, if you fell and hurt yourself in the middle of the night, you wouldn't call us until morning, and I can't allow that to happen."

"Then I don't see how we can solve this problem."

Brenda's gaze shifted to the floor as Herschel made himself comfortable, wedging himself between my left leg and the side of the chair. "Let me work on it," she said thoughtfully.

"Okay."

She scrutinized my face. "You look wiped. But did you learn anything today to help with your investigations?"

"Only that it looks like someone deliberately slammed that SUV into me and my bike."

"Oh my God," Brenda said, appalled.

"I don't mean I was specifically targeted, just that it was a malicious thing to do. Witnesses weren't able to provide the cops with a license number, so whoever did it as a lark is likely to get away with it."

"What kind of sick person could do that?"

I yawned. "You just said it—a sick person." I closed my eyes and must have fallen asleep, because when I opened them again, it was Richard who sat on the couch, holding a glass of Scotch, just staring at me.

"Why are you looking at me when I'm asleep?" I asked, still groggy.

"I wasn't watching you—I was watching the cat."

"Herschel," I told him for the millionth time, which caused my boy's ears to twitch in my direction.

"Whatever," Richard said, and sipped his Scotch.

"Why?"

"Brenda put me in time out."

"She's punishing you?"

"It sure feels that way," he muttered and took another sip. "She thinks I need to at least get used to looking at the cat—Herschel," he corrected himself.

I reached over to pet the little guy's head, which usually made him purr—but not then. He stared intently at Richard as if he knew he could unnerve him by just doing it.

I looked at the mantle clock; part of me was surprised to see it was almost six. Then again, Richard had that glass of Scotch, which meant happy hour had commenced.

I yawned. "What have you been up to all afternoon?"

"Genealogy."

"I didn't know you were interested."

"Not ours—Alice's."

"How far back?"

"Not back; forward. I wondered if she had any living relatives we might be able to talk to."

"And?"

"After her mother's death; her father remarried."

"We already knew that, right?"

"Yes. His second wife was much younger than him."

"By how much?"

"Almost thirty years."

"You say that like you disapprove. You're thirteen years older than Brenda."

"Hiram's new wife was only a year or two older than Alice would have been."

I shrugged. "I guess you're right; that is kind of creepy. What else?"

"They had two children: Arthur and Thelma. They'd be elderly now. I've been able to track down the last known address of the son and his children, but not the daughter. She got married and had a daughter, then seems to have dropped off the face of the earth."

Herschel stood and yawned, as if our topic of conversation had bored him. He walked across my lap.

"Where's he going?" Richard asked, sounding panicked.

"Probably to get something to eat or go to the can."

Sure enough, Herschel jumped down and sashayed off in the direction of the kitchen. Richard set his glass down, grabbed my crutches, and practically yanked me out of the chair. I stumped along after my cat.

CP sat in her highchair, smearing a gummy cookie through her hair, while Brenda sliced a tomato for the salad she was preparing. She looked up as the male parade entered the kitchen. Herschel seemed to glide through and into the butler's pantry, with Brenda suddenly in hot pursuit. He entered the craft room and she quickly shut the door behind him.

I looked at my brother, whose brow glistened with sweat. I just couldn't understand how a small cat could cause that kind of reaction. Still, I had to cut Richard some slack.

Brenda returned to the kitchen and resumed her salad-making.

"Any chance I can have a drink?" I asked, as much a distraction as a true request for libation.

Richard turned and stepped up to the liquor cabinet

while I took my usual seat at the table and struggled to get my leg onto the other chair.

"Ja-Ja!" Betsy called and offered me her cookie.

"No, thank you," I told her and the baby seemed confused by my refusal to accept her spit-soaked gift. "You were telling me about Alice's survivors," I reminded Richard.

"Yeah."

Richard freshened his own drink and brought me mine before taking his seat. "Do we want to bother to approach people who never met the sibling that died before they were born?"

"There's a chance they were told about Alice."

"And if they weren't?"

"It can't hurt to ask. Maybe a phone call would be better than approaching them in person."

"You said Alice's parents were disappointed she wasn't born a boy. There's a chance her father didn't talk about his first child to his second family."

"That would be despicable," I said, glancing to my left to take in Richard and Brenda's pride and joy—my little Cherry Pie, Betsy Ruth—who wasn't exactly at her best while caked with cookie goo.

"It happens," Richard said reasonably.

"Do you have contact info for these people?"

He nodded.

I'd made cold calls, hundreds—maybe even thousands—of times when I was an insurance investigator. It wasn't my favorite part of the job. Still, if that's what it took....

"Hey, Jeffy, with everything else that went on today, I forgot to mention that your friend Dave called while you were out. He wants you to call him back."

"I'll do that tomorrow," I said, feeling too weary to listen to yet another diatribe against Maria. "What time do you guys pick up the new car tomorrow?"

"We're all going to get the car," Brenda said

"I don't need to go," I protested.

"Didn't we have a similar conversation a few hours ago?" Brenda asked.

"I'll be bored out of my mind."

"Charge your phone. If nothing else, you can play hangman or tic-tac-toe on it," Richard said. Boy was he out of the gaming loop.

"I'd rather take your iPad."

"That could happen."

"Then we all agree," Brenda said: A statement, not a question.

"I guess." I sipped my drink and noted that Brenda hadn't poured herself a glass of wine. Was she going to hold it against Richard and me that we did imbibe? The specter of Richard's and my alcoholic mother seemed to hang over us far too often. I decided to ignore the disparity. "What are we eating tonight?"

"Nothing fancy. In fact, I thought it might make a change to have a cold supper."

"Which is?"

"Tuna mac salad, deviled eggs, tossed salad, and green Jell-O."

"Jell-O?" Richard did not seem pleased.

"It's Betsy's favorite."

"Sounds good to me," I said. I wasn't fussy, but I bet Richard would have preferred a steak and a baked potato with sour cream.

"How soon are we going to eat?" Richard asked.

"Are you in a hurry?" I asked.

"There are a few more genealogy websites I want to check to try to track down Alice's half-sister."

"I'll need to visit Alice again soon, too—if only to update her on what we're doing."

"Updating a ghost?" Brenda said, shook her head, and stepped over to the cupboard to grab three dinner plates.

"She might not be real to you, but she's real to me."

"I just never met a ghost before."

"Well, I have," Richard said, "and it's weird."

"I hope I never do," Brenda said. "It's just too creepy."

"Not all ghosts are creepy. Most of them are just sad. And speaking of those of the netherworld, I'd like to go visit Sophie sometime soon."

"I'd be glad to go with you. I'd like to see her again."

"No. You wouldn't be welcome."

"Why not?"

"If you go with me, she won't be there. I'm just not sure how I can get there on my own. I wonder if I could drive with my left foot."

"No!" Richard said.

"It's not the driving so much; it's getting in and out of the car by myself that worries me."

"You're not driving," Richard said emphatically. "I'll take you to the bakery."

"And what will you do while I'm there?"

"I'll sit in the car."

"And what if a cop sees you sitting in the car parked on a side street in the dead of night? What will you tell him—or her?"

Richard didn't seem to have an answer.

"I guess you could drive around until Jeffy calls you," Brenda suggested. "But what time are we talking about?"

"After midnight. Sophie's never been available to me before that."

"Are you up to it tonight?"

I shook my head. "No. Maybe tomorrow—depending on how tired I am after going to the car dealership." I lowered my voice to a mutter. "Where I don't want or need to go."

"Shut up," Richard whispered, looking at his wife out of the corner of his eye.

"Maggie and I talked today," Brenda said, changing

the subject.

This time both Richard and I turned in her direction.

"Even though her house isn't officially listed, the real estate agent she chose asked if he could show the place this evening."

"Is that a good idea?" I asked.

"He felt the couple might like the house and could possibly put in an offer."

"But Maggie said she still had a lot of work to do in the duplex's lower unit."

"She might be willing to give them a concession so that updating it is their headache and not hers. They might want a fast closing, too."

"Wow." Life was charging ahead while I was stuck in convalescent mode. It made me feel inconsequential.

"It'll be nice if Maggie lives closer," Richard observed as Brenda set the bowl of mac salad on the table.

"It will for me. We might be able to do lots more girl-friend stuff." She went back to the counter to grab the deviled eggs. "You know, I've only been to her house a couple of times. It always seemed so far away."

"Tell me about it," I said. I'd had to drive out to Clarence for nearly two years on a regular basis.

Brenda brought the salad and then fetched the dressing and a bowl of croutons. "Dinner is served." She sat down and we started doling out portions and passing bowls back and forth. I put a minuscule amount on my plate as our conversation had kind of killed my appetite. Brenda's new car—Maggie plunging ahead with her life without me. Too much was happening around me, and the stinking cast and brace on my leg and the whole healing process kept me from being a contributing member of society. And yet, as I poked at the food on my plate, I had a feeling that that was about to change in the not-too-distant future, and I was pretty sure it wouldn't be for the better.

SEVENTEEN

The logistics of getting the four of us up and out the house to make the trip to the car dealership the next morning seemed almost as overwhelming as what the entire Barnum and Bailey Circus must go through to get the big top up and ready for a show.

Brenda and Betsy took the lead in her Altima, while I rode shotgun with Richard in the Mercedes. He figured the whole ordeal would take about an hour. I knew the dealership would have Wi-Fi, so it made sense to leave the car and sit in the service area while Richard, Brenda, and CP (strapped in her stroller), consummated the deal.

As planned, Richard had brought along his iPad so I could surf the net and entertain myself, while the local all-news channel blared on the sixty-inch plasma TV bolted to the wall across from me.

I hadn't really had a plan for what I would do to kill that hour, and surfed the net while half-listening to the local sports and weather reports. The news cycled every ten minutes or so, and I'd missed the headlines. But it was a familiar name that caught my attention and made my head jerk up.

"The victim, David Morris, was taken to Sister's Hospital and was pronounced dead—"

"What! What!" My stomach did the proverbial flip-flop—but the report ended and I'd missed whatever else the newscaster had to say.

The news wouldn't cycle around for another ten minutes and instead I focused on the iPad, Googling the station's URL, feeling panicky. Dave—dead? No. There were probably fifty Dave Morrises in the area.

Then why did my gut feel knotted?

My fingers fumbled as I typed. Sure enough, the headline 'Man Stabbed at Convenience Mart' practically jumped out at me. The fact that the victim's name was mentioned meant that the next of kin had already been contacted. *The victim, David Morris, of 41 Reinwalt Street in Williamsville, was* ....

Jesus. It was Dave. My friend Dave. My co-worker.

Dave was dead.

I was going to call him after we got home. I was going to—

My cell's ringtone sounded.

I dug into the pocket of my sweats and for a crazy moment figured that the news had got it wrong. It would be Dave calling—

"Jeff?"

Not a man's voice. Maggie.

"Maggs?" I croaked.

"Oh my God! I can't believe it. I've sold my house!"

"What? What?" I couldn't seem to take in what she was saying.

"My real estate agent just called. He sold my house—and for the asking price! Can you believe it?"

"No," I managed. I still wasn't sure what she was blathering about. I still hadn't processed Dave being stabbed.

Stabbed to death.

Stabbed to death at a convenience store.

I looked back down at the tablet that still sat on my lap.

"This is great news," Maggie insisted.

"Yeah."

Silence. Then, "You could sound the least bit happy for me."

More silence.

"What?" I asked, still dumbfounded.

"Have you been drinking or something? How many pain pills did you take this morning?" she accused.

"None. Why do you ask?"

"Because you sound weird. Maybe we should talk later—after you've had a chance to sleep it off."

"What?" I asked again.

"I thought you might look at this as good news, but I can see that—"

"Maggie!"

"I'll talk to you later," she said tersely and hung up on me.

I lowered the phone, stared at it for long seconds, and then stabbed the end call icon. Pocketing the phone, I still couldn't seem to process our all-too-brief conversation and turned my attention back to the tablet.

Dave had ridden his bike to the convenience store to get a quart of milk. The photo that accompanied the story showed the plastic quart bottle had ruptured, its contents puddled on the asphalt behind yellow crime tape.

According to the store's video, Dave had exited the premises and had unlocked his bike when he was approached by a guy in a hoodie. They spoke for a few seconds and then the guy lunged, which must have been when he'd attacked.

The victim was slashed twice and stabbed once in the chest. He was taken by ambulance to Sister's Hospital and pronounced dead on arrival.

My God ... Dave was dead.

I sat there, feeling numb, feeling sick at heart.

A goddamn mugger had killed my friend.

The TV news cycled around to the story, and this time I heard every word, but it wasn't as up-to-date as the version I'd read online.

I stared vacantly at the tube as the sports and weather repeated again.

Dave was dead.

But how dead? Dead and gone like my parents? Like Shelley? Or dead like Alice and Sophie, who no longer lived, but were still of this earth.

Should I go to the morgue? Would they let me see him? Did the dead lie dormant for a while before seeking … what? Closure? That's what Alice sought. I never could figure out why Sophie hadn't moved on. Was it because she felt she had to look after me? She didn't—but I didn't want to lose her, either. I depended on her.

But Dave … *dead.*

I switched off the iPad and closed the cover, wishing I could get away from that damned TV.

I don't know how long I stared at my hands, but eventually a nudge at my shoulder caused me to look up.

"The van's out front. The service guys are putting Betsy's car seat in now. Come and have a look." Then Richard seemed to notice that something was wrong. "Are you okay?"

"Dave was murdered last night."

"What?"

I nodded toward the TV. "I saw it on the news and confirmed it online."

"Oh my God," he whispered.

"We need to go see Bonnie Wilder."

"Sure," he said without hesitation. Then he looked over his shoulder. "Brenda was hoping we could go out to lunch to celebrate."

I looked at the clock on the wall. It was almost twelve thirty. "Oh, shit."

"I hate to disappoint her, but—"

"No. If she wants to celebrate—and have an hour out of harness—I'm not going to stand in her way. It can wait an hour or so before we see Detective Wilder."

Richard nodded. He grabbed his iPad and gave me a hand to get up. I realized then that I was going to have to suck it up and not depend on him and Brenda so much. The pushback would be brutal, but I had to do what I had to do.

My resolve solidified. I was determined to find out who had run me down and killed Dave, and I had a pretty good idea of where I needed to look, too.

Lunch wasn't as much of a celebration as Brenda had hoped, which made Richard feel guilty for not telling her why his brother was such a stick in the mud. He'd helped Jeff get into the Mercedes before walking back to the new minivan.

"Brenda—" he began.

"What on earth is wrong with Jeffy?" No doubt about it; she was not pleased.

Richard let out a breath. "He didn't want to spoil your celebration—"

"Epic fail," she said succinctly.

Jeff had barely looked at either of them during the meal. He'd hardly touched his sandwich, but had gulped two beers at the family restaurant where they'd gone for lunch. Brenda had agreed to take his leftovers home for later.

"You weren't much better," Brenda accused.

"I'm sorry. The thing is ... while we were closing the deal on your car, Jeff heard on the TV news that his friend Dave was murdered last night."

"Oh my God!" Brenda cried, instantly distressed.

"Yeah. Jeff's pretty shook up."

"Oh, Richard, you should have told me."

"Yeah, well—now you know. Could you call Maggie? Jeff got a call from her and now she's pissed at him because he wasn't as overjoyed as her about selling her house."

"I'll call her as soon as I put Betsy down for her nap."

"Thanks. We're going to see Detective Wilder of the Amherst PD."

"When will you be home?"

"I don't know. I'll call."

"Okay." She leaned forward and kissed him. When she pulled back, her expression was somber. "We need to talk about the implications of Dave's death—you, me, and Jeffy."

"I know," he said. "Lock the door when you get home."

"I will."

She kissed him again, got in the van, closed the door, and started the engine. She gave him a half-hearted wave as she pulled out of the lot. Richard watched her go, then walked back to his own car. He got in and Jeff reached over to shut the passenger side door.

"You told her?"

"Yeah."

"I'll apologize when we get home." Jeff shook his head. "All I seem to do these days is apologize."

"Brenda was very upset to hear about Dave. She's going to call Maggie and smooth things over."

"It pisses me off that Brenda even needs to do that."

Richard started the car. "Moving is stressful. Maggie is making a major life change."

"Yeah, and is pissed because I'm not able to help her pay the freight."

"You can't do what you can't do." He put the car in gear and headed for the exit.

"Even worse, I can't give her the life she wants."

"What do you mean?"

"I would love to wake up every morning with Maggie by my side, but I can no longer live the life she does—which is working in an office five days a week—nine to five; steady employment. I'm not capable of it. She doesn't seem to want to understand that."

"Does this mean you guys are at an impasse?" Richard asked as a break in the traffic presented itself.

"On one level, yes. But that's one level. I happen to believe we'll get through this, but it's not going to be easy. It's actually kind of good to have this cast between us," he said, indicating his incapacitated leg. "It buys me—us—time."

Richard drove east, heading once again for the Amherst PD. "What are we going to say to Detective Wilder—that is if she's even on site?"

"She may not be the detective in charge of the case. But even if that's so, I hope she can get me in to see Dave at the morgue."

"No."

"Yes. I can sometimes talk to the dead."

"So far, it only seems like you can talk to those who've been dead for decades, not the newly deceased."

"I hadn't thought of that. I guess it also depends if a person is at peace when they die. The restless spirits I've been in contact with all had unfinished business. Dave could have felt that way. He wanted me to look into Maria's past—and present."

"But just because he was suspicious of her doesn't mean she's a villain."

"You're right. But he interacted with Maria on a daily basis when they changed shifts and was definitely wary of her. My reaction to her touching my glass was toxic. I trust that interpretation."

"Will you tell Detective Wilder about it?"

"She's listened to me before."

Richard wasn't sure how to broach the next subject,

but it needed to be said. "Our fledgling business may be DOA."

"Why?"

"Brenda's worried that both you and Dave were targeted. Dave's dead. What if whoever took him out decides you're still a threat?"

"That idea has occurred to me."

"Yeah, well—we've got a baby to think about."

"You know I'd never do anything to endanger CP."

"I do. But you have no control over what other people are going to think about what you—we," he corrected, "investigate. That's why I want to concentrate on cold cases."

"I get that. But I wasn't poking around into anything when someone decided to pick me off my bike. Dave wasn't actively doing anything out of the norm, either."

"That you know of."

Jeff's answer was subdued. "Yeah. If my so-called accident and Dave's murder are connected, and if there's still a threat out there, what am I supposed to do? I can't do nothing."

"If you weren't laid up—I might suggest a trip out of town for a couple of weeks."

"And what would that accomplish in the long run? If I came back, I might still be a target; and if not me—you, Brenda, CP, and Maggie."

"Maybe Detective Wilder will give us a different perspective."

"I sure as hell hope so." Jeff was quiet for a long few moments. "If Maria is behind all this, what could possibly be her motive? The Whole Nine Yards was never a huge success. Tom's only been scraping by for the past decade. And it astounds me that not only does she get hired, but brings incredible prosperity to the bar in only days."

"Research," Richard said. "Before we can even bring

up her name to Detective Wilder, we need to know a hell of a lot more about Maria."

"Then maybe we should just go home."

"I thought you wanted to see if something of Dave was left behind."

"If he hasn't moved on, he'll still be around tomorrow."

"I guess you're right," Richard said. "Okay, home we go. But we're going back to security mode—like we did when Brenda was being stalked."

"That's totally appropriate. In fact, though they weren't all that effective the last time you hired a guard, it wouldn't hurt to go for that extra level of protection once again."

"I'll make the call as soon as we get home," Richard said, taking the next right, which would take them back to Main Street.

"If we do end up opening a consulting firm, from time to time we might want to have a staff of hired protectors on call, depending on the situation."

"I hadn't given it any thought."

"There are all kinds of ways we could build the business. We might want to expand in several different areas."

"I'm surprised to hear you say that. I wasn't sure you had any real interest in this little endeavor."

"I'm interested, but right now I'm more of a liability than an asset."

"Are you kidding? Your experience as an investigator is our biggest asset."

Jeff didn't acknowledge the compliment. Instead, he stared straight ahead, his expression pensive.

Richard's ringtone broke the quiet. He dug for the phone in his left pants pocket and tossed it to Jeff. "It's Brenda."

Jeff tapped the talk icon. "Brenda?"

He listened for a moment. "Wait, wait!" he said, then tapped the speaker feature. "Say again."

"I'm sitting in the minivan in our driveway. The window to the door up to Jeffy's apartment is broken."

"Get out of there right now!" Richard hollered.

Brenda said no more, but they could hear the sound of tires spinning on the asphalt as she must have shoved the van back in gear and taken off.

Richard clutched the Mercedes' steering wheel as they waited for Brenda to come back on the phone. "What do you think?"

"I think Brenda and CP need to take a nice trip to Philly to visit her sister, Evelyn, until we can figure out what the hell is going on."

"Richard?"

"Brenda, where are you?"

"Parked around the corner and two blocks down from the house. What should I do?"

"Hold tight. We're almost there," Jeff said.

"Call nine-one-one and tell them what you saw. Ask if you can speak to Detective Wilder, and if you can—tell her about Dave," Richard said.

"Okay." She sounded remarkably calm.

"Don't get out of the car. And keep it locked."

"Will do." The connection was severed.

Richard risked a glance at his brother. "Now what?"

"I'm sorry, Rich. I don't know what to say about this whole shitty mess."

"Neither do I."

"What the hell could Dave and I have done to make someone hate us this much?"

Richard's fingers held the steering wheel so tight, they were white. "I have no idea. But we're sure as hell going to find out."

EIGHTEEN

The back of the minivan was packed nearly to the ceiling when we finally pulled out of Richard's driveway. Richard had personally called Evelyn to ask if Brenda and CP could stay with her indefinitely—there was no way he was risking either of their lives for a situation we didn't understand. And so each of us packed a bag or two, Brenda collected Herschel and put him in his carrier, packed his litter box, food, and our computers, and we all headed for the airport.

Once Brenda and CP were dispatched (with six bags, the baby's car seat, and carry on), Richard and I headed downtown for one of the best suites the Hyatt Regency had to offer. His top criteria was valet parking, so that theoretically, no one would mess with the van. Since Brenda had only picked up the car earlier in the afternoon, there was a good possibility Maria—or whoever else was menacing us—wouldn't know what we were now using as transportation. That would change. We might end up renting a car in a day or two...if we couldn't figure out what was going on before then.

Richard and I both spoke with Detective Wilder on the phone. She agreed we were being prudent to take such precautions, but also reminded us that a broken window and then jimmied door to my apartment didn't mean I was being stalked. Since I didn't crawl up the steps to check it out, I had to take Richard's word that nothing had been messed with.

Between the two of us, we managed to arrange for Brenda's and CP's flight, book the hotel, call in a locksmith, get the window fixed, pack, and arrange for a twenty-four hour guard on the house all within a four-hour window. I felt half dead by then, having had no time to rest during the day. Once at the hotel, Richard bummed a wheelchair and had a bell cap take me up to the suite, along with another to bring up Herschel, his supplies, and the rest of our baggage.

It was nearly eight by the time all but Herschel and our computers had been moved into the bedrooms and the bell caps left with hefty tips, leaving Richard and me to stare at each other.

"Now what?" I asked from the club chair where I'd been deposited.

"First things first."

"That would be setting up Herschel's litter box and getting him some water. He's been in that carrier for almost two hours."

Richard grimaced.

"I'm sorry about this, Rich. Maybe you should have just booked us adjoining rooms."

"No, the suite will work better." He glared at the carrier, where Herschel was pawing at the metal grate that separated him from freedom. "I don't like this situation, but I'm not going to let a ten-pound cat get the better of me."

"Seven pounds," I clarified. "At least that's what he weighed the last time I took him to the vet." Herschel's carrier was six feet from me on the floor. No way was I going to be able to maneuver close enough to let him out—not with a cast and crutches. Damn, we'd forgotten to pack the gripper Maggie had given me. I looked around the room. "Maybe we can rent a wheelchair for the time we're here? The doorways are wide enough—

and it could make it a lot easier for me to navigate. Plus, it would give my poor bruised armpits a rest."

"We'll add that to the list of things to do." Richard got up from his chair, walked over to the carrier, and stood before it, glaring at my cat for long seconds. "I don't like you."

"*Brah!*" Herschel replied, as though to say, "Same to you, buddy!"

Richard bent down and opened the carrier's door. A wary Herschel took his time before stepping out of it. He looked around, as though getting his bearings, and then slowly walked around the perimeter of the room.

"He's mapping the area," I said.

"What?"

"Memorizing the room—rooms," I amended. "It's what cats do. He'll have this place figured out in no time. If you'll hand me that bag, I'll take out a bowl and can of food and get it ready for his dinner."

"Why should he eat before us?" Richard asked.

"Herschel doesn't have fingers to pull the tab on a can. Besides, we can call room service."

A reluctant Richard complied. He'd shut the door to his bed and bath rooms, and with my instructions, set up the litter box, water, and food bowls for my cat in my bathroom. Once that was done, he sat down with the room service menu.

"I did a lot of travel in my old job and used room service a lot. I found it best to order sandwiches, since anything else usually came up stone cold," I told him.

"We're got a microwave and a fridge."

"What happened to my sandwich from lunch?"

"It sat in the car for hours and got tossed."

"If that menu has a ham and Swiss club sandwich, I'll take it on rye."

Richard studied the entrées on offer. "Sorry, ciabatta roll only."

"So be it."

"I've had a few good room service meals over the years. I'll risk getting the strip steak. I'll call it in, and we can set up the computers while we wait."

"Good idea." Of course we weren't going to do the grunt work in that regard. Richard was twelve years older than me, but he was better able to crawl around the floor and get the strip plugs going and fire up my crappy printer.

Half an hour later, we were both connected to the Internet, which was what we were going to need if we were to do some cyber snooping. A knock at the door let us know that our dinners had arrived. The bell cap who'd wheeled me up less than an hour before pushed the linen-clad cart inside, and Richard rewarded him with yet another generous tip.

Richard pushed his chair closer to mine and set our meals on the coffee table. He'd ordered a couple of beers, although I knew he'd also packed the kitchen booze to bring along. He picked up his silverware. "This wasn't how I pictured my last meal of the day."

"Me, either." I picked up a potato chip from my plate and crunched it. "Brenda should be getting into Philly in about an hour."

"She wasn't happy about leaving us."

"I got that feeling."

"I'm pretty sure she never got a chance to call Maggie."

"Yeah. I guess I should do that right after we eat—but I'm going to have to crash pretty damn quick. I've never felt so tired—or hungry—in my life." The latter was a lie, but it sounded appropriate.

Richard opened the little plastic container of sour cream and slathered it on his baked potato. "We need to figure out a plan of attack—or at least where we want to direct our inquiries."

I picked up one of my sandwich quarters. "Should I call Sam Nielsen—" a friend who worked as a reporter at the *Buffalo News*, "—and have him look into Maria's background, or would your friends in California have a better shot at it?"

"I have confidence you and I can look into this. This is our test case—to see if we have what it takes to solve—"

"Crimes?" I offered.

"Cases," Richard corrected.

"We still need to figure out why Alice Newcomb came to my attention."

"Then perhaps that should be where you concentrate your efforts."

"Why?"

"Is there a chance she and Maria are somehow connected?"

"Alice died at least fifty years before Maria was born, so I don't see how that can be."

"And you won't—unless you look," Richard observed. "Don't you think it's odd that these two problems surfaced so close together?"

He had a point, but a big part of me didn't want to believe they were connected, although I have no idea why. I took a bite of my sandwich and chewed before swallowing. I was so friggin' tired, I wasn't sure I could even finish that one triangle of sandwich before I would need to fall into bed and give in to the exhaustion that pulled at every muscle in my body and in my mind.

I took another bite of my sandwich, chewing slower and slower. I had to take a slug of my beer before I could even swallow it. I put the rest of it back on my plate and sat back.

"You looked wiped," Richard said, set his fork, aside and stood. "Let's get you to bed and then I'll call Maggie and smooth things over."

"No; eat your dinner."

He reached for my crutches, handing them to me. "No way. I know from experience that if you fall asleep where you are, I'll never be able to get you up. I can nuke the rest of my dinner once you're in for the night."

"Thanks."

The evening's ablutions were abandoned. I hit the john, pulled off my sweatpants, and hit the sack. I'm pretty sure I was asleep before Richard even turned off the light.

I awoke at the crack of dawn—literally. It was five thirty-six and Herschel was wedged next to my chest. I'd slept straight through. I hated to disturb the little guy, but nature's call was pretty urgent. It took me a full minute to remember where the hell I was and why. Thankfully, Richard had left my crutches within easy reach. Five minutes later, I entered the suite's living room, surprised to find Richard already dressed and seated at the desk, his laptop's screen flashing.

"You're up early," I said, startling him.

"Room service should be here any minute now. I ordered a bunch of stuff. We'll have more than enough to start the day."

"Thanks." First things first. "Did you talk to Brenda last night?"

"It was after eleven when she called. She was happy to see her family. Apparently a whole mob showed up to greet her at the airport—but she wants us to wrap this up ASAP so she can come home."

"I can't blame her."

"I spoke to Maggie, too. She felt terrible when I told her about Dave. She'd like you to call her sometime today."

"Can do. Did you tell her our situation?"

"Sort of."

"What does that mean?"

"That you'll need to explain why she can't visit you for the foreseeable future, and why Brenda and Betsy went to Philadelphia."

"Not a problem. But damn, now I really feel like I'm abandoning her. And if she's sold her house, now even Brenda can't help her find something else fast."

"Perhaps one of her sisters can do that."

"Irene is a bitch who'll only find fault with everything she does and denigrate me. Sandy's a militant soccer mom. I doubt she'd be willing to carve out a second to help Maggie. Whatever you do—please don't become a friggin' helicopter parent. I'd hate to see every second of CP's life scheduled so she never has a moment to actually be a kid. God knows neither of us had a decent childhood; let's make sure she does."

"Brenda and I are in complete agreement on that account."

I nodded toward his computer. "What are you working on?"

"I've signed up for every service I could Google that can connect us to public information, as well as a few genealogy sites."

"Which makes me glad I've been actively working to hide my Internet presence."

"I could probably hack into any database I please, but I'd prefer to use public sites as much as possible."

"I'm still astounded that you would even consider hacking in any way, shape, or form."

"As I've told you, I don't have a problem if it's done in the name of justice."

"It sounds like you think of yourself as a superhero."

Richard shook his head. "Most likely, anything we uncover would never have to be taken to court."

"You're thinking ahead—to a time when we concentrate on cold cases—not about our current situation. If

Maria Spodina is behind my accident and Dave's murder, I want whatever we uncover to stick."

"I'm keeping that in mind."

A knock sounded at the door. Richard got up, walked across the room, and checked the peep hole before he opened it.

"Your breakfast, sir," the bell cap said.

Richard stood back to let him in. Once the cart had been pushed into the room and near me, the bell cap turned to face Richard. "Will you need anything else, sir?"

Richard reached into his pocket and pulled out a wad of cash, peeling off a ten and handing it to the bell cap.

"Thank you, sir."

Richard followed the guy to the door, then closed and locked it behind him. He moved to stand before the cart, poured coffee for both of us, handing me mine, and then plunked a croissant and a Danish each on two plates, again, handing me mine.

"Thanks. I've decided to be paranoid," I said, and took my first sip of coffee.

He took his seat at the desk once more. "In what way?"

"Maria seems to be a step ahead of us. If she finds out we're here, she might try to get at us."

"What do you suggest we do?"

"First, that this should be our last room service meal. As you pointed out, we have a microwave and a fridge. We can fend for ourselves."

"Do you think we should move every few days?"

"I hope like hell we figure out what's going on before we have to do that, but yes." I pulled apart my croissant and took a bite. Nice. "Have you come up with anything since last night?"

Richard nodded. "Maria has definitely been misrepresenting herself."

"In what way?"

"She may have started out as a bar maid, but she owns several commercial parcels of land in the area."

"Such as?"

"Areas that are up and coming."

"You only have to look at Main Street to see a lot of that happening."

"And speaking of Main Street, guess who owns the property next to the Whole Nine Yards?"

"Maria?"

Richard nodded. "At least the shell company she seems to own does."

"She's got a shell company?"

"It took a bit of digging, but I eventually traced it back to her social security number."

The property next to The Whole Nine Yards had been a florist that had gone out of business and sported a FOR SALE OR LEASE sign for more than a year. "When did she buy it?"

"Six months ago. It and the property behind it and the bar."

"It's starting to make sense now. It sounds like she intends to develop the whole block."

"And the stumbling block is your familiar little bar," Richard said, "which is owned by Tom Link."

"Who would never sell. But what if he suddenly married? Tom's a middle-class guy—"

"Who undoubtedly would never think of asking for a pre-nup."

"Goddamn," I said, feeling heartsick. "If I tried to warn him, he wouldn't listen to me."

"Probably not."

The whole situation troubled me. "Why would Maria think Dave and I are—were—a threat?"

"I'm puzzled by that, too." Richard looked thoughtful. "Maybe because you'd both been working for Tom for a while. Hell, Dave worked there for a decade, right?"

"Yeah."

"If Maria was going to have any influence on Tom, it stands to reason that getting rid of his long-time employees would make her indispensable to him."

"You've got that right," I said, thinking of the bar's recent prosperity. I shook my head. "How could Tom be so friggin' stupid?"

"How long has he been alone?" Richard asked.

"A long time," I conceded.

Richard shrugged. "Imagine if you'd been lonely for years and suddenly a very attractive—much younger—woman showed interest in you?"

"I'd be suspicious as hell."

"But that's *you*. Not Tom."

"Yeah," I had to agree. "What can we do to stop her?"

"I'm not sure we can. We could probably assemble a credible case against her, but Tom might think it's just sour grapes on your part. And now that Dave's dead, it's your word against a pretty young woman who's probably whispering sweet nothings in Tom's ear."

"How Goddamn pathetic."

We spent the next few minutes in silence, sipping our coffee and eating our continental breakfasts. I was the first to break the quiet. "I need to connect with Alice today, if that's okay."

"I agree. But we also need to do more research on her and her half-siblings.

"We haven't got much else to do this morning," I offered.

Herschel wandered into the living room, making a beeline for Richard, as though knowing—and taking great pleasure in the fact—that he'd be freaked out.

"I never unpacked last night," I said, as a distraction.

"As you said, it might be prudent to move out of here tomorrow and go somewhere else."

"Paranoia doesn't suit us."

"I keep thinking about Dave. Seeing that cast on your leg makes me feel like we need to take whatever precautions we can. I'm glad Brenda and Betsy are safe, hundreds of miles from here."

I was, too.

I ate the rest of my croissant and put a dent in my Danish before I got up and lured Herschel back to the bathroom in my part of the suite and fed him, and then Richard helped me get ready for the day. It was six-thirty when I sat down before my computer and went to work.

The ride to the cemetery was quiet. After all, what did Richard and I have to discuss? Still, I had a feeling the subject of security would raise its ugly head the moment we passed under Forest Lawn's big granite gates.

I'd learned a lot during the past couple of hours and hit pay dirt when I'd tracked down and spoken to Alice's niece—daughter of the half-brother Alice had never known existed. What she'd told me was hearsay, but at that point, it was all I had.

Richard braked as he turned into the cemetery's main entrance. "I can't leave you alone this time. It's too dangerous, considering your current condition."

"And I'm not certain Alice will show up if you're in the vicinity."

"Then so be it."

I wasn't going to win should I argue. Still…. "Perhaps you could back the car up so that you can keep me in sight, but not be too close."

"I was thinking the same thing. Still, a sniper…." He let the sentence hang.

Thanks for that, bro.

Not!

We drove along the cemetery's roads until we came

to the same stone bench where I'd encountered Alice on two previous occasions. Richard handed me my crutches, looking all around us. I moved to and settled on the cold stone memorial. "Take out your phone," he directed.

I did. "Go."

He nodded, looking distinctly unhappy. He got back in the minivan, started the engine, and backed up at least a hundred yards from where I sat, pulled off the road, and parked.

It was my turn to look all around me. Snipers? That was a scary thought, but Maria wouldn't have had a clue that our destination that morning would be Buffalo's biggest cemetery.

Unless, of course, she already knew where we'd set up base camp and followed us.

"Alice?" I called. I admit it; I was feeling antsy. I wanted to get this over with as soon as possible. "Alice?"

"Shhh!"

I heard her—I just wasn't sure where the sound had come from. "Where are you?"

"Here!"

I looked around me, but saw no one, and then the top of a brunette head slowly rose over the far edge of the stone bench's armrest until I could see her blue eyes.

"Why are you hiding?"

"Because of that car." She nodded up the hill toward Brenda's minivan.

"I'm sorry. But my brother insists on being able to see me. It appears that someone might be trying to kill me."

"Why?" she asked, sounding distressed.

The situation was far too convoluted for me to go into with such a guileless spirit as Alice. "It's complicated. Why don't you come and sit beside me?"

"I'm fine here," she assured me.

As crouching for any length of time wasn't going to be painful for her, I decided not to push it. "I've been investigating what happened after you died."

"And?" she asked, sounding apprehensive.

"You know your mother passed away just short of two years after you were killed."

Alice nodded sadly.

"What you don't know is that your father remarried."

More of Alice appeared over the armrest, her mouth open in disbelief. "No!"

"Yes. In fact, his new wife was much younger than he was. Just a couple of years older than you when you died."

Alice looked crestfallen. "How could Papa be so disloyal?"

"Loneliness?" I suggested. "He had two more children. You had a half-brother, Arthur, and a half-sister, Thelma."

"No!" she protested.

"Yes."

Alice's mouth was a thin line. "So, Papa finally got the son he always wanted."

"I'm afraid so."

Alice's eyes filled with ghostly tears. "My Papa forgot about me and Mama, that's why he isn't here with us."

"We don't know he forgot you. His much younger wife probably decided to have him buried in Williamsville."

"Why so far away?" she cried.

"He sold the home you lived in and that's where he and his new family lived."

"That's not right. My Papa should have been buried here with me and Mama!"

"I'm sorry, but that's not what happened."

I waited a minute or more until her sniffles began to quiet before I continued. "Your brother, Arthur, is dead. I spoke with his daughter, your niece, Deborah, this morning."

"I have a niece?" Alice asked, still sniffling.

"You have a number of nieces and nephews."

"What did she say?"

"That your father told your brother and sister about you. When they were little, they used to pray for your soul."

That information didn't please her. "Why didn't I know that?"

I shrugged. I had no clue how all this worked—if indeed it did work. "Your brother told his daughter that you were murdered."

"I was!" Alice insisted.

"But apparently your father believed that you were killed because you did not heed his warnings to stay away from speakeasies. That you defied him." I couldn't say more. The old man had told the children from his second family that Alice had died because she was not a "good girl."

Bastard prick.

"I *did* drink gin. I *did* dance until the wee hours. But I *never* disgraced my Papa."

Was she talking about having sex? She'd had a beau—but had they ever consummated their relationship?

I didn't need to know.

"Your niece told me that your beau was found near your body and that he'd been badly beaten, but that he couldn't remember what happened to the two of you once you left the club."

"Do you think that's the truth?"

"I don't know. I'm still waiting to hear if my brother and I can read the police reports."

Alice's expression was decidedly unhappy. "What does all this mean for me?"

I'm sorry, but I don't know," I admitted.

Alice's face scrunched up as more tears filled her noncorporeal eyes.

It took several long minutes before she was able to speak coherently once again. "How do we move forward?"

"As I said, if I can read the police reports, it may give me another perspective. But I'm also a little confused about what brought me here to seek you out."

"I've thought about that, too. I'm sorry, but I have no answers. I'm just grateful that you found me." Alice pursed her lips. "You said someone wanted to kill you. Why? You seem like a kind gentleman."

"Thank you. It's a long, convoluted story."

"If you need someone to talk to, I have all the time in the world. I've had decades and decades of time to spend with no one to talk to. If I could help you in any way, I would do so with a loving heart."

A loving heart. That was what I needed about then. Brenda had a loving heart and was out of the picture. Maggie had a loving heart, but was preoccupied by all that had happened to her. The only other person I had to talk with was Richard.

Wait—and Sophie. How could I forget her? I needed to connect with her—and later that night.

"Thanks, Alice. Maybe I'll know more by the time we next speak and then I can tell all. Okay?"

She nodded.

We looked at one another for a long moment. "I should get going.

"When will I see you again?" she asked.

"Tomorrow. Maybe the next day. It depends on what I find out."

Again she nodded.

"I'm going to call my brother now."

"Very well. Until we meet again," she said, and began to fade into nothingness.

Once she'd gone, I hit the contacts list on my phone and tapped Richard's name. He picked it up on the first ring. "I'm ready."

He didn't reply, but I heard the minivan's engine come back to life. Seconds later he pulled up in front of me. "Let me see if I can get in by myself," I said.

"Are you sure?"

"Yeah."

It was a struggle, but I did get in, although I had to toss the crutches one at a time over the passenger seat. Shutting the door took even more effort. By then I was sweating profusely and thankful I could depend on my antiperspirant. Without Brenda around, it might be a while before I could take another shower.

"I didn't see her," Richard said, as he steered the van toward the cemetery's exit.

I looked over at him. "What?"

"Alice. If she showed up, I couldn't see her."

"She showed up, but she also crouched behind the arm of the bench. She didn't want you to see her, but it obviously didn't matter."

"What did she have to say?"

"She wasn't happy to hear her Papa had remarried and had another family. I have a feeling that we're going to find out even more unsavory information about her beloved Papa, which will crush her."

"You've got a theory?"

"Half-baked. But my gut tells me it'll be confirmed either when we read those case records or talk to someone else about the case."

"Which reminds me; while you were chatting with your ghostly friend, I got a call from Detective Wilder. The cops in District B found the old files on Alice's murder. The detective convinced them to let us take a look. We can't take them with us, but we can at least read them."

"If nothing else, we can take pictures with our phones."

"And, of course, we can take all the notes we want. They're expecting us in half an hour."

I nodded. Already I was starting to feel wiped. The thought that someone might want me dead weighed heavy on my mind, adding to the feeling. We had a long day ahead of us and a lot to accomplish.

"Okay," I told Richard, "let's roll."

NINETEEN

During the ride to the police station, Jeff shared the rest of his conversation with Alice, which seemed to be devoid of any tangible leads.

"It seems like we're going nowhere fast," Richard grumbled.

"In cases like this, it takes thousands of pieces of apparently trivial information to figure out what in retrospect seems like an easy solution."

"I spent almost three hours surfing the web this morning to try to get the goods on Maria and came up with damn little. I think it's time to be a little more aggressive."

"Aggressive how?"

"You know what I'm talking about."

"Hacking?" Jeff asked, disapproval coloring his tone.

"Not necessarily. There are all kinds of legitimate companies—and individuals—who run credit and other checks on people. Why shouldn't we be one of them?"

"Are you suggesting we set up a shell company to try to cover our tracks?"

"Not necessarily, but it isn't that hard to do, either. Someone like even Maggie has reason to check credit ratings and the criminal backgrounds of potential renters."

"Please tell me you don't intend to use her as a shill," Jeff demanded.

"Of course not. But all that's needed is a social security number to do a detailed background check, and we've already mined that info on Maria."

"Even that was obtained surreptitiously." Jeff shook his head and turned his attention back out the passenger side window. "We've pretty much decided Maria is behind all my and Dave's bad luck, but we haven't got tangible proof that it's true."

"I trust your insight. Right now, it's *you* who seems skeptical."

"I am."

"We haven't looked into Maria's friends and relatives. We could also talk to people at the other bars she owns."

"And if we're already targets, that screams 'come and get us.'"

Richard clutched the steering wheel in an effort to quell his frustration. "What about asking your reporter friend from *The Buffalo News* to do some of the legwork? We could pay him on the side."

"I'm sure his editor would see that as a huge conflict of interest."

"Only if he was doing a story on Dave's death—and it wasn't Sam's name attached to the story that ran in this morning's paper."

Jeff didn't comment.

"Okay," Richard began again, "we could have a security firm make inquiries on our behalf."

"And what does that say about us as we aspire to be a security firm? Either we look incompetent, or like a couple of chickens."

"Until we hang out a shingle, we're just a couple of averages joes off the street," Richard countered.

"Try telling that to Brenda," Jeff said with just the hint of mirth in his voice.

Richard braked for a light and glanced to his right. Jeff still looked out the passenger side window. Irked as he was at his brother being obstinate, Richard could tell something about Jeff's posture seemed very wrong. "Hey, are you okay?"

"No, I'm not."

The light turned green and Richard stomped on the gas. "Talk to me."

For a long—a very long—time Jeff said nothing. "I hate to say it, but with everything that's happened, I'm scared shitless."

"You and me both," Richard said, and then realized his brother wasn't being flippant. "I didn't mean to blow you off. Tell me what's up."

"Everything's sliding out of control. Banishing Brenda and Betsy to Philadelphia; us hiding in a hotel; telling Maggie I can't talk to her, and for what? Because some crazy bitch wants a stinking piece of real estate?"

"It's a temporary situation," Richard tried to assure him.

"Is it?" Jeff countered.

"Yes," Richard said reasonably. Up ahead was a chain grocery parking lot. Richard braked and pulled into the lot, steering into a slot far from the store. He put the van in park but kept the engine running if only to power the air conditioning. "What's wrong?"

Jeff said nothing, his hands clenched in fists on his lap—the skin taut and pale. For a terrible few moments Richard feared his usually stoic brother might explode in rage. But then Jeff shook his head—not unlike a wet dog—and seemed to sink in on himself.

"This damned leg cast has me feeling vulnerable—a lot more vulnerable than when I had my head caved in and my arm broken. This time I can't run away in a dangerous situation. I really can't defend myself at all."

"What are you saying?"

Jeff finally faced him, his expression grim. "I want to buy a gun."

"No."

"Yes! It's not like I don't know how to use one."

"I know that, but it would take forever to get a permit and—"

"Hey, I've had a permit for more than a decade. I reported my last gun as stolen, and I've kept up with the paperwork. I can legally buy another gun today."

"No!" Richard said again. "We're not going to bow to the lowest common denominator."

"So says Mister-I-can-hack anything."

Richard made an effort to hold his temper. "There's a big difference between garnering information and potentially shooting a projectile that can kill or maim."

"When push comes to shove, do you want to be defenseless?"

Richard didn't answer. He'd been shot a little over two years before. He never wanted to experience that again, nor be responsible—in one way or another—of inflicting that kind of misery on someone else. "So you're prepared to kill—?"

"To save you, me, Brenda, Betsy, or Maggie? You bet your ass I am."

Richard let out an exasperated breath. "I don't think it's going to come down to that."

"Yeah? Tell that to Dave. Oh, wait—you can't. He's dead."

There was no way to refute that statement. Still, Richard needed to deflect the conversation—to get them both back on common ground.

"We've got options, not the least of which is hiring bodyguards."

"Who'd hole us up in some godforsaken place while we go stir crazy."

"You're already stir crazy," Richard pointed out.

"You've got that right. And never in my life have I felt so paranoid."

The air conditioning continued to blast. Jeff had

again turned away and Richard felt at a loss as to how to rectify the tense situation. "What do you want do to?" he asked finally.

"I don't know." Jeff was quiet for a minute or more before speaking again. "Maybe I need to do what I already proposed. I need to see if I can connect with dead Dave."

"And if you can't?"

"Then we're back to square one."

It felt as though Richard had gone back in time to his former job in California, having to deal with obstinate foundation board members who put up barriers against avenues of research he and other staff members wanted to aggressively pursue. He had never considered putting Jeff in that same category.

The air conditioner continued to roar.

"Okay," Richard said in his most placating tone. "Then it seems to me that your first priority needs to be trying to connect with Dave."

Jeff turned to look at him. "What do you propose?"

"That we call Detective Wilder and see if she can get us in to see Dave at the morgue."

"By now his body has probably been released to an undertaker."

"Then maybe we can go to whatever funeral parlor his body's been sent to."

"Okay."

Richard reached into his pocket and pulled out his cell phone. "I'll call Bonnie Wilder right now and see if she can arrange it."

"And what do we do in the interim?"

Richard shrugged. "It may be a couple of hours before she gets back to me. "Depending on how long it takes to read Alice's case files, we could play tourist."

"Why?"

"Why not? I've been back in Buffalo for more than two years, but there are a lot of places I haven't checked out."

"Give me a for instance."

"Hot dogs at Ted's. I haven't had a beef on weck at Charlie the Butchers. I haven't visited the Carousel Museum."

"Are you sure you want to do that kind of stuff with me and not Brenda?"

"If I like the places, then I know Brenda won't be disappointed. I'll enjoy sharing them with her."

Jeff shrugged. "I guess."

"Then it's settled. But first I'll call Detective Wilder." He glanced at the dashboard clock. "Then again, if we don't leave now we're going to be late getting to the police station to see Alice's records."

"Yeah," Jeff said and let out what sounded like a defeated breath, turning his gaze out the passenger-side window.

"For what it's worth," Richard began, "I'm scared, too."

Jeff turned to look at him "Good. If you're scared, theoretically you'll be more careful."

"Only theoretically?"

"Yeah."

Richard made no reply. Instead, he moved the van's gearshift back into drive and pressed the accelerator, steering for the lot's exit.

Detective John Destross slapped a thin file folder down on the drab steel-and-Formica table. I looked up at him and frowned. "Is that all?"

He shrugged. "That's all we found in the archives."

"Has anyone looked at this file in decades?"

Again he shrugged. "Not to my knowledge. Do you need anything else, Mr. Resnick?"

It was obvious the detective thought the whole exercise was a waste of time—ours, his, and the world at large, and yet I couldn't blame the guy. If I hadn't met Alice—talked with her—I would have been just as skeptical.

Destross left the conference room and I saw Richard pass by the open door, cell phone pressed to his ear, presumably talking to Detective Wilder. He didn't look happy, but I needed to ignore him for the time being and concentrate on the file before me.

I folded back the aged and stained manila folder to expose yellowing onion-skin sheets that had been typed a generation or more before I'd been born.

Thanks to talking to Alice, Richard's notes, and what I'd gleaned from Forest Lawn's website, I pretty much knew the basic facts surrounding Alice's death. The seven or eight sheets of paper in the file didn't give me much more, and in fact seemed to concentrate more on the assault against her boyfriend, Joe Campbell.

According to Alice's beau, the couple emerged from the Blue Moon speakeasy, just a little before midnight, and a little tipsy, and headed for his car when they were accosted by several men dressed in black with dishtowels tied over their faces and brandishing handguns. Alice and Joe were herded into the alley behind the bar and when Joe jumped forward to defend his lady, he'd been knocked unconscious.

Okay. But if that was true, and he was no longer a threat, why did the attackers need to strangle petite Alice? Yessiree—Alice's death was looking more and more like a mobster's hit. Had somebody been angry with her presumed rumrunner father enough to murder Alice? If so, had the old man retaliated in kind? Considering the thugs had wielded handguns, why had they strangled and not just shot her? Not only was there no mention of a sexual assault, but Campbell had not been fleeced of his wallet. Alice's purse was found near her body, containing a comb, lipstick, and twenty-one dollars. There was no mention of the possibility that Alice's death could be tied to illegal activities.

Something was very fishy about Mr. Campbell's sworn testimony. He claimed he couldn't remember anything after being whacked on the head. Okay, I could identify with that, having also been the victim of a mugger with a baseball bat. But it didn't entirely ring true, either. Within weeks, I'd started remembering more and more of the incident. Had Campbell done the same and just didn't bother to report it, or was he scared enough to keep his mouth shut?

The lack of follow-up by the police department was equally as troubling. Had someone been paid off to make sure no one ever investigated Alice Newcomb's death?

I'd read most of the pages by the time Richard finally finished his call and joined me in the conference room.

"So?"

Richard sat in the chair across from me. "As we suspected, Dave's body has already been released to the funeral home."

"And?"

"I don't know. Detective Wilder said she'd call to see if we could get in to see him. She brought up an interesting question: what if Dave's family decides to have him cremated?"

I hadn't thought about that possibility "I suppose if he was a restless spirit I'd still be able to connect with him."

"Have you ever connected with a dead person who was cremated?"

"Yeah. Madam Zahara." Otherwise known as Bridget Madison. "But it seems to me the dead are usually stuck in one place. Sophie's only at the bakery. Alice is only at the cemetery. Madam Zahara's spirit clung to the house she'd last lived in, but I'm pretty sure that would have been the case even if her ashes hadn't been scattered in the yard. If Dave isn't at the funeral home, I have no idea where he'd be. And so far no restless spirits have come to me—and I don't want them to, either."

Richard indicated the pages before me. "Are you done with them?"

"No, but you can read what I've already gone through." I slid the pages across the table.

Ten minutes later I'd finished going over all the sheets. I thought about all I'd read, waiting for Richard to catch up. Finally he looked up.

"Talk about a shoddy investigation."

"My thoughts exactly."

"It's almost as though someone didn't *want* Alice's murder to be solved."

"The cops here in Buffalo turned a blind eye to a lot during Prohibition," I pointed out. "Did you notice there were virtually no interviews with Alice's family and friends? Not even the other couples who'd spent the evening with Alice and her boyfriend."

"Do you suspect a cover up?"

"Yeah. Remember Alice's niece said her father portrayed her as 'not a good girl.' Rumrunners and their suppliers had plenty of turf wars. Alice's father could have been one or the other? She couldn't tell me exactly what kind of business her father was in, but that they had plenty of money during the great depression."

"I don't know," Richard said. "You'd think if someone killed his only child, the guy would be out for blood. I sure as hell would be." And Richard had only been a dad for eight months—not twenty-three years like Alice's father.

"Yeah, but you're forgetting something; the guy wanted a *son*. Back in the day, cigars were handed out at the birth of a boy. Half-hearted smiles and talk about the next time around often followed the birth of a daughter."

"Then the guy was an ignoramus."

"Probably," I agreed, thinking about poor sweet Alice.

Richard looked down at the papers in front of us. "Do you think we need to make copies?"

I shook my head.

Richard nodded and collected the papers, settling them back into the folder. "I've been thinking paranoid thoughts," he admitted.

"How so?"

"Our phones. I propose we make like terrorists."

"In what way?"

"We head to Walmart and buy a couple of those cheap smart phones and load them with a thousand minutes each. That way we can still communicate with Brenda, Maggie, and whoever else we please, but Maria—or whoever—won't be able to track us. That is, as long as we don't log onto any social media with them.

"Sounds like a plan. Maggie was pretty upset this morning when I told her I might be incommunicado for a few days."

"Pay phones would still be better—if we could find them. We just have to hope Brenda's and Maggie's phones haven't been compromised."

"You can always call Evelyn's landline to talk to Brenda, and I can call Maggie at work. There's no way Maria could tap into numbers she doesn't know about."

"Don't be so sure," Richard warned.

As he was pretty much a computer expert, he was probably right.

"So what's up next?" I asked.

"We get the phones, contact Detective Wilder and our loved ones—and then eat lunch."

"And then?"

"Punt."

And apparently punting wasn't going to include me buying a gun. But I had a pretty good idea of how I might obtain one. I would call upon my reporter friend, Sam

Nielsen. He'd once loaned me an unregistered gun. When I didn't return it, he'd never said a word. I don't know why he side-stepped the law, and I never asked. But I was willing to bet he'd have no problem taking me to a place that legally sold guns, especially after what had not only happened to me, but Dave, too. It was something I intended to pursue.

I had no plans to end up like my former co-worker: dead by unknown attackers.

TWENTY

Walmart was not a place Richard was familiar with, but he disappeared inside for almost forty-five minutes and bought a couple of cheapie phones to tide us over during the crisis. Another purchase Richard made was a nanny cam so that he could set it up in whatever hotel we inhabited for the foreseeable future. He figured he'd download the app to our phones later that day when he installed the camera. Just a couple more pieces of the security puzzle we needed. After that, we were ready for lunch, which was damn fine. We nixed Charlie the Butcher because we couldn't get a beer there, let alone anything stronger, and we ended up at a Buffalo institution: Schwabl's, for their classic beef on weck. Yes! Mi-T-Fine.

Neither of us were in a hurry to get back to the hotel, where I'd left a do-not-disturb sign on the door of my side of the suite so that Herschel wouldn't be spooked by strangers wielding vacuum cleaners and dusters.

Instead of visiting a more commercial tourist attraction, we drove to Buffalo's waterfront and called our ladies. Richard took a walk while I laid low in the minivan, wishing all the windows were tinted. After conversing with Maggie, who sounded pleased to hear from me, I knew someone else I needed to speak to—and yet, I knew Sophie wasn't likely to be available until at least midnight.

It was nearly four when Richard hit a grocery store and bought a ton of food for supper and the next day's breakfast before we headed back to our hotel. By then my leg ached like it was about to fall off and I was so friggin' tired I could barely keep my eyes open, desperately needing to crash. As soon as I hit the bed, a lonely Herschel was only too glad to plaster his furry body against me after Richard relieved me of my phone so he could download the nanny cam software and set up the camera.

I didn't emerge from my room until almost eight thirty. Richard's iPod was plugged into a hotel clock radio pumping out some somber piece of classical music while he sat in front of the living room's desk in front of his computer. He hadn't waited for me to start Happy Hour and had already broken out the Scotch bottle.

"Welcome back to the land of the living," he said.

"Thanks." I planted my ass on the couch, hauled my broken leg onto the coffee table, and realized I hadn't completely shut the door to my bedroom. Herschel wandered into the room and jumped onto the window sill to look at the outside world. Richard gave him a wary look and then grabbed his drink, taking a healthy swig.

I looked at my brother with what I hoped was a hopeful expression. "I'm kind of thirsty and too bloody tired to get up and make myself a drink."

Richard showed good grace by not rolling his eyes and got up, tossed ice in a glass, then poured bourbon and a splash of club soda into it before refreshing his own drink. He handed me the glass and gave me back my new phone, which I pocketed.

"Thanks." I took a hit of that liquid gold and let myself relax…but only so much. I needed to bring up what could be a potentially sore subject. "I'd like to connect with my friend Sophie tonight."

"I got that feeling," Richard said, glancing at my cat with peripheral vision.

"We've got to establish some parameters around that."

He turned back to face me. "Which means?"

"I'm not sure you'd be welcome at the bakery."

"Why wouldn't I?"

"Because Sophie's told me on a number of occasions that she's only here on this earth for me."

"But I've met and spoken to her in the past. Why wouldn't she talk to me now?" He sounded offended.

"I'm just telling you my perception of how things might go down. If we go in together and she doesn't show up—you have to go."

"And leave you vulnerable?"

"Yeah. Believe me, I'm not thrilled at the prospect, but I don't get to make the rules—and Sophie said she doesn't, either."

"So there is a supreme being calling the shots?" Richard asked, and I wasn't sure if he was hopeful or skeptical.

"Not that I've been told." I sipped my drink and looked around the room seeing no evidence of the tiny camera Richard had bought earlier that day. "Am I on Candid Camera right now?"

He shook his head. "I won't turn it on until we either leave to go out or go to bed."

"Where is it?"

"On the top of my monitor." He pointed.

I don't think I would have seen the thing if he hadn't indicated where I should look. I could only hope someone entering the room would be as oblivious.

"Are you hungry?" he asked.

"I will be pretty soon. I'd like to enjoy my drink first."

He frowned. "Okay."

Was he hungry?

"I'd like to call Brenda and say goodnight to Betsy. Do you mind?"

"Not a bit." I was already plotting my next move—which didn't include him.

Richard got up, grabbed his drink, and headed for his half of the suite. "I'll be back in a while."

"Take your time." There was someone I wanted to contact, as well.

Once the door closed behind him, I pulled my new cell phone out of my pocket and punched in a number. It wouldn't be familiar, so I wasn't sure if my call would be answered and was prepared to leave a message. I didn't have to.

"Yeah?" Sam Nielsen asked warily.

"Hey, Sam, it's me—Jeff, your paranoid friend."

"Paranoid?" He sounded confused.

"Yeah. It turns out that someone is trying to kill me—at least, that's what I think. And I'd be more than happy to share the details with you because if I'm murdered, I want you to follow through to catch the bitch behind it."

"A woman wants to kill you?"

"Yeah. I'm hoping you'd like to hear the whole story. But more than that, I need your help to procure a gun."

"What for?"

"Because there's a woman out there who wants to kill me," I reiterated.

"Why?"

"Because I work—I mean I worked—at The Whole Nine Yards."

"I'm confused."

"And I don't blame you. I can't explain it all now, but I'd be glad to tomorrow. And I really need to buy a gun for protection. I have a permit, but I need your help to snag the paperwork and take me somewhere to buy one."

"Why?

"I can't drive. I sort of got hit by a car and I'm on crutches."

"You got hit by a car?" he asked, aghast.

"Hit and run. Except for a busted leg, I'm pretty much okay."

"Why won't your brother take you to buy protection?"

"Because he's a doctor who got shot. He's sort of prejudiced against them."

"I can see why."

"Yeah, but despite his qualms I need to protect us—and especially me. If you're available tomorrow, I'd appreciate your help."

"And what do I get out of the deal?"

"Besides helping a friend? One hell of a story—but only if you keep me out of it."

Silence.

It lengthened.

"Well," he began, "if nothing else, I'm willing to listen."

"Great. The only thing is…I need a little subterfuge."

"In what way?"

"Send me an email asking me out to lunch. I can't let Richard know that I contacted you."

"Why not?"

"Just because," I said with the hint of an edge creeping into my voice.

"Oh, all right."

"Do it as soon as we get off the phone, will you?"

"Okay, okay," Sam said, sounding annoyed. "But if the story that comes out of this isn't print worthy, you'll owe me—big time."

"I get that."

"Anything else?" he asked

I eyed the still-closed door to Richard's half of the suite. "I really need this to happen tomorrow. Is that a problem?"

"I'll have to rearrange a few things but, yeah, it can happen."

"Thanks, Sam. I really appreciate this."

"Appreciation is one thing; paying forward is another."

"Right. I'll call or email you back in a while. Thanks."

The connection was broken.

I put my phone away and guzzled my drink. I set the empty glass aside and leaned back against the couch trying to look like I'd been cooling my heels for the past five minutes. The door handle to Richard's bedroom rattled and he emerged looking grim-faced.

"What's wrong?"

He went straight to his make-shift bar, plunked more of the wet hotel ice cubes into his glass and poured himself a generous portion of the breath of the heather. "Brenda's antsy. She wants to come home."

"Did something happen?"

He sat back down on the computer chair. "Betsy had a bad afternoon. She was fussy; probably cutting a new tooth. Evelyn is tutoring a couple of high school students for their end-of-year finals and Brenda and the baby were banished to the backyard. It started to pour and Brenda ended up standing in the garage for twenty minutes during a thunderstorm. The baby howled the whole time."

"Aw, crap."

"Yeah."

After hearing about Brenda's day, suddenly I needed another drink, too, but I wasn't about to ask Richard to make one. I'd just have to suffer. "Would Brenda be happier in a hotel?"

"I asked her that. Her relationship with her family is still rather tenuous. She doesn't want to rock the boat."

Yeah, I could understand that. I didn't envy Brenda having to deal with that crap, and it was all my fault—just because some demented woman wanted to get rid of me. And at that point we were still only dealing in speculation. But I hadn't bullshitted Sam; I wanted to get a gun pretty damn quick. And as I'd told Richard, I was prepared to use one to save myself or those I loved. That said, I hated the thought that I might actually take someone's life. But when push came to shove, my goal was protection, not predator.

My phone pinged—a text message. I consulted it. Good old Sam. "Hey, I just got a text from my buddy Sam. He wants to have lunch tomorrow."

Richard looked up. "Oh, yeah? Does he know about your leg?"

"Of course. I emailed him the other day."

Richard accepted my lie without question. "I suppose he wants to involve you in another one of his stories."

"There's not much I can do like this," I said, indicating my case. "I mentioned being home bound. Maybe this is a mercy lunch."

"Maybe." Richard still seemed distracted. The good thing about that was he might not give this sudden invitation much more than a passing thought. At least I hoped so, because it just occurred to me that Sam wouldn't have known my new number unless I'd called to tell him. Luckily, Richard was too preoccupied to think of it, either.

I texted a reply, which took a few minutes since I don't like to text and the cheap phone's tiny keyboard made it doubly frustrating. We went back and forth a couple of times before I spoke to Richard again. "He's going to pick me up here at the hotel tomorrow at eleven thirty. Are you okay to get lunch on your own?"

"Of course. I downloaded a book about Buffalo during Prohibition. I want to read it and maybe contact the author, so the timing is good. But we should think about changing hotels as of tomorrow or Friday."

"I agree."

"Will you tell Sam your troubles?"

"Of course. He may be able to help. He hasn't disappointed me yet."

Richard nodded thoughtfully, sipping his Scotch. My stomach growled. We needed to eat and Richard needed to stop drinking if he was going to drive us to Sophie's bakery later that evening.

"So what's for supper?"

He seemed to brighten at the mention of food. "I got everything you like."

"Aw, you didn't have to do that."

"As Brenda likes to say, you don't eat enough to keep a bird alive. You're looking kind of gaunt."

"I am?"

He nodded. "You need to bulk up."

"I hope you got something you like, too."

"Definitely." He got up to rustle up our makeshift meal. "Oh—" He turned back to face me. "Would you like a refill?"

Did I! "Yes, but just one. I want to be sharp when I speak to Sophie."

His cheerful demeanor evaporated at the mention of my psychic mentor. Was it because he might not be welcome or that he'd have to curb his alcohol consumption to go there? I wasn't about to ask.

Richard made me another drink and Herschel abandoned the window to come sit beside me on the couch. We didn't talk much as Richard set Chinet plates and plastic cutlery next to my leg on the coffee table. He brought out plastic containers with transparent domed lids that would constitute our feast. Yeah, he'd gotten a couple of things I liked, but the majority of items on offer were what Brenda favored. I didn't point that out. I only had to look at his forlorn expression to see how much he missed his wife and baby girl.

We doled out mashed potatoes, gravy, roast beef, and squash. Richard nuked mine first. We ate in silence with the still morose music playing in the background.

Eating off a coffee table sucked. I wanted to go home—even if it was temporarily in Richard's house and Brenda's craft room. I wanted my real life back. I still had at least four if not six, weeks left in the damn cast and brace, but I also had a feeling this situation would resolve itself pretty quickly.

The question was ... would I live to see the cast removed?

TWENTY-ONE

As I suspected, the bakery was dark when Richard drove by at just past midnight. That wasn't unusual. Often I'd have to ring the bell a couple of times before Sophie showed up. I just wasn't sure she'd show up at all if I had Richard in tow.

I was nearly certain we hadn't been followed from the hotel, which let at least part of me relax. Unfortunately, my stomach seemed to be tied in knots and I wasn't sure why.

"You'd better drop me off."

"We've talked about that," Richard said.

"Yeah, and we have differing opinions on the subject."

"Let's just see if Sophie will show up before we discuss alternatives."

"Fine." But now that we'd arrived, I knew there'd be no welcome mat out for my brother.

Richard parked the van on the side street and got out, waiting for me to extricate myself. He appeared to be pretty confident as we approached the bakery's entrance. He reached out and pressed the doorbell, which we heard ring inside.

We stood there in silence for at least thirty seconds before he pressed the bell again. Another thirty seconds went by—I counted—and still no light went on in the back of the shop.

I shifted position so I could lean against the building.

"How long do you usually have to wait before she shows up?" Richard asked.

"Not this long."

He tried ringing the bell again, and again we waited.

"Didn't you say that sometimes she doesn't show at all?"

"Yeah, but she'll know I got hurt. She'll want to see me now."

He rang the bell again.

I wasn't going to suggest he leave.

We waited.

"Okay," Richard said, conceding defeat. "I guess I can sit in the car for a couple of minutes and if you're still standing outside the bakery in five minutes, we'll go back to the hotel."

"Right. And if I'm not?"

"Call me when you're ready to be picked up."

"Will do."

He turned and, with slumped shoulders, headed back toward the minivan. No sooner was he out of sight when the light in the back of the shop flashed on. Sophie hurried forward, looking distraught. She unlocked the door.

"What have you done to yourself?" she demanded, taking in my scabby face and the cast that poked out of the end of my sweatpants.

"I didn't do a damn thing; it was done to me."

"Come inside," she said, holding the door open for me. She usually led the way to the storeroom where she held court, but this time she followed me.

I let myself fall onto my usual folding chair next to an ancient, tippy card table and set my crutches aside.

"Is hot chocolate okay?" Sophie asked.

"It's fine."

She put a pan of water on the electric burner on the shelf above the sink, then bustled to put powdered cocoa into a couple of cracked mugs. She didn't seem to want to face me until she could offer me a little comfort, even if it was only cocoa. I took that opportunity to check out my phone. As I suspected, it said no signal available. Was that because I was situated in a pocket where time stood still? I didn't know and wasn't sure I *wanted* to know.

Finally Sophie determined the steaming pot was hot enough, poured the water, stirred the chocolate, and brought the cups to the table. She sat down. "Now, tell me what happened."

I did, leaving out the scarier parts, but I could tell she knew I was holding back. She often seemed to know exactly what I was going to say even before I said it.

"So," I said after finishing my recitation. "What's new with you?"

"Fretting after you," she said with disapproval, "and with cause, because you haven't told me the worst of it."

"I don't want you to worry."

Her glare was laser sharp.

I let out a breath. "My friend at the bar died."

"Was killed," she corrected, "and now the person who did it is after you."

"It's a possibility," I admitted, trying to downplay the threat.

"And there's more," she accused.

"Oh?" I wasn't sure what she meant.

"Your brother has plans. *Big* plans. Plans that will put the two of you in continual danger."

I shook my head. "You're exaggerating."

Again with the laser glare.

"We're going to concentrate on cold cases," I explained. "Old unsolved cases. Cases where the possibility of running into trouble is extremely limited."

"Is that what you believe?" Why the hell did she sound so angry?

"Yes." For the most part.

She shook her head. "I know you want to please your

brother—you feel you owe him a lot. But you do not owe him your life."

Oh, yes I did—and several times over. "I'm taking steps to keep us safe."

"Buying a gun?" she practically shrieked, getting angrier by the second. "And worst—the worst of all—you intend to *charge* people for using your gifts?"

I had a feeling that might be her biggest beef.

"I need to make a living," I said calmly.

"Charlatans hang out a sign that says 'psychic for hire!'"

"Who says I need to tell people about my—" I could barely stomach to say the words, "my gift." I considered what I could do—could sense—to be a major pain in the ass. It wasn't fun. It was often frightening. Employing it often gave me excruciating headaches. Doing it for a living—calling on that so-called gift on a regular basis—wasn't what I wanted to do for the rest of my life. It had taken me two years since the mugging to get where I was. If I was going to have to work at solving cold cases, I hoped the job would end sooner rather than later.

Sophie wouldn't look at me. Her focus was fixed on the mug on the table before her. "I am so disappointed in you."

How disappointed?

She looked up, as though hearing my unspoken question. "If you do this, I don't know if I will be here for you anymore."

A threat or a promise?

I said nothing.

I loved Sophie.

I loved Richard.

He was alive.

She wasn't.

"I wouldn't like that."

It was her turn to say nothing.

I looked down at my cup. It was empty.

"You should go," she said, her voice devoid of emotion.

I wanted to say more—to explain how I wasn't keen on Richard's business plan, but I also knew she wouldn't listen.

I grabbed my crutches and got to my feet. She rose from her chair, too.

I hobbled out of the storeroom and into the shop, pausing at the door. "Can I kiss you good-bye?"

Sophie didn't answer, and I stood there waiting for long seconds before she reluctantly offered me her cheek. I gave her a quick kiss. For the first time, she didn't give me one in return.

"I love you, Sophie Levin."

"And I love you, Jeffrey Resnick."

"I'll come by when all of this is over."

She shrugged, again saying nothing.

"See you."

I shoved my shoulder against the plate glass door and pushed. This time she didn't hold it open for me. Once it swung shut behind me, I turned. The shop was dark, with no sign of Sophie, and no sign I'd ever been inside.

I leaned against the door, fished for my phone, saw that I could get a signal, and hit the call icon. Richard picked up immediately.

"I'm ready."

"I'll be right there."

I hit the call end icon, stuffed the phone back in my pocket, and waited. Seconds later, Brenda's minivan appeared. I shuffle-hopped around the front, opened the door, tossed the crutches over the top of the passenger seat, and maneuvered myself inside. Shutting the door, I reached for the seat belt.

"Well?" Richard asked.

"I've been disowned."

"What?"

"Sophie doesn't approve of our plans to go into business. She disowned me."

"I hope you're kidding."

I shook my head. "I'm beat. Let's go back to the hotel."

"Sure," Richard said quietly.

We didn't talk any more that night.

TWENTY-TWO

The sky was overcast when I awoke the next morning, its gray nothingness reinforcing the way I felt. I tried not to think about my conversation with Sophie the night before, and instead concentrated on what I needed to do that day—which was pretty ambitious. I only hoped Sam could give me as much time as I needed to accomplish everything that had to be done. It was, after all, still a work day for him.

Richard was reading and I left him to it, making sure Herschel was shut up for the day before I left the room and headed for the elevator.

I planted myself on a bench just outside the hotel's lobby which, considering Maria could literally be gunning for me may have been a dumb move, but being cooped up in the car or in the hotel had me feeling vaguely claustrophobic. I didn't have long to wait as Sam was a couple of minutes early. I'll admit that seeing his black SUV gave me a momentary scare as it pulled up beside me and the power window on the passenger side rolled open.

"I was about to say 'hop in,' but then I remembered you're on crutches. Need help?"

"I wouldn't mind."

So Sam left the vehicle running, got out, and circled around to help me into the car. It was a lot taller than Brenda's new minivan, but luckily there was a handhold so I could haul myself into the passenger seat while Sam tossed the crutches in back, slammed both doors, and got back in.

"Where to?"

"My place in Amherst. I need you to climb the steps and retrieve my gun permit. Then you can take me anywhere that legally sells guns."

"There's a sports shop at the mall."

"Suits me."

He pulled out of the hotel's parking area. "Okay, but start talking. I want to know everything that's going down."

It took the entire drive to LeBrun Road to tell Sam what I knew and suspected about Ms. Maria Spodina and Dave's death, including the fact that my bank accounts had also been decimated.

"Aren't you jumping to conclusions?" Sam asked.

"I trust my gut."

He nodded, conceding my point.

A gray sedan emblazoned with a Bison Security logo blocked the end of Richard's driveway. A uniformed guard sat behind the wheel, but got out when Sam pulled up behind it.

"This is private property," the burly guy dressed in gray said. He had shoulders like a linebacker and a nose that had been broken at least once. "Can I help you gentlemen?" His voice and demeanor was gruff—no nonsense.

"Yeah, I live here," I said.

"You got some ID?"

It was a struggle to fish my wallet out of my pocket, but I handed him my license, which he scrutinized before checking a list on a clipboard, and then handing it back to me.

"I need to pick up something—or at least my friend will retrieve it for me," I said, jerking a thumb in Sam's direction.

"I'll move my car," said the guy, whose name tag said Tony Barber. "Do you want the accumulated mail?"

"Yeah, thanks."

"I'll get it for you."

We watched as he moved the car, and then Sam pulled right up to the door that led to my apartment. He rolled the windows down and I handed him my keys, telling him where to find my gun permit. He disappeared up the stairs and Tony appeared in front of the SUV's passenger side window with a stack of envelopes, magazines, and circulars. "Thanks."

Tony nodded and went back to his cruiser.

I sorted the envelopes into piles, and opened what little mail had arrived for me. Included in the stack was a nondescript envelope that harbored my new credit card. I'd been hoping it would arrive, as I had nothing else to use to pay for the gun. If push came to shove, I meant to ask Sam to buy it for me and let me pay him later. I pulled out my cell phone and activated the card, shoving it into my wallet and pocketing it.

Sam exited the stairwell to my apartment and got back in the SUV. He handed over my keys and the paperwork. "Looks like you made a hasty exit."

"Yeah. Richard grabbed my printer and some clothes and that's about it."

"Is all this intrigue—with you guys bailing on your homes and all—really necessary?"

"If my friend Dave hadn't been murdered, I might have a different answer, but—yeah. I'm scared shitless," I admitted.

Sam nodded, did a K-turn, and pulled out of the driveway. I gave a half-hearted wave to the security guy as we headed back toward Main Street and, then turned east. "Have you got any idea of what kind of gun you want?" Sam asked.

"A semi-automatic should do."

"Why?"

"A gut feeling doesn't hold much weight with law enforcement."

"Yeah, but you've got a rep for being right."

"Sometimes."

"More than that," Sam said. "In fact, if you weren't so busted up, I'd ask you for some help with—"

"And that's another thing," I interrupted him. "Richard thinks we ought to exploit my little psychic tricks for fun and profit." Crap, now even I was using the "P" word and calling what I could do a trick. Maybe Sophie was right. Maybe we were being frivolous with something that had proven dangerous to me on way too many occasions.

"You wouldn't charge an old buddy like me for your services, would you?"

"I'm still wrestling with the idea of charging at all. Would that be bad karma?"

"I don't believe in karma, so I'm not the one to ask."

I wasn't sure I believed in karma, either.

I changed the subject. "If we're heading to the mall anyway, I'd like to hit a clothes store."

"What for?"

"It'll be hard to pack heat without drawing attention while wearing a snug t-shirt."

"Okay. But I haven't got unlimited time, you know?"

"I figured as much. I pretty much know what I want to get in both departments, so I'll make it as quick as I can."

"Thanks."

Sam launched into a detailed description of his latest series of articles for the paper, but I only half-listened. I had too many other things on my mind. I was beginning to feel antsy. Something was going to happen—and soon.

I only wish I had a clue about what that would be.

Not only did we hit the mall's big box sports shop and national chain department store, but we stopped at a Subway and got sandwiches to go. Sam dropped me off at the front of the hotel and made sure I made it through the front door before he burned rubber. He was way late getting back to work.

Richard was asleep on the suite's couch when I arrived back at our hotel room at a little after two. The maids had apparently come and gone, and the door to my room was open. Herschel sat on the arm of the sofa, right above Richard's head, which I was sure would freak out my brother when he awoke. I tried to be quiet as I struggled through the door, hanging onto a large Macy's bag. I hoped the new, oversized Aloha shirt ablaze with big pink flowers I now wore would do a good job of hiding the holster where the semi-automatic with the ten-round clip in it hung on my right hip. I had a couple of other clips at the bottom of the bag, and had stashed two in the minivan before I'd come upstairs. I wanted to make sure that no matter where I was, I'd be well armed.

Richard awoke with a start, saw Herschel looming over him, and let out a yell, startling the cat, who jumped onto him. He hollered again, and Herschel sprang off his's abs like they were a trampoline.

"Damn that cat!"

"How did he get out?" I asked, leaning back against the door to close it.

Richard sat up, rubbing his eyes. "The maids. I was on the computer and they went in your room before I could stop them. The woman said he got out, but he must have been hiding here in the living room. I left the door to your room open hoping he'd go back inside."

"A lot you know about cats," I muttered.

He glanced at the bag. "What did you get?"

"Something to wear besides just t-shirts." I sat down on the chair he usually used and hauled my leg up on the coffee table. I plucked at the lapel of my shirt. "What do you think?"

"It's a little loud—not your usual style. And don't you think it will draw attention to you? Attention you might not want."

"I hadn't thought of that," I agreed.

"I hope you bought something a little more sedate, because you're going to need it."

"Why?"

"Because Dave's wake is tonight."

Aw, crap.

"I'm assuming you want to go."

"No, I don't ... and, yeah, I do. What time?"

"It's seven to nine."

"Let's go on the early end—just to get it over with."

"Do you think he'll ... be there?" Richard asked.

I shrugged, knowing what he meant. "I don't know." I opened the large bag and pulled out a black shirt. I hadn't thought about wearing it to a wake—I just liked the pattern of little palm trees woven into the fabric. "Will this do?"

Richard nodded.

I set it and the rest of the stuff back on the floor and pulled out my sub. "Is there any pop in the minibar?"

"Yeah." He got up to retrieve it. "You were gone nearly three hours; what else were you doing besides clothes shopping?"

"Sam listened to my story first, and then I listened to what he's got going. Oh, and I stopped by the house and picked up the mail. It's at the bottom of the bag." I went to retrieve it, but he gestured for me to forget it, opened the tab on the can, and handed it to me. "I'm sure there's nothing of any importance."

"I got my credit card, which is how I got new shirts."

"I was on the phone with your bank this morning."

"Is my money going to make a return visit?" I asked hopefully

"Not likely."

Great. And I now had a seven-hundred-dollar balance on my new credit card and no job to pay it off. If I couldn't use my psychic gift, just how did Sophie think I was going to make a living in the next couple of months?

I unwrapped my ham and every-kind-of-vegetable-they-stocked sub and offered half to Richard. He shook his head. "I had something from out of the fridge." He made a face, and I figured he was getting tired of eating in.

Richard watched as I polished off half of my sandwich. I wrapped up the rest of it for later and he put it into the fridge before again joining me.

"What have you got planned for the rest of the day?" I asked.

"I still have more reading to do. And I want to invest some time in more genealogical research. I've made some progress finding the last of Alice's descendants. Another hour or two of searching websites and I should have it nailed down."

"Couldn't your friends in California do it a lot faster?"

"I've already imposed on them far too much this last year or so. If we're going to go into business, we have to be willing to do the research we need on our own."

I nodded. And he was right; the whole Alice thing wasn't our main concern. We could afford to put it on the back-burner if we had to.

Now that I'd eaten, I felt logy and ready to fall into the sweet abyss of sleep. I needed to be sharp when we went to Dave's wake because I had a feeling that an important exchange of information would take place there. Maybe from someone—or two—in attendance ... or maybe from Dave himself, should he still be attached to this earthly plane.

"I'm going to need to crash for a while," I told Richard. "I'm sure once I do, Herschel will join me. Feel free to shut the door."

He nodded. "And tomorrow we're moving to another hotel. We've been here far too long."

"Agreed."

He nodded toward the bag. "Want me to take that to your room?"

"If you wouldn't mind."

He got up, grabbed the bag, and headed for my half of the suite. I was glad to be following him. I didn't want him to see the bulge from the gun on my hip. I'd take it off in the bathroom and stash it in a drawer until later. But I also knew I'd holster it again before heading for the funeral parlor. I had a feeling I might need it sometime quite soon.

TWENTY-THREE

Although we arrived at the Delaware Avenue location of Amigone Funeral Chapel at precisely seven o'clock that evening, I was surprised at how many cars were already parked in the lot. It looked like Dave was going to get a good sendoff. No doubt the word had gone out and former patrons from the bar—and the people who inhabited the rest of his life—had shown up to pay their last respects.

Richard hadn't said much since I'd awakened from my nearly three-hour nap. Since I can't tune into his emotional spectrum like I can with others, I presumed he was probably bummed by being separated from Brenda and Betsy. I hadn't heard from Maggie and I figured we were both due for some quality face time with our loved ones after we left the funeral parlor. And I hoped we might seek out something better than take-out to eat, too. I sure was missing Brenda's home cooking.

Richard got out of the van and stood before the passenger side door as I got out. He seemed rather tight lipped, but retrieved my crutches from the backseat and handed them to me. "How do you want to play this?" he asked, looking around as though to scope out a threat.

"By ear. But I do think I'll learn something significant."

"Good. How long do you think this will take?"

I shrugged. "Maybe half an hour."

He nodded. "I might not stay inside the whole time. I might come back to the car to work on Alice's genealogy some more."

"Are you okay?" I asked, noting the sweat on his brow. The temperature was warm, but not sweltering.

"Let's just get this over with." He nodded toward the chapel's door.

We headed for the side entrance and the addition to the former brick two-story home. Richard held the door open for me to enter. It occurred to me that Dave might not be the only client on display that night, but I only saw his name on the small sign outside the door to our right.

The room was pleasant enough, with soft green walls and a neutral carpet, and already filled with a number of people—mostly men—many whose faces were familiar to me. I looked around until I saw a closed coffin against the far wall. Nowhere did I see my incorporeal former workmate and must admit it was with a conflicting air of relief and disappointment.

"I'll add your name to the guest book," Richard said, and let me forge ahead to meet and talk with several of the guys I'd known for the past two years at the bar. They'd been sorry to hear I'd been hurt; they were shocked that Dave had been killed, and wasn't that just terrible luck?

Luck? I didn't think so.

Richard hung with me for a couple of minutes before he excused himself to find a john. I took the opportunity to gravitate to the receiving line, and seemed to be the last one in it.

A slim woman of about thirty-five, dressed in a black-and-white floral dress, stood next to a guy in a gray suit and a darker gray tie. He looked terribly uncomfortable; she looked sad, yet resigned.

Finally, it was my turn to introduce myself. "Hi. I'm

Jeff Resnick. Dave and I were co-workers at The Whole Nine Yards."

"Yes, he spoke of you often. I'm Susan Lynden, his sister. And this is my husband, Bill."

Still clutching the handholds of my crutches, I didn't offer her my hand. "Nice to meet you."

She offered me a wan smile. "Dave liked you. He was thrilled to have a new biking buddy." She eyed the cast poking out of the right leg of my sweatpants. "I was sorry to hear about your accident."

It was my turn to force a smile. "Thanks."

"Dave thought you guys had a lot in common."

Oh, yeah? I wasn't sure what, and she didn't elaborate. Instead, she shook her head. "He had such a bad streak of luck these last couple of weeks."

"Oh?" I asked, my gut tightening, my fingers clutching the crutch handholds just a little tighter. Had that been what Dave had wanted to talk about when I'd blown him off days before?

"His bank accounts had all been hacked. His credit cards were compromised. He was fighting with his bank trying to clear it up."

My mouth went dry. Just. Like. Me.

"Did he report that to the police? Have you mentioned it to them?"

"Yes. I guess they'll be looking into it, but I don't see how it connects."

Should I tell her about my own predicament? I looked into her sad gray eyes and decided she didn't need another brick added to her shoulder, but I would call Detective Wilder the minute I left the funeral home. It couldn't be a coincidence that we'd both been hacked— that we'd both been attacked, and yet I still couldn't figure out why. It couldn't be because Maria Spodina wanted that small corner of real estate on Main Street in Synder. It just didn't make sense because why would she see Dave and me as a threat?

My gaze shifted to my left and I saw Tom—Dave's and my boss—enter the room. He was dressed in jeans, a buff-colored cord jacket with suede elbow patches straight out of the nineteen eighties, a blue shirt and a green tie, looking much older than the last time I'd seen him.

Tom saw me, and headed over to intercept us.

"Tom," I said more or less in greeting, "This is Susan Lynden, Dave's sister. Susan, this is Tom Link, Dave's and my boss."

"I'm so sorry for your loss," he said, and offered his hand, which she dutifully shook.

"It was a shock," she admitted, not at all warming to Tom. Dave must have told her how he'd been demoted and his feeling of betrayal after Maria's arrival at the bar.

"Dave was a great employee. All the guys loved him."

Susan nodded, but her gaze drifted over to the coffin and her lips pursed. She looked like she was about to cry. Her husband came to her rescue. "Honey, would you like to sit down for a while?"

Susan nodded, and Bill gently grasped her arm and led her to one of the rows of seats that faced a lectern. A box of tissues sat on a nearby seat, and he handed it to her.

"It's a damn shame about Dave," Tom said, his gaze straying to the coffin, too.

"Yeah," I said, shifting on my one good leg. I'd been standing a little too long. "Did you come alone?"

"Yeah. Maria's taking care of things at the bar. We hired another two bartenders yesterday. Gotta keep up with the trade," he said, but there didn't seem to be any pleasure in his voice.

"Something wrong?" I asked.

Tom looked away from the casket. "Things at the bar … they're just not quite …" He seemed to struggle to come up with the correct verbiage, then settled for the obvious. "...right."

"How so?"

He shrugged. "What happened to you—what happened to Dave. It seems rather coincidental."

"Does it?" I pushed.

"You don't think so?"

"No, I don't."

He frowned. "Who would want to hurt you guys?"

"You tell me."

"You don't think I had anything to do with—?"

"No," I cut him off. "But think about everything that's happened in the past few weeks."

Tom frown deepened. "I've done nothing but think about it ever since I heard about Dave's murder."

"Have you spoken to anyone about it?"

"No."

"Not even Maria?"

"You can't think she's got anything to do with what happened to you guys."

"Why not?"

Tom looked appalled. "She's a great little gal."

"She's hardly a gal. What do you actually know about her?"

"Just that she was a wildly successful bartender at The Double Helix before she came to work for me."

"She was more than just a bartender there—she owns the place."

Tom's eyes widened.

"And that's not all she owns."

"Such as?"

"Most of the block around your bar."

His eyes narrowed with suspicion. "How do you know?"

"Public records. Remember, I once made my living as an investigator."

A blush rose up Tom's neck until it stained his cheeks.

"What are you saying?"

"Just that you should watch your step. Don't make any rash decisions—like a sudden marriage proposal."

Tom's eyebrows shot up. I'd definitely hit a nerve.

"You're way out of line, Jeff."

"Am I?"

"Yes."

"Fair enough. But please don't mention our conversation to Maria. I'd hate for her next attempt on my life to be successful."

I looked at the casket, then glanced around the room but didn't see Richard. "I've got to go."

"Take care," Tom said, but I wasn't sure how sincere the wish really was.

I turned and headed for the exit. I had a feeling I'd just lost a friend, and worse, may have made an enemy.

Out in the parking lot, I headed for the van, but stopped some ten feet from it. I could see Richard sitting in the driver's seat, but his arms were folded over the top of the steering wheel, his head resting on them. My stomach did a somersault and, panicked, I shuffle-hopped as fast as I could, thinking the worst, and wrenched open the passenger door. "Rich?"

Slowly, he turned his head to look at me through bloodshot eyes.

"What's wrong?"

His voice was strained. "I think I've been poisoned."

"What?"

"I need to get to the ER."

My mind was spinning. "Should I call for an ambulance?"

"No, I can drive. We're not far. Get in."

My mouth went dry, my hands shaking as I tossed my left crutch over the passenger seat, grabbed the handhold just inside the passenger side door, hauled my left ass cheek onto the seat, shifted my other crutch in and over my head, and pulled the rest of me inside. I grabbed the door, slamming it. "What can I do?"

"Nothing," he said, and turned the key in the ignition. His brow was beaded with sweat.

"When did this start?" I asked as the van lurched forward.

"I felt rocky most of the afternoon. When we got inside the funeral home, I had to go to the men's room where I literally lost my lunch." He looked both ways before pulling out of the lot and headed for Sisters Hospital.

I buckled my seat belt. "What did you eat today?"

"Leftovers from the fridge in our room."

"Food poisoning?" I asked.

"I don't know."

"Nobody could have gotten to it. I mean, you were there all day."

"I left the cleaning women alone for a few minutes just to get away from the sound of vacuuming. One of them could have put something in the food. I should have known better than to leave the room." He braked for a light and I could see his fingers were wrapped so tight around the wheel they were bloodless.

"Do you think Maria got to one of them?"

"I wouldn't underestimate her."

Hadn't I intimated the same to Tom just minutes before?

The light went green and his foot slipped from the brake onto the accelerator, jolting us forward. "Can you make it to the hospital?"

"I haven't got much choice," he said, sounding worse by the moment.

Could Maria have bribed one of the hotel workers to taint the leftovers in our fridge? Most food poisoning takes a day or two to show up. What would they have used? Something chemical? A bio agent?

I felt the gun on my hip dig into me. What good was

it as a form of protection against something like poison?

Richard turned onto Kensington Avenue. My nails were biting into my palms as I caught sight of the hospital up ahead, but instead of pulling up to the doors of the Emergency Department, Richard bypassed that driveway and chose the big lot adjacent to it. "What are you doing?"

"I can't leave the van in front of the ER—you can't drive it away."

"The hell I can't!"

"Bullshit." He pulled into the first empty slot and nearly hit the car ahead of us. He shoved the gearshift into park and turned off the engine, yanking out the electronic key.

"Can you walk all the way to the entrance?"

"What choice have I got?" he said, but already he sounded exhausted. He opened his door and oozed out of the van. I had a harder time getting out and grabbing my crutches. He waited for me, then pressed the fob and locked the van before shambling forward. I couldn't do a damn thing to help keep him upright, and he stumbled against the cars as he made his way across the lot, with me struggling to keep up with him.

A line of ambulances were parked nearby and he made the first one his target, leaning against it until he made it to the next one and the next until he practically stumbled to the big glass doors. He triggered the magic eye and the automatic doors whooshed open. A line of the walking wounded waited to be seen at reception. This could take some time.

"Go sit down in one of the chairs. I'll stand in line for you."

"Bullshit,"' he said again, and bypassed the queue, moving to the left to lean against the counter behind the receptionist.

"I'm sorry, sir, but you'll have to wait your turn," one

of the women dressed in scrubs behind the desk said.

"I'm Dr. Richard Alpert, I don't have my ID with me, but I'm affiliated with the hospital. I think I've been poisoned."

The woman turned to her keyboard, her fingers dancing across it.

"Rich, this isn't like you."

"This is the first time I've been poisoned. There's a bloody hand, a swollen foot, and a bad rash in line. They can wait an extra few minutes, where I might not have that luxury," he managed. His breathing was growing labored.

The woman pulled up a picture of Richard on her computer—the same one that was on the ID card he usually wore on a lanyard around his neck when he visited the hospital for a meeting or on the rare occasion when he called on a patient.

"Hang on, Doc. We'll get a chair and come get you," she said, motioning to the security officer nearby, who grabbed an empty wheelchair. Another of the scrubs-clad women came around the desk to commandeer it. Seconds later, Richard was whisked inside the ER with me left standing there like an asshole.

"Are you with the doc?" the first woman asked.

I nodded dumbly—shook myself, and answered, "I'm his brother."

"Why don't you wait in one of the chairs?" She nodded to the room at large. "We'll call you when he's settled."

"Thanks."

"Here," the security guard said, handing me a laminated visitor's badge, which I clipped to my shirt.

The place was fairly crowded, and I had to search for two empty seats before I could get settled on one of the hard plastic chairs and haul my right leg up on the other. Why in hell did hospitals everywhere provide such crappy seating for those who had to wait for loved ones? My heart was pounding but I was pretty sure it was from worry and not exertion.

I'd sat in an ER before, scared shitless my brother would die after he'd been shot trying to protect me. After he'd tried to save Gene Higgins' life, attempting to staunch the flow of the guy's life blood with no latex gloves between him and possible infection, Richard had lived with the specter of HIV for six months.

Oh, yeah—I knew about worry.

There was nothing but a wrinkled copy of the morning's paper around—which I'd already read—and the large-screen TV bolted to the wall, which had been set on mute, as entertainment. Should I call someone?

That didn't seem like a good idea, at least when I had no news—good, bad, or indifferent—to share. I'd just scare Brenda and Maggie by reporting Richard's whereabouts, and we really had no idea if he'd been poisoned. Maybe he had appendicitis. Hell, I'd been sick as a dog and puked myself empty when mine had gone south half a lifetime before. Maybe Richard had guessed wrong. Then again, he was a doctor. He knew what to look for when assessing poison over appendicitis.

Goddamn Maria. She'd obviously found where we'd set up our base camp and had infiltrated it. It was bad enough that she'd targeted me—and killed my co-worker—but now she'd gone too far by going after my brother, who had never done anything to hurt her. Hell, Dave and I were in the same boat. She'd attacked us with no provocation simply because she'd seen us as a *potential* threat. How ruthless were her attacks against people who'd actually been hostile toward her?

Ten minutes went by.

Twenty.

Thirty.

Forty.

"Relative for Richard Alpert?" a voice called out.

It took a moment for me to react, then I swung my leg off the chair, made a grab for my crutches, and hauled myself to my feet as the woman gave yet another call. "Coming!"

She waited for me to make my way to her, eyed my crutches but made no comment. "If you'll follow me." She punched a big square button with a wheelchair symbol on it that opened the double doors leading to the ER's inner sanctum. I followed her through the large room filled with men and women in scrubs, past patients lying on gurneys in the aisles, to treatment room eleven where a drape of swirling pastels had been pulled to give the glass-enclosed cubicle some privacy.

"There you go," she said and moved aside to let me enter, then abandoned me.

I stepped into the room crammed with all kinds of medical monitors and found my brother lying on the gurney clad in a hospital gown looking like death warmed over, wired for sound, and with an IV running into the back of his right hand.

"You look like shit," I said, and his eyes opened at the sound of my voice.

He turned his head toward me. "I feel like shit," he said and sounded that way, too.

Yet another uncomfortable plastic chair was wedged between a monitor and the wall. I took it. There was nothing for me to prop my leg up on. "What's the verdict? Are you going to live?" I asked, half afraid to hear the answer.

"It's a good possibility."

Thank God, I said to myself, despite the fact I was pretty sure I didn't believe in such a deity—although it seemed my brother did.

"What's next?"

"Observation. If I had someone to take care of me, I

could probably leave in a couple of hours."

"But I won't cut it as a caretaker," I said unnecessarily.

"Unfortunately, no."

Neither of us spoke for a couple of minutes. Meanwhile, the monitor to my right continued to beep in time with Richard's heartbeats. The place made me feel vaguely queasy. After all, I'd been a patient in one of the rooms down the aisle just a few weeks before.

"So, what do I do next?"

He let out a long breath. "You could go back to the hotel."

"Where I'm probably not safe."

"Or you could stay the night here with me."

"And sit in this chair?"

He shook his head. "They'll find me a room. They can bring in a recliner for you. I've still got some pull around here, you know."

"Thank goodness for small favors."

"Very small," he agreed and closed his eyes.

The muffled ringtone on Richard's phone sounded from somewhere nearby.

"Oh, shit. It's probably Brenda. I'm late calling her."

I scrambled to figure out where the sound was coming from, found a white plastic bag with Richard's clothes in it, and came up with the phone just as it stopped chirping. "Shall I call her back?"

"Only if you let me do the talking."

"And what if some nurse or tech comes in while you're on the phone?"

"I can tell her I'm at the ER for another reason?"

"Such as?"

"Don't look for trouble," he warned.

I hit the call icon and handed him the phone. He seemed to be steeling himself, and when he spoke, he'd plastered a smile across his lips and almost sounded like his usual self. Almost. Brenda must have detected it right away. "Nothing's wrong. Jeff and I had to go to Dave's wake, and while we were in the neighborhood, I decided to stop at the ER to visit Rob McIntyre. He was on a break, but—"

I knew the bullshit was going to pile higher and higher and tried to tune out the rest of the conversation—which was not that easy to do when there was nowhere to go, and nothing to do.

Finally, the exchange wound down. "Yeah, I love you, too. And I hope you can come home in a day or two. I'll call you in the morning. Bye." He handed me the phone.

"Did she believe you?"

"Not a chance. I wouldn't be surprised if she shows up tomorrow morning on the first plane in from Philadelphia."

"If it's any consolation, something's going to happen—and soon."

"Like?"

I shrugged. "I don't know. But something." Again, I could feel the weight of the gun resting against my hip. I didn't know what was coming at me down the pike, but there was a good possibility my new gun was going to see some kind of action. I just didn't know what or where.

TWENTY-FOUR

Being able to nap in a recliner had been a godsend at Richard's house, namely because he'd spent some decent bucks on a comfortable chair. The chair the hospital supplied me that night could have doubled as a torture device. It wouldn't go back all the way, and the cheap plastic was probably hygienic, in that it could be scrubbed if soiled, but it was hot and stuck to my sweaty skin. Hospital routine never seemed to vary, and some tech or other seemed to come into the room about every twenty minutes or so, waking both of us when they took vitals or performed some other invasive act.

Of course, lying awake half the night gave me plenty of time to think about our next move, not that I came to any real conclusions. We were fucked. We weren't safe in our hotel room, and I didn't know what else to suggest except the one obvious thing; we should leave town, too. And go where?

But thanks to my funny feelings, I also knew that something was going to happen that day that would blow everything apart.

I didn't have long to wait to find out, either.

I must have conked out around dawn, for light peaked around the edges of the curtains and the sound of a TV greeted me as I opened my eyes.

"Good morning," Richard said. He sat propped up in his hospital bed, looking rumpled and stubbled, but better than he had the night before.

"I've had better," I said, feeling achy and grumpy. I hadn't had a pain pill in forever.

The local all-news channel was squeaking on the tiny speaker that doubled as the combination TV remote-call button-bed control. The station's meteorologist was gushing about what a beautiful day we had in store for us—not a chance of rain.

"When can we get the hell out of here?" I asked.

"The resident on duty will be around in an hour or two. There's paperwork that has to happen, too. I'm guessing we'll be out of here by lunchtime—if we're lucky."

"Luck hasn't been in abundance of late," I commented, and the weather segued into a commercial. "And neither has food. I'm starved."

"You're better off going to the cafeteria to find something edible."

"I've got no money," I reminded him.

"I do."

I nodded. The poor schmuck always had to pick up the slack.

"By the way, I felt so crappy yesterday I never had an opportunity to tell you what I learned from the book on Prohibition here in Buffalo. In all the US, Buffalo was only second when it came to ignoring the eighteenth amendment."

"How so?"

"There were approximately eight thousand speakeasies in the area."

"You're joking."

He shook his head. "You could cross the Niagara River to get a legal drink, but everybody and his brother also tried to smuggle it in. And if they weren't doing that, they were making bathtub gin or beer."

"I'll bet it tasted like swill."

"You're right, but if it didn't poison you, you could still get lit."

It didn't sound all that appealing to me, but I'd been legally able to buy a beer on my eighteenth birthday— just before the rules had changed.

"Interestingly enough, there was a paragraph about Hiram Newcomb."

My interest piqued. "Oh, yeah?"

"He was known as one of the most ruthless of the rumrunners, also known as hard-fisted Hiram."

"Did it mention Alice?"

He nodded. "Newcomb considered her collateral damage—the bastard fuck."

I'd never heard Richard use that expression. That it was delivered with such vehemence was telling. "And what about the genealogy you've been working on?"

"I'm not sure. I've come up with a couple of scenarios, but there's a missing link."

"Any ideas on where to go?"

Before he could answer, yet another tech entered the room to take Richard's vitals. It seemed like overkill when he was obviously on the mend. By the time the guy left, I'd lost track of our conversation. My stomach grumbled, reminding me I needed to get something to eat. I cast around for my crutches.

"I know it's an inconvenience, but I was wondering if you could go down to the van and retrieve the paper-work," Richard said. "Playing with it would give me something to do during the next couple of hours."

"Is it something I can carry?"

"You can take my clothes out of the plastic bag and stick them in the closet. Stuff the file folders in it and it can hang it from your wrist."

Yeah, and it would probably bang into my leg or crutch and trip me up, but it was the least I could do for the poor guy. "Sure."

A commercial ended and the newscaster returned with a story about a fire overnight. Richard started on about needing a cup of coffee when, recognizing the front of the building ablaze on the TV before us I leaned forward. "Oh, my God. It's The Whole Nine Yards!"

Richard shut up, fumbling with the controller in his hand to crank up the sound.

"—fully engulfed when firefighters arrived," the reporter on the scene went on.

"Goddamn that Maria!"

"Fire officials believe arson was the cause—"

"Of course it was!" I practically shouted at the TV.

"Poor Tom," Richard said.

We watched in horror as the rest of the all-too-quick report finished up.

"That bitch," I grated, so angry I could spit. But why was I surprised? She'd already committed murder to get what she wanted. "I told Tom not to talk to her—I *told* him!"

"When?"

"Last night. At Dave's wake. I intimated that she was responsible for my accident and Dave's death—and I told him to watch his back. I'll bet he went straight to her to have it out."

"And she burned his bar to the ground?" Richard asked, incredulous.

There hadn't been much left when the last shot of the bar had been shown at the end of the report. Just a smoldering pile of rubble.

"Surely the cops will start adding things together now," Richard said. "She can't get away with everything she's done—or had someone else do for her."

"You think?" I asked, not at all sure that the legal system would be able to nail the likes of Maria. The fact that the bank couldn't trace where my money had gone meant she was in cahoots with highly skilled hackers and who knew who else? She hadn't become successful by backing down when things weren't going her way.

"What are we going to do?" Richard asked.

I didn't hesitate. "Retreat. At least until I can stand on my own two feet again."

"Where?"

"That's a good question."

"I don't want to go to Philadelphia."

"And neither do I."

"How about Martha's Vineyard or Nantucket? I've always wanted to try summering there. We could rent a house—maybe Maggie could come and stay a few weeks, too."

"That would be nice. But we've got too much to wind up first, not the least of which is getting my cat out of that hotel before Maria does him in, too."

"I can have Bison Security take care of getting our stuff and Herschel, too."

Hey, he'd just called my cat by his name. Progress!

A young woman dressed in maroon scrubs entered the room with a tray. "Breakfast."

I knew what would be on offer for Richard; a can of ginger ale, and something bland and dreadful. "I'm going to hit the can and then the cafeteria," I said, reaching for my crutches.

"Would you get my phone for me? I'd like to call Brenda and run the whole Nantucket thing past her and then contact Bison Security."

"Sure thing."

I stopped at the room's miniscule closet, grabbed the bag containing his personal effects and rummaged until I found his phone. I gave it to him. He set it down and turned his attention to his uninspired meal. I shuffled back to the closet, grabbed the bag and his keys, and then headed out the room and down the hall.

After making a pit stop, I found the nearest bank of elevators and started the long journey back to the emergency room and the parking lot where we'd left the minivan the evening before.

The day was bright and already hot. It would be a scorcher. Hard to believe Dave would be buried in just a few hours. That the place we worked was history. That so many lives had been damaged or destroyed in just a few short weeks. Yet a sunny day always made things seem less hostile—more friendly. Safe.

And on that day, a total sham.

I approached the minivan, fumbled for the fob in my pocket, and pressed the auto unlock. Obediently, the button on the door jumped upright. I opened the passenger side door and slid my ass onto the seat, leaving the crutches, standing outside the vehicle. I pulled my right leg mostly in and twisted to retrieve the file folder of pages. I did a quick look around the parking lot, saw no sign of a threat, and turned my attention to the pages on my lap.

Richard's work was always meticulous, and what he'd done to trace Alice's family tree was exemplary. He'd even constructed a graphic showing the family line, which he began with her parents. It was the side line of grandchildren where there were still a few question marks.

I shuffled through the pages, skimming through the notes he'd made. It looked like he'd found the names to plug into his graphic, but hadn't had a chance to do so before we'd had to leave for the wake the evening before.

I leaned back in the seat and the gun reminded me it was still there, and that if caught off guard I wouldn't be completely helpless to protect myself.

I read through the list of names and short bios Richard had written. The last piece of the puzzle had been tracking down Hiram Newcomb's granddaughter and her issue. Marlena Buchanan had left the Buffalo area in her teens and had apparently met and coupled with several different men, for each of her children had different last names. Batina M. Randall, Christopher V. Bowman, and Ryan W. Harper.

I read the names over several times. Something about them bothered me, but I wasn't sure what. And then a cold shiver ran through me.

Batina M. Randall.

I remembered the job application Dave had handed me weeks before where he'd scribbled Maria's personal information, along with her social security number. B. Maria R. Spodina.

No. It couldn't be.

And yet.... I traced my index finger over the name. It was Richard who, days earlier, had suggested there might be a connection between Alice's appearance and the goings on at The Whole Nine Yards. Why the hell hadn't I listened to him?

Alice had no idea why after decades of nothing, she'd suddenly found someone she could talk to—me. I'd had no idea why I was drawn to Forest Lawn to find her. To find out who'd killed her. And here was the missing link that bound us both together—a family tie.

Alice's own father had been responsible for her death.

Maria had been responsible for Dave's death, my accident, and I had no doubt the arson at The Whole Nine Yards, too.

Had Hiram Newcomb's ruthlessness been passed down the generations, manifesting itself in his great granddaughter? And if so, how the hell could I stop her?

Perhaps it was time to tell Alice the whole sordid story. She deserved to know the truth. At least one of us deserved some kind of closure.

The keys on the ring in my pocket dug into my leg—all but the minivan's electronic key, which was smooth and rounded on all sides.

Forest Lawn Cemetery was just around the corner. I

could drive there in less than five minutes. Okay, it wouldn't be easy, but all I had to do was drag my ass—and leg—across the van, plant myself in the driver's seat, and I could use my left foot to press the van's gas and brake.

It was a stupid idea. It was dangerous. The lack of common sense and anger were a potent combination. I could drive to the cemetery, and I didn't even need to get out of the van to speak with Alice. And I had my gun. I could do it.

I hauled the crutches inside the van, pulled the door shut, and struggled to maneuver myself across the center console and into the driver's seat. It wasn't exactly a comfortable position, since my broken leg was stretched across the small space and into the foot well of the passenger seat, but my left foot was quite capable of working the controls. Yeah—of course it could.

Shoving the key into the ignition, I started the engine.

TWENTY-FIVE

Driving with your left foot isn't as easy as you'd think. And driving with your broken right leg stretched to the max across the floor at an acute angle makes driving with your left foot even harder. Thankfully, I didn't have far to go. I drove like a granny with people honking and swearing at me, but in less than five minutes had made it to Forest Lawn Cemetery once again.

I eased the minivan through the Delaware Avenue gates and began my round-about journey to Alice's grave—or at least nearby. No way was I walking up that little hill and falling on my ass when I had no backup. In fact, it had been really stupid of me to pull this stunt in the first place. If I didn't end up dead, I was sure Richard would be out for my blood. But sometimes you do things knowing the risks—and hoping against hope that things will work out. Crossing my fingers just then would have inhibited my driving, but it might have been worth it.

I still didn't know how things could possibly work out, but Alice was the key to everything, and it was time for me to tell her all I knew.

As always, the cemetery was peaceful, and pretty much deadly quiet. I passed a couple of cars parked by the side of the road with people taking pictures of the Blue Sky Mausoleum. An older couple tended a grave in Section B, while some workmen weed-whacked monuments in Section E. I'm sure there must have been more people around, but I sure didn't see them.

I steered the minivan over the hill and saw the familiar bench where I'd perched on the other occasions when visiting Alice. I wasn't sure she'd appear unless she knew I was alone. I pulled off the narrow road and cut the engine. I hit the power window control. Obediently, it retreated.

"Alice? Alice! It's me, Jeff. I'm alone. You can come out now."

I looked around. She'd always appeared from the west side of the bench, but I waited and nothing happened.

"Alice?"

I waited a little while longer, but still she was a no show. It looked like I was going have to leave the damn van after all.

I wasn't sure I could safely get out of the driver's side, and scooted over the console to the passenger side, fighting against the crutches in residence in that small space. I managed to get the door open, set the crutches against it, and ease myself out of the van. But before I got out, I checked my gun, making sure the safety was off. If something bad went down, I'd have no time to do it later.

Once on my good foot, I tucked the crutches under my arms, moved around so I could shut the van door with my ass, and started for the bench. Alice usually appeared within a minute of me sitting down, and I hoped that would be the case just then, too.

I crossed the road and flopped onto the hard stone bench, but kept the crutches close at hand. Leaning forward, I retrieved my gun from the holster, setting it on the bench behind me, hoping the wrinkled, oversized shirt I'd slept in would keep it hidden from view.

"Why did you drive here?" Alice demanded, standing not three feet from me.

My heart nearly exploded from my chest at the sound of her voice. "Don't scare a guy like that!"

"Well, you scared me driving up in that vehicle. Where's your brother?"

"In the hospital. Someone tried to poison him."

"Poison?" she practically gasped.

"That's not the least of everything I need to tell you."

Her eyes widened. "You found out who killed me?"

I nodded. "It won't be easy for you to hear what I have to say."

Alice sat down on the other side of the bench and primly folded her hands on her lap. "I don't suppose I ever thought it would be."

"I'm not sure where to start."

"The beginning usually works best," she suggested grimly.

I nodded. Still, what I had to tell her would be painful. I thought carefully about how I should convey the information.

"Sometimes the people we love do bad things," I began. "I loved my wife very much, but she was into drugs."

Alice's eyes widened. "Did she smoke—" She stopped herself, as though what she was about to say might be considered vulgar. "Reefers?"

I couldn't help myself; I laughed. "If only that was the extent of it. She did many bad things, including stealing and prostitution."

"Oh my goodness! What did you do?"

"I tried to help her, but she wouldn't let me. She was eventually killed by someone who took advantage of her."

"And you're telling me this because someone took advantage of me?"

"Not in so many words." A shiver ran through me, a distinct feeling of apprehension, although I couldn't have said why. I eased my hand behind my back, curling my fingers around the butt of the gun.

"It seems your papa was involved in the illicit liquor trade," I continued.

"That can't be!" Alice protested. "Mama would never have allowed it."

"I'm afraid it's true. And unfortunately," I said in my kindest tone, "that wasn't the worst of it."

Alice looked skeptical.

"In fact, his closest rival threatened your papa. He warned that if your father undercut him again, he'd do something terrible. He promised to kill you in retaliation."

"No!" Alice protested.

"Your father called his bluff. Two days later, you and your beau were ambushed outside of the Blue Moon speakeasy."

Alice shook her head, her lower lip trembling. "No, that can't be. My papa would never...." And yet she didn't finish the sentence, her expression souring. Maybe she *could* envision her father betraying her—something she might never have wanted to believe.

She gasped, which seemed odd as ghosts don't need to breathe. "Did—did my mama know?"

"I don't know. But I heard she died of a broken heart, so ... it's possible."

"That's a sad story," came a voice from behind me, dripping with sarcasm. "But why are you talking to yourself in the middle of an empty cemetery?"

I turned to face Maria, taking in the sneer that curled her upper lip. Somehow I wasn't surprised by her presence. "This place isn't empty. The dead are all around us—but not all of them went quietly into oblivion."

"Dave Morris did. They're about to bury him, you know, although not in this cemetery."

I did know that. I started to lean forward when Maria's voice stopped me.

"I wouldn't move if I were you, Mr. Resnick."

Her right hand rose up to reveal a gun—the mirror of my own—and she aimed it straight at my face. "Ah-ah-ah," she warned. "Please put your hands in the air so that I can take that nasty weapon away from you."

"What makes you think I have a gun?"

"Because I keep tabs on everything you do, Mr. Resnick. Ever since the day you had my brothers ejected from The Whole Nine Yards."

"The obnoxious college guys?"

She nodded.

"One of them was driving the SUV that hit me," I guessed.

Again, she nodded. "That was Chris."

"And the other—Ryan?"

"Is a computer whiz. He made it easy for me to follow your—and Dave's—every move online. For example: I know you went to a sporting goods store yesterday and made a six hundred and forty seven dollar purchase with your newly issued credit card, which had been activated only forty-two minutes before that transaction. The cast rather limits your mobility, so I took an educated guess that you didn't buy any kind of exercise equipment."

She sounded so damned smug. I had no doubt that Chris had also stabbed Dave to death.

"If you'll lean forward, I'll just relieve you of that little piece of hardware."

It was hard to argue with that deadly steel aimed straight at my nose. I did as she said and Maria stepped forward, shoving the barrel of her semi-automatic against the carotid artery in my neck. She grabbed my shiny new gun and tossed it onto the ground in front of the stone bench.

Alice had disappeared the second Maria had revealed herself, but when I saw movement out the corner of my eye, I knew she'd returned.

"That woman can't see me," Alice whispered.

I nodded ever so slowly.

"Is there anything I can do to help?" she asked, sounding desperate.

I could only shrug. Then I thought better of it. "I could finish my story," I said, not sure if I was speaking to Alice or Maria.

"Go ahead," they said in unison.

"Hiram Newcomb's second family probably never knew of his Prohibition ties. All they knew was that they had money. He was a respected businessman in the furniture trade. His second family wasn't nearly as financially savvy as he. They all inherited, but each of them squandered the cash." And here was where I had to take a bit of poetic license. "When it came to the next generation, there was nothing left to leave."

"You've got that right," Maria said. "My mother was abandoned by her family when I was conceived out of wedlock. The old-fashioned fucks wouldn't lift a finger to help her, so she left Buffalo to find her fortune elsewhere."

"And did she find fortune?" I asked.

Maria didn't answer.

"Is this horrible woman related to me?" Alice asked, appalled.

I swung my head in her direction and nodded.

"What are you looking at?" Maria demanded.

"Your great Aunt Alice. Alice Newcomb. Surely you've heard of her."

Maria laughed. "She's legendary—as the most moronic female who ever lived."

"Hey!" Alice protested, not that Maria could hear her.

"What were you told about Alice?" I asked.

"Ever heard the phrase 'too-stupid to live?'"

"I was not stupid!" Alice declared. "I did very well in school. My mama and papa hosted a wonderful party for me on my high school graduation. I was fifth in my class!"

"What makes you think Alice was stupid?" I asked Maria.

"She never figured out how her father made his money. Apparently she was clueless about a lot of other stuff. She was kind of the family imbecile."

"Imbecile!" Alice protested. "My papa would never call me that."

"Are you sure?" I asked.

"Sure of what?" Maria said.

"Alice, please show yourself. It would be a whole lot easier on all of us."

"What are you talking about?" Maria demanded. She sure got pissed easily, which I guess wasn't surprising.

"I don't know if I can," Alice declared.

"Try," I implored.

"Try what?" Maria demanded.

Alice squeezed her eyes shut and clenched her fists.

I heard a pop, and then a gasp—from Maria.

"Who the hell are you?"

"I'm Alice, and I'm not stupid," my flapper friend declared.

Maria turned an angry glare on me. "What the hell?"

"Maria, meet your great, great aunt."

"Bullshit!" Maria said.

"No, really. This is Alice. She's a ghost."

"No way."

"Way," I said, feeling just a tad smug. How many ghosts had I communicated with during the past couple of years? "Alice, is there anything you want to say to Maria?"

"Yes," Alice said, indignantly. "Why did you hurt my friend, Jeff?"

I turned back to Maria. "I wouldn't mind hearing that answer, too."

"What the fuck? This is bullshit!" Maria declared.

"You are a foul-mouthed woman," Alice practically spat. "An embarrassment to my entire family—past and present!"

"You ain't heard nothin' yet," I muttered, and once again Maria's gun rose to zero in on my nose.

"Shut up!" she shouted.

A cloud passed in front of the sun, dimming the light. Alice rose to her full height, full of indignation. "What kind of woman did my Papa marry that begat the likes of you and your horrible brothers?"

"Someone with a stronger spine than the one from whom you were weaned," Maria grated.

Whom? Maria at least had good grammar.

"My mother was a kind and gentle person," Alice asserted.

"Another chump," Maria said with scorn.

"You are *evil*," Alice said, sounding hurt and confused.

"Why, because I can identify an idiot when I see one?"

"Why have you come here?" Alice demanded.

Maria's lips curled into a mockery of a smile. "To kill this stupid jerk," she said, waving her gun in my direction.

"What did he ever do to you?"

"He's too smart for his own good. His boss, Tom, actually *listens* to what he has to say. "

"And because I warned him about you, you destroyed his business by arson?" I accused.

Maria laughed. "He rebuffed my advances. If I could have married the jerk, it would have better served me. I wouldn't have had to pay a penny for The Whole Nine Yards. So instead, I destroyed his business. Now that it's worthless, I can buy it for pennies on the dollar," she practically crowed.

"Why?" Alice implored. "Why would you do something so terrible?"

"Because I'm my great grandfather's great grand-daughter." Maria lurched forward and grabbed one of my crutches. Hampered by the cast and hobbled by the brace, I couldn't move fast enough. She hauled off and whacked me on the back—knocking me off the stone bench. I fell face-first to the ground, my top front teeth digging into the dirt.

Alice screamed and was suddenly at my side. Though I couldn't seem to catch my breath, I looked up to see her eyes were wide with horror—but she wasn't looking at me. "You are *despicable*," she screamed at Maria. "Hitting an injured man like that. You're worse than my papa ever could have been."

"You obviously didn't know your papa," Maria sneered.

Alice stood, ramrod straight. "Something should be done about you. Something should be done about *all* people like you!"

"And what can *you* do? You're nothing in death—just like you were a nothing in life."

I spit out dirt as Alice's eyes widened until they seemed to grow to an obscene size.

From out of nowhere came a strong wind that rustled the leaves on the trees. The sky above us darkened as the sun was totally obliterated by angry gray clouds that seemed to boil.

"What the hell?" Maria yelled over the rising gale, but the fury of the unexpected storm muffled her words.

Movement to my right startled me. Sweet, petite Alice's usually pretty features had morphed into a malevolent caricature of the young woman I'd known in death. But worse, she seemed to be expanding, growing larger and larger into an opaque, amorphous blob with blazing red eyes that advanced toward Maria, exuding a malevolence I hadn't thought her capable of.

Maria stumbled backward in panic. "The dead can't do anything to the living," she asserted as though trying to convince herself.

The thing that had once been Alice said nothing, still advancing on her quarry with murderous fury. The force of her rage washed over me, the howling wind that circled around me was horrific—like a hundred wailing sirens, accompanied by thunder and flashes of blue-white lightning. Tree limbs snapped like matchsticks. I tried to raise myself on my elbows, but the buffeting wind kept me pinned.

Maria fired her gun, spraying the entity with what would have stopped flesh and blood, but the projectiles sailed right through what was left of Alice Newcomb.

Maria shrieked again as the unearthly entity swooped over her, as though consuming her.

The screams abruptly stopped.

Panicked, I needed to get the hell out of there. Drenching sheets of rain pummeled me as I groped around until I could grab my crutches and began to crawl toward the van, dragging my useless leg along, afraid to look behind me.

I'm not sure how I managed to get back inside the van, entering via the passenger side door. The driver's side was drenched where I'd left the window open. Still, I pulled my muddied self into the sopping wet seat, started the car and hit the window control, which sealed off the rain, but the wind continued to yowl. Was that what a tornado sounded like? The descriptor 'like a freight train' was right on the money.

I dug into my soggy sweatpants pocket and pulled out my phone. No signal. I wasn't sure what to do. Should I just leave Maria where she lay? I still couldn't bear to look to my left and, absurdly, turned the windshield wipers on high, which manically thumped against the glass.

I wiped the wet from around my eyes and realized my

hand was shaking. The cast on my foot was saturated. I'd have to get it replaced, but when was that likely to happen?

Working up my courage, I looked through the driver's side window, but the glass was so beaded with rain I couldn't make out anything but vague shapes outside in the gloom.

I must have sat there for two or three minutes, finally noticing that the shaking traveled from my hand and reverberated through my entire body. The windows had fogged, and I switched from AC to heat. It took less than a minute for the front window to clear, and as it did, the rain abated. Up ahead, I could see the sky had begun to clear, leaving a patch of blue among the scattering clouds. I turned off the windshield wipers and looked out the driver's window.

I couldn't see Maria. Where she should have been was a heap of leaves from a very thick limb that had been wrenched from the maple overhead.

There was no sign at all of Alice Newcomb.

TWENTY-SIX

It's amazing how many things you take for granted when you have a broken leg. Like standing under a shower for ten minutes and letting the warm water sloosh off you; jumping in the car to get a six pack of beer; walking across the damned room without the aid of crutches.

Getting rid of that accursed knee brace meant freedom of a sort, but the cast was replaced by a walking boot, which made me feel like I wore one of Frankenstein's discarded shoes. If I had to walk any great distance, I'd use a cane, but that wouldn't last too long. (I hoped.) Technically I still wasn't supposed to drive, but I found I could ditch the boot and wear a loose sneaker and make short trips—but not when my stick-to-the-rules-of-healing brother was anywhere near.

Best of all, my cat and I got to go *home*.

The day I got my boot, Richard drove me back from the orthopedist's before helping me to pack up and move back across the driveway to my own digs. I waited until just after midnight to head to the bakery to visit Sophie. She wasn't there, which wasn't totally unexpected, but I was disappointed. After all, Richard and I had not yet gone into business—and since Sophie and I had last spoken, I hadn't used my so-called gift to do more than avoid phone calls from telemarketers. I still clung to the hope that her threat to abandon me had been just that—a threat. Only time would tell.

I wish I could say that I had a peaceful rest of the summer, but that wouldn't be true thanks to my physical therapy regimen, but my goal was to eventually walk without a limp and I decided to do whatever it took to accomplish it.

And then there was Richard.

He'd been livid with me taking off in Brenda's day's-old minivan, risking life and limb to drive it, as well as possible assassination, and worst of all—for buying a gun. He refused to let it come into his house and insisted I buy a gun safe for it. Of course, he ended up paying for the safe—as well as the gun, because I never did get back the money that been hacked from my bank accounts. My tab at Casa Alpert kept rising and rising.

Two good things did come from my enforced residence in the big house. CP came to love Herschel—who let her pull his tail, and smother him with wet kisses—and Richard learned to tolerate him. Upon his return from the hotel, my cat was given free rein to roam the Alpert pseudo-mansion, although usually he stuck pretty close to me. It was rather a shock one afternoon when we sat together in the living room to realize that Herschel sat on Richard's lap while my scared-of-cats brother absently petted him. It happened more than once—whether Richard wants to admit it or not.

Ironically enough, it turned out Maria *hadn't* poisoned Richard. He had the food in our hotel room fridge tested, and his leftover mashed potatoes had simply gone bad, Of course, that was after Brenda and CP had arrived back home. As Richard had predicted, Brenda had taken the very next flight and returned to Buffalo, arriving at home via a cab no more than ten minutes after we'd made it back to the house. By then, hours had passed since Maria's untimely death. No surprise, the autopsy determined she'd been crushed to death. But I'll never forget Alice's terrible fury and I wondered if she'd literally scared that evil woman to death before the limb had a chance to take her out. Meteorologists were stumped as to how a localized microburst had hit the cemetery with virtually no warning, and I sure as hell wasn't going to offer an explanation. Since my gun obviously hadn't been fired, and Maria's fingerprints on it substantiated my story, the police returned it to me within days.

Maggie bought a bungalow in Tonawanda, not far from her sister, Sandy. The whole deal took less than two months. I didn't see much of her during the entire packing process, and can't say I'm sorry I missed it. But it was the second lonely summer we'd been forced apart. It almost felt like we were back at square one again.

Richard continued to ferry me around the city to my doctor's appointments. He also took me to visit Dave's grave, but like at the funeral home, there was no trace of my biking buddy. He was lost to me forever and I felt like a heel for blowing him off so many times before his death. If only I'd listened.... But the truth was, even if I *had* spoken to him that last time he'd called, I may not have been able to stop someone as determined as Maria Spodina from getting her way.

The fire at The Whole Nine Yards *was* officially declared arson, but that wasn't the worst of Tom's troubles. Before she'd had the building set ablaze, Maria had canceled Tom's insurance on the place. With no capital to start over, the property had been put up for sale and immediately snapped up by a developer who hoped to obtain the rest of the block when Maria's estate was finally settled—which could take years. A heartbroken Tom left the state, leaving no forwarding address.

That one person could wreak such havoc still astounded me. So far, the cops hadn't been able to get enough evidence to arrest Maria's brothers for the crimes they'd committed on their sister's behalf, but Detective Wilder promised she and her brother officers in other jurisdictions wouldn't give up.

As I mentioned, Richard hadn't pushed me to make a decision on us going into business, but now that I was out of the cast and brace, I expected the subject to come up yet again. I was pretty sure what the answer would be: an extremely reluctant yes.

The gardens along the fences in Richard's yard hadn't suffered due to my enforced inactivity, thanks to the landscaping firm he'd hired to take care of them, but I felt like I'd missed out on the entire summer.

The sun was beginning to set on that early September evening when Richard sauntered into the backyard in his beige Dockers, looking like a golf pro in his green Izod shirt—or maybe like a country club waiter, since he held a sweating beer bottle in each hand. He climbed the steps to join me on the deck behind his house.

"What's up?" he asked, handing me one of the bottles.

I shook my head and leaned back in the wooden Adirondack chair that was comfortable to sit in, but hell for someone with a bum leg to get out of. "Absolutely nothing."

He sat down on one of the chairs and took a sip of his beer.

"You've got something on your mind," I guessed.

"And no doubt you know exactly what it is."

I took a sip of my beer, admiring a patch of pink, dark pink, and white cosmos that swayed in the light breeze along the east fence. I'd introduced them to the garden just days before my accident—attack. The thirty-six plants had taken nicely, and I decided I'd plant three or four times that next year.

"You want to end the boredom. You want to go back to work. You want to feel useful again."

"Is that so bad?" he asked.

I turned to face him. "No, because I feel the same way.

I won't guarantee you that I'll do this for the rest of my life, but I'm willing to give it my honest best."

"And what about the money?" he asked, sounding wary.

I let out a breath and then took another sip of my beer. "Sophie's right. There's no way I can ever charge someone I help using this so-called gift of mine. Somehow it wouldn't be right."

"What are you trying to say?"

It was hard—damned hard—to articulate what needed to be said. "This isn't how I pictured my life going." My throat tightened, and yet I wasn't going to succumb to an embarrassing display of emotion. No way.

"What do you mean?"

"I worked hard most of my life to be independent of you, and now I'm stuck."

Richard said nothing.

"My father told me that your family owed me. But now I feel like it's more that you own me."

"Jeff!" Richard protested.

"Listen to me. He was right to some degree, but I don't hold it against you. You never...." But I couldn't go on, because for most of the time I lived in that house back when I was a teen, Richard was too preoccupied with his job to care about me. It was benign—not calculated—neglect.

But he couldn't let it go. "Then we need to clarify the money thing."

I shook my head.

"Yes, we have to. What do you need to live on?"

I let out a weary breath. "I don't have a figure. I'll only take what I need to get by."

Richard nodded. "I'll set up a checking account and a credit card."

"Whatever," I muttered.

"But there's other business we need to discuss."

I looked at him and took another swig of my beer. "Such as?"

"Office space. I don't want potential clients coming to the house. It just doesn't feel right."

"I agree, but aren't you jumping the gun?"

"I've scoped out a few sites in Snyder and Williamsville. Nothing fancy. Just a couple of rooms, a small reception area, a conference room, and a john. Maybe we could go look at them tomorrow."

"Sure." I wasn't exactly overflowing with excitement.

Richard reached for his wallet and extricated a business card, handing it to me. It said:

R & A Insights
Jeffrey Resnick
716-555-1234

"It's just a dummy. We'll add the address and a real phone number as soon as we get established."

He must have printed it up on his computer on special linen stock, but it looked nice—professional. "I like it."

Richard smiled, but then his expression grew pensive. "I heard from Bonnie Wilder. She has an unsolved case that's stumped the Amherst cops for years. She wondered if we'd like to take a look at the files."

"What's it involve?"

"A missing child."

Our first consultation had involved a missing boy. I'd found him—dead. It had been a sobering experience, but it had helped the child's mother find closure and move on.

Sophie once told me that what I really wanted to do in life was help people. She had me pegged. Helping people resolve old conflicts with good old detective work would be satisfying work—more satisfying than pouring drinks. Richard offered me a way to do it with—almost— no strings attached. He'd never pulled a guilt trip on me.

Well, not really. Would I be stupid to let an opportunity like this slip away?

Hell, yes!

"Okay. Tell me all about it."

ABOUT THE AUTHOR

The immensely popular Booktown Mystery series is what put Lorraine Bartlett's pen name Lorna Barrett on the New York Times Bestseller list, but it's her talent -- whether writing as Lorna, or L.L. Bartlett, or Lorraine Bartlett—that keeps her there. This multi-published, Agatha-nominated author pens the exciting Jeff Resnick Mysteries as well as the acclaimed Victoria Square and Lotus Bay Mystery series, and now the Tales of Telenia fantasy saga, and has many short stories and novellas to her name(s). Check out the links to all her works here: http://www.lorrainebartlett.com

If you enjoyed **Shattered Spirits**, please consider leaving a review on your favorite online review site.

Thank you so much.

18587373R00179

Printed in Poland
by Amazon Fulfillment
Poland Sp. z o.o., Wrocław